SERGEI

Roxie Rivera

Night Works Books
College Station, Texas

Roxie Rivera/Night Works Books
3515-B Longmire Dr. #103
College Station, Texas 77845
www.roxierivera.com

Publisher's Note: This is a work of fiction. Names, characters, places, and incidents are a product of the author's imagination. Locales and public names are sometimes used for atmospheric purposes. Any resemblance to actual people, living or dead, or to businesses, companies, events, institutions, or locales is completely coincidental.

SERGEI (Her Russian Protector #5)/Roxie Rivera. -- 1st ed.
ISBN-10: 1630420034
ISBN-13: 978-1-63042-003-1

DEDICATION

For my fellow fine, fabulous and feisty big, beautiful women. May we all be so lucky as Bianca!

ACKNOWLEDGMENTS

Believe it or not, this is a book I was on the fence about writing. I had always wanted to tell more stories in the universe I created for the *Her Russian Protector* series but I wasn't sure anyone else wanted to read them but me!

Thankfully, I had so many readers reach out to me and ask for the books in this world to continue. I appreciate your encouragement so much—especially yours, Jayha Leigh!—and hope that Sergei and Bianca's love story fills you with the same sort of breathless excitement and happiness that it gave me while I wrote it.

Roxie Rivera

CHAPTER ONE

I *really* hated weddings.

Sipping my champagne and nibbling on the richly flavored and exquisitely decorated wedding cake, I silently acknowledged the thought was damn near blasphemy in my field. A dress designer and wedding boutique owner who groaned every time an embossed and gilded invitation dropped into her mailbox? It wasn't good for business.

Poking at my cake, I conceded it wasn't the actual wedding ceremony I disliked. Earlier in the evening, I had cried like a baby when Ivan and Erin exchanged vows. Seeing the pair make promises to each other for the life they intended to build together had touched me so very deeply. The tender moments the newly married couple had shared throughout the night left me yearning for the same thing.

It was the receptions that really ruined weddings for me. Now entering my mid-twenties, I seemed to have reached a point where it was no longer acceptable to attend a wedding solo. Without a plus-one on my arm, I suddenly earned *that* pitying look. It made my damn skin crawl.

"You look awfully pensive," Vivian Kalasnikov remarked as she slid into the empty seat next to me. Dressed in one of the strapless, chiffon bridesmaid gowns, my friend looked absolutely stunning. Her dark hair and light eyes popped against the vibrant shade of fuchsia. The diamond accents under the bust glinted in the light cast off from the flameless candles and chandeliers decorating the grand ballroom of the downtown Houston hotel.

With my longtime friend, I dared to be honest. "I'm just thinking that I need to find some more men to add to my dating pool. This business of attending weddings alone is for the birds."

She arched one of those wing-shaped eyebrows. "Maybe it's time to consider doing the opposite."

"How's that?"

"Maybe you should think about whittling down that list of men to two or three that you might get serious with, you know? Or maybe it's time to start all over and find someone new and exciting with real potential."

The mere mention of someone new and exciting filled my head with images of one extremely tempting man. Even now, sitting in this crowded ballroom and surrounded by hundreds of revelers dancing the night away, I innately sensed his presence. He loomed somewhere behind me, near one of the tables where a group of rowdy men had congregated to exchange wild tales. Every now and then a burst of laughter punctuated by a loudly spoken Russian phrase or two would erupt from that general direction. Each time, I buried the intense desire to sneak a glance at *him*.

As if reading my mind, Vivian smiled knowingly. "You

know he's dying to ask you to dance, right?"

Even though she'd nailed me, I feigned confusion as I reached for my flute of champagne. "Who?"

She rolled those bright blue eyes at me. "That might work on someone else, Bianca, but it doesn't work on me. You've had your eye on Sergei since December."

Her comment spurred the memory of the chilly night Vivian and Nikolai had been attacked. Learning my friend had been kidnapped had been such a punch to the gut. The memories of the panic-filled days that followed as I waited for any news on Vivi's return were shoved aside by those of Sergei shadowing us that night during dinner and later at Faze, Houston's hottest nightspot.

The giant Russian with dark hair and dark eyes had taken my breath away from the very first moment I'd spied him. In high school, I had dated a couple of basketball players so I thought I knew tall men but that was before Sergei. With the broadest, sexiest shoulders I had ever seen, he had to be nearly seven feet high. He had a strong aquiline nose and a sinful mouth that tempted me like no other.

And that was bad. Really, *really* bad.

Feeling Vivi's pointed stare, I shrugged and sipped my champagne. "I'll admit to looking at the merchandise, but I'm sure as hell not about to try it on or take it home with me."

"I don't know," she said a bit conspiratorially. "I think my curiosity would get the better of me."

I snorted rather indelicately. "Please! Those moon-eyes of yours for Nikolai have made you blind to every other man in creation!"

Smiling and not even attempting to deny my assertion, she glanced just to her right and easily zeroed in on her husband. As if connected by some sixth sense, the devastatingly handsome Russian cast a smoldering gaze her way before returning to his conversation with two men I didn't recognize.

A longing pang squeezed my heart. God, I wanted that. I wanted a man to look at me as if I was his entire world, as if he couldn't breathe without me.

Beside me, Vivian took a drink from the glass of clear, fizzy soda she'd brought with her. I'd never known her to be a fan of the lemon-lime flavored drink and ticked another box on the list in my head. Earlier that morning, I had rushed over to her house to let out the bust of her bridesmaid dress. In all the years I had known Vivian, her weight hadn't fluctuated once yet this morning her bosom seemed to have swelled a full cup size.

I'd been taking in and letting out wedding gowns and bridesmaid's dresses since high school so I had easily put two and two together. More than one panicked bride had called either me or my mother into her dressing room on her very special day to make adjustments for a baby belly that just happened to make its debut at the most inopportune moment.

As far as I could tell, Vivian's tummy remained flat and toned but that full C-cup she now sported? Oh, that was an undeniable clue. Add to that the glass of wine she hadn't touched during dinner and the caffeine-free soda in her hand now? There weren't many scenarios other than pregnancy that fit the bill. Even so, I didn't ask her to confirm my suspicion. Certain she had her reasons for keeping the news quiet, I tamped down my curiosity.

The sight of Benny Stepanov waddling toward our table brought a twitch of amusement to my lips. The empire waist of the bridesmaid dress and wispy, light chiffon enhanced her rounded figure. Heavily pregnant and due any day, the petite Latina lowered her body into a chair with a loud sigh and rested a hand on her belly. "My dogs are barking tonight!"

"Well, why are you wearing heels?" Vivi demanded with a humorous glint in her eyes. "Erin told you to wear flats. She wanted you to be comfortable and to take it easy."

"Have you seen how tall my husband is?" She gestured toward the imposing blond. Arms crossed and a grin on his handsome face, Dimitri exuded raw sexuality and power. I wasn't surprised she was already expecting their first baby. With a man like that heating up the sheets, how could any woman resist his charms? "I'd like for us to have a picture or two where both of our heads are in the shot, you know?"

"So sit together," Vivi pointed out the obvious. "I bet Dimitri would love to have you sitting on his lap."

Benny laughed and pointed to her belly. "I'm pretty sure that's how I got into this predicament."

Amid our giggling, excited shouts drew my gaze. Yuri Novakovsky had snatched up Erin right under Ivan's nose. She squealed with laughter as the billionaire magnate rushed off with her and Dimitri, Sergei and Nikolai blocked his path. The custom of stealing away the bride and ransoming her back to the groom made me grin. I had been to so many weddings over the years and had assumed I'd seen it all—but I had to give it to these Russians. Their customs and celebrations were so sweet and lighthearted and they *really* knew how to throw a party.

"Erin looks gorgeous, Bianca. That design is perfect for her." Benny shot me an approving smile. "The lace is amazing."

"Thank you. That touch was one of my mother's suggestions." I considered the gown hugging Erin's willowy frame. The design had been a tricky one because Erin had wanted so many different things—a sweetheart neckline, dropped waist, chapel train that could be bustled, beading and lace. "She wasn't an easy bride to please but I'm so thrilled with the way the gown came together."

"Will this design be available to other brides?"

I shook my head at Benny's question and let my gaze drift to the intimidating, tattooed fighter who had won Erin's heart. "No, I promised Ivan that no other woman would ever wear a dress like hers. He wanted this one to be especially for Erin and always hers."

"Aw," Vivian said with a sappy smile. "Could that guy be any freaking sweeter? I mean, you look at him and he's, like, the scariest man on the planet and then he does something so romantic like that! Erin is so lucky to have him."

"Yes, she is," I murmured a bit enviously.

Out on the dance floor, Ivan gathered Erin's smaller body to his and wrapped those brutally strong arms of his around her in the most protective embrace. I sensed she missed her older sister Ruby something fierce but the incarcerated pill addict and thief had popped positive on a random inmate drug test a few weeks earlier so any chance of her earning early release and probation had been scuttled.

Erin had been at my boutique for an early morning fitting when she'd received the call from her sister's lawyer. Though we were friends, we were nowhere near as close as I was with Vivian, but I hadn't let that stop me from hugging her and letting her sob on my shoulder as the years of pent-up frustration and hurt her older sister had caused rushed to the surface.

I still remembered the pained look on Ivan's face

when he had suddenly appeared in the fitting room. Apparently their lawyer had called him with the update on Ruby's situation. He had instinctively known that Erin would need him and come right to her. When he swept her up into his arms and called her his angel in that gruff, accented voice of his, I had understood why Erin loved him so much.

As Ivan's thick, heavily tattooed fingers sifted through her hair while they danced, I decided they were probably the most mismatched couple I'd ever met, but there was no doubting the deep and unshakeable love they shared. Flushed with happiness, Erin burrowed against Ivan's chest and closed her eyes as they swayed together.

While I tried to suppress the sadness that threatened to ruin such a great night, the universe seemed determined to dash a little more salt in that wound. Dimitri and Nikolai strode toward the table and joined their spouses. Nikolai actually slid his arms around Vivi and dragged her onto his lap so he could nuzzle her neck and whisper lovingly to her in their shared language.

Across the table, Dimitri hauled Benny's aching feet onto his lap and removed her high heels while gently scolding her and massaging her calves. Benny smoothed her hand down the curve of her big baby bump and remarked that their little girl was kicking up a storm. When Dimitri reached out to feel his daughter's kicks, the expectant parents shared a look that made my heart freaking ache in my chest.

Deciding I'd had just about enough of the universe rubbing my face in the one thing my otherwise happy life lacked, I reached for my clutch. Before I could even open my mouth to bid everyone goodnight, a shadow fell over me. I didn't have to glance up to know that it was *him*.

All seven feet of Sergei Sakharov dropped into the

empty chair next to me. Instantly my traitorous body reacted to the tremendous amount of body heat radiating from his huge frame. The faint smell of eucalyptus tickled my nose, and I had to fight the urge to inhale deeply, to imprint the very scent of him in my lungs and brain.

Casting a stealthy sideways glance, I took in the sight of him in that tuxedo. I didn't think that any man had ever made the classic black and white ensemble look so good. His tailor had fit him to sheer perfection.

Nikolai addressed him in Russian and Sergei answered back with a laugh while tugging free his bowtie and unbuttoning his collar. Inspired by the sight of him undressing just that tiny bit, I refused to let my mind travel along the rather naughty path it wanted to follow.

My heart stuttered wildly when he slid his massive arm along the back of my chair and leaned closer. Unable to avoid meeting his gaze, I shyly glanced at him. Those dark eyes of his ensnared me, made me want to slide a little closer so I could count the amber flecks in his irises. His sensual mouth curved, and it was all I could do not to finally give in to the desperate urge to kiss him just to see if it would be as amazing as I expected.

"You having a nice time?" That deep baritone voice of his made the womanly core of me clench with desire.

"Yes. You?" Somehow I managed to get out two words without stumbling over them.

"I love weddings."

"Really?" I let a little skepticism invade my tone.

He gestured around us. "When was the last time you saw people having this much fun?"

I considered his question. "Vivian's wedding."

"Exactly." His fingers brushed my bare upper arm. "Would you like to dance, Bianca?"

God, the way he said my name, his Russian accent

stretching out the syllables and rolling over the vowel sounds, made me want to give in and break my number one dating rule. I wanted to hear him saying my name *all* night long—but I didn't dare cross that line. My late brother's face flashed before me, reminding me of exactly why Sergei was all wrong for me, and I gently shut him down.

"I can't." Lifting my clutch, I gave it a little wave. "I was actually on my way home when you sat down."

"So soon?" Vivi piped up from beside me. "But the night is still so young, and Erin hasn't tossed her bouquet yet."

I turned my head and gave her a look that made her smile guiltily. I knew *exactly* what she was doing but it wasn't going to work. "I have to pick Mama up for church in the morning and get there early enough to get into my choir robes."

Sergei's fingers drew a slash across my skin. "You sing at church?"

I turned back toward him and tried to ignore the way his touch made me throb in all the right places. "Yes."

"Then I'll have to come listen sometime."

My eyebrows arched toward my hairline as I tried to imagine Sergei in one of the pews of my childhood church. Boy, would he stick out like a sore thumb!

"If you're ready to leave, I'll drive you home."

"No, thanks." I had a bad feeling I wouldn't be able to fend him off with a handshake the way I had when he'd taken me home that frigid December night when he was Vivian's bodyguard and driver. "I have my car here."

"Maybe you should let him take you, Bianca," Vivian interjected very unhelpfully. "He could check your house and yard for that prowler."

Sergei stiffened and the flirtatious slant to his mouth

vanished. His jaw visibly tightened and his big hand cupped my arm. "Is someone bothering you?"

If he had been a wolf, his hackles would have raised as he turned fiercely protective...of *me*. Surprised by his reaction, I quickly explained, "It's nothing. Really." Judging by the hard set of his jaw, he wasn't buying it. "Look, I just thought I saw something the other night."

"And Monday night and last Thursday," Vivi butted in again. "The neighborhood watch guy knocked on her door to let her know he'd seen someone running out of her backyard too."

If Vivi hadn't been sitting on her husband's lap, I would have pinched her for being so dang intrusive. Instead, I had to face Sergei who wore an expression of utter irritation. "It's nothing."

"It doesn't sound like nothing. It sounds like someone is trying to break into your home or attack you."

"It's fine. I called Kevan—"

"Who is Kevan?"

I didn't miss his gruffness. "He's a guy I date sometimes. A police officer," I added.

Sergei grunted with annoyance. Lowering his voice, he slid a little closer and asked, "Why didn't you call me?"

My eyes widened. Was he for real? Not wanting to let everyone in on my personal business, I whispered a bit harshly, "Why in the world would I call you?"

Something flashed in his dark eyes. Hurt? Frustration? Why in the world did the thought of hurting his feeling make my stomach ache so badly?

"We're friends," Sergei insisted.

Were we? I tried to decide if our relationship fit that category. Sure, I spent a lot of time in his company but that was only because Nikolai trusted Sergei to keep Vivian safe. I called Sergei her shadow for a reason. They were practically joined at the hip which meant that, technically, over the last few months, I'd had dinner with Sergei more often than I had any of the men I had dated.

And—if I was being completely honest with myself—I had enjoyed those evenings when he was sitting nearby or driving us around Houston. Beneath that rough exterior, he could be such a sweetheart. That scared me more than anything. He possessed so many of the qualities I wanted in a man but the package was all wrong. He was much too dangerous for me and too damn sexy for his own good.

Even now, I couldn't fathom why this man—this outrageously handsome and sculpted model of male perfection—seemed so intent on getting closer to me. The experiences of my teenage years warned me that a guy like Sergei only wanted one thing from a girl like me. Some part of me feared this was all a setup for some colossal joke or even worse.

Maybe I was simply an itch that needed to be a scratched, a curiosity that demanded to be satisfied. I didn't think my heart could handle getting trampled under that huge foot of his if it turned out he was simply wondering what it would be like to date a fat girl or if he was trying to figure out if the stereotypes about big girls in bed were true.

"Bianca?" Sergei prompted, his voice even lower and softer. "Aren't we friends?"

Meeting his questioning gaze, I couldn't lie. "Yes, we're friends."

The tight lines around his mouth relaxed. "Then let me help you."

Certain his brand of help was the very last complication I needed, I reached out and patted his cheek. "I'm a big girl, Sergei. I've got this."

He covered my hand with his, the heat of his palm searing my skin. I marveled at the way our hands looked together, his tan skin a few shades lighter than mine and his fingers so long and thick and mean-looking. "This isn't a game, Bianca. You could get hurt."

His gentle warning scared me but I refused to back down. "I won't."

Tugging my hand free, I rose from my chair and bent down to peck Vivian's cheek. Whispering hotly against her ear, I said, "You are on my list."

She gave me a hug. "I had to try. Besides, we both know you'll forgive me."

"We'll see." I caught her husband's amused gaze and touched his shoulder. "Good night, Nikolai."

"Good night, Bianca. Be safe."

"I will."

After bidding farewell to Dimitri and Benny, I skirted the edge of the busy dance floor on my way toward the exit. Ever the glamorous, jet-setting couple, Yuri and Lena happened to whirl by me. Lena stepped away from Yuri and engulfed me in a big hug. The diamonds dripping from her ears and adorning her neck felt so cold against my skin. As of now, her ring finger remained bare, but I had a feeling Yuri would be changing that very soon.

I visited the valet station and headed outside to wait for my car. Though I had left the reception early to escape the sight of so many canoodling couples, it seemed futile now. Everywhere I looked, couples held hands, laughed, made out and whispered sweetly to one another. By the time my silver sedan rolled up to the curb, I was ready for a glass of wine and a hot shower.

After tipping the valet, I slid behind the wheel and fastened my seatbelt. Throat tight, I eased on the gas, pulled away from the hotel and tried not to think about the empty house that awaited me—and yet another long night alone.

* * *

Sergei leaned back in his chair so he could watch Bianca leave. Despite his frustration at her constant rejection, he had to admit that this view was incredibly nice. The curve-hugging dress she wore highlighted some of her very best assets. Even now, his fingertips burned with the memory of caressing her silky brown skin. He had wanted to do so much more when he slid close to her chair, but he hadn't dared to push.

Every time he saw her, Bianca Bradshaw blew him away. This girl was class all the way. She managed to look so fucking sexy but without ever crossing the line into trashy or cheap. Tonight, she wore a simple and unadorned black dress that she somehow made hotter than the skimpiest lingerie. Did she have any idea how damned beautiful she was?

He bit his lower lip as he imagined what it would be like to peel that dress from her body and discover all the soft, warm delights beneath the fabric. That sweet, plump ass of hers had been made for a big man like him. Those swinging hips made him ache with desire. He imagined her straddling his lap, his hands cupping that amazing ass while her thick thighs cushioned their coupling.

He wanted her. He wanted her so badly he could fucking taste it. Since the moment he'd spied her coming into the restaurant that late December night to meet with Vivian, Sergei had been blind to every other woman on the planet.

But Bianca wanted nothing to do with him.

Watching her embrace Lena, Sergei wondered what the hell it was going to take to convince Bianca that he was dead serious about her. She wasn't a passing fascination for him. He had played the field enough in his thirty-one years to know that she was different, that what he felt for her was *real*.

He rubbed the back of his neck and remembered Vivian's warning a few months back that Bianca wouldn't go for his type. Fully aware that she had lost her brother in a senseless act of violence, he understood why Bianca shied away from men who weren't strictly on the right side of the law. Though he owned part of a successful construction business, Sergei remained firmly in Nikolai's pocket. He did whatever his boss asked of him without question—and that wasn't going to work for Bianca.

She was unlike any woman he'd ever dated. There was the obvious issue—she didn't want anything to do with him. Grudgingly, he admitted his ego had taken quite a hit over that one. He'd gotten used to women tripping over themselves to go out with him. The right glance, the right smile and a few sweetly spoken words and he was assured of a date with any woman he wanted.

But none of that worked on Bianca.

He'd always acknowledged that she was out of his league. Maybe it was time to accept that she was *too far* out of his league and would never see him as anything other than the big, dumb, mobbed-up bodyguard who watched over her friend.

"Seryozha."

Hearing Vivian call him by his childhood nickname made him smile. Over the last few months, they had grown incredibly close. He thought of her as the little sister he had never had and she had admitted to viewing him as an older brother now.

Tearing his gaze away from Bianca's backside, he glanced at Vivian and asked, "Yes, Mrs. Boss?"

She grinned at his teasing reply and waved a smartphone at him. "I think Bianca left this behind."

Nikolai snorted softly and rubbed Vivian's arm. "No, I think my wife means that she stole it out of Bianca's purse while they were hugging."

Vivian narrowed her eyes at her husband. "Stole is such a harsh word, Kolya. I *borrowed* it."

Nikolai swept his fingers along her jaw. "Because?"

"Because Bianca has some creep peeking in her windows and she's too stubborn to let anyone help her." Vivian slapped the phone down on the table. "Take it, Sergei. Ride to her rescue on your white horse. I mean— SUV."

Sergei stared at the phone Vivian had taken from Bianca. It was an underhanded trick but he was a man out of options. Before he reached for the phone, he glanced at Nikolai who gave a small nod of encouragement. Feeling a flutter of hope in his chest, he snatched up the device. "Thank you, Vivian."

She shooed him with her hands. "Well—go on. If I know Bianca, she's going to crack open a bottle of wine about twenty steps inside that front door. If you catch her after that first glass, she'll be in a good mood and might even invite you inside."

He laughed as Vivian suggestively waggled her eyebrows. "I'm not going to get my hopes up. I'll be lucky if she doesn't slam the door in my face."

"She won't."

"I wish I had your confidence."

A short time later, he drove the streets of the historic neighborhood where Bianca lived and replayed their short conversation. He couldn't believe how blasé she had been about the prowler situation. He refused to even think about this Kevan guy she had asked for help.

A police officer. Of course. A man who was everything Sergei could never be for her. The very thought of Bianca seeking aid from some other man frustrated him. He wanted to be the one she thought of when she was frightened or needed help. Hell—at this point, he would take being the man who mowed her lawn or fixed a leaky pipe!

Navigating the old streets, he conceded Bianca might be right about the prowler situation. Maybe it was nothing. It could be a teenager cutting through her yard to sneak into his house late at night or something else equally as innocent.

Or maybe it wasn't. She was a single woman living alone in a neighborhood known for its spacious homes filled with antiques. Granted, she had purchased her home in a tax sale at a deep discount as a fixer-upper. He doubted she had much in the way of expensive furnishings and knickknacks but a thief might not know that.

If someone was casing her place, Bianca might be on a short-list of marks for an upcoming robbery run. He'd known enough men who ran in the B&E crowds to know that many of them preferred to hit a string of high-end houses in a night to improve their odds of success and evading the police.

The thought of Bianca being terrorized by a home invasion soured his stomach. He pressed a little harder on the gas and made up his mind that he would ask around in the morning to see if any of the usual suspects were planning something in this neighborhood. He didn't care what it cost or how many favors he had to call in or extend. He would do anything to protect Bianca—whether she wanted his help or not.

Pulling up to the sidewalk in front of her large corner lot, Sergei killed the engine and studied her home. The Queen Anne needed a new roof and some paint but it had good bones. He had never been farther than the front door but what he had glimpsed of the interior needed a lot of work. From the conversations he had overhead between Vivian and Bianca, it seemed she was trying to do most of it herself. He had a feeling Bianca was in way over her head.

He unlatched and pushed open the gate, running his fingers over the iron scrollwork with appreciation. It clanged shut behind him, the sound so very loud in this still, quiet neighborhood, and he winced. Heading up the sidewalk, he noted the pavers that needed replacing and the spotty landscaping. An idea began to form, one that might prove to Bianca that he was worth more as a man than his shady connections.

At the door, he rang the bell twice and knocked. While he waited for her to answer, he tried to think of something witty. He wouldn't lie to her about how the phone had come into his possession. Vivian would probably kick him in the shins before their next run for ratting her out, but he'd been on the receiving end of worse. He wanted nothing but the truth with Bianca, even when it was something as small as this.

When she didn't answer, he knocked again, louder this time, and started to reach for the doorbell. Just as his fingertip pressed the button, a panicked scream ripped through the house and turned his blood cold. Another shriek of terror followed a second later.

Gripped by his protective instinct, Sergei tried the door handle but it was locked. Desperate to reach Bianca, he took a step back to examine the solid wood door and its frame. He judged the weakest spot, inhaled a deep breath and planted his foot against the spot just to the side of the lock. A satisfying crunch erupted so he slammed his foot against it twice more. The door flew inward and nearly off its hinges.

As he raced into Bianca's house, he heard a loud thump upstairs. Rushing toward the stairs, he leapt up them two at a time. "Bianca!"

CHAPTER TWO

I shouldn't have waited to have that glass of wine. The nice buzz from my favorite Shiraz might have softened the blow of just how bad my attempt at renovating this bathroom had really gone. Standing there under the spotty, stuttering spray of tepid water and examining my embarrassing failures as a DIY home remodeler, I just wanted to cry.

The rainfall showerhead leaked horrendously. I'd clearly missed a step during the installation. Eying the rattling faucet with trepidation, I wondered how many more uses it had before it finally died. The low temp and pitiful amount of pressure snaking through the pipes convinced me a plumbing problem was brewing. I cringed at the thought of how much it would cost.

Running my fingers along an uneven seam of grout, I reluctantly admitted that the pretty tile I had painstakingly applied earlier in the week would probably have to be ripped out and redone. Not that it would take much work to tear the tile from the wall. Just touching that section now made it wiggle precariously.

With a sigh, I stepped forward to rinse the soapy lather from my body. When I turned to rinse my back, I accidentally knocked my elbow against the wall—and dislodged that entire strip of tile. I gasped and tried to catch the tiles hooked together by a mesh backing but they landed right on my foot. I shrieked with pain and yanked my foot free.

Bad move!

Losing my balance, I flailed wildly for anything to stop my fall. Grabbing the showerhead, I managed to steady myself for a fraction of an instant before the damn thing came right off in my hand. A blast of lukewarm water splattered my face. I lurched back to escape the spray and began to tumble out of the tub.

Panicked, I screamed and grasped the shower curtain and liner in one final desperate clutch but it wasn't enough to save myself. The plastic rings popped loose, and I was in free fall.

"*Oof!*" I hit the floor hard. Thankfully the plush bathmat cushioned my fall but I still winced as pain lanced my bottom and back. "Ow!"

Over the whirring rush of water spilling into the tub, I thought I heard a crack of thunder. The sound confused me because the skies were clear and there hadn't been even the slightest chance of rain in the forecast. Another loud boom and then another met my ears. What in the hell?

And then I heard the unmistakable sound of Sergei's voice.

"Bianca!"

Still dazed by my fall, I wondered if I was hallucinating. Why would Sergei be yelling for me? Why would he be inside my house?

"Bianca!" It sounded as if a bull was running up the

stairs and barreling down the hallway. Those heavy footsteps echoed in my bedroom. Without warning, the bathroom door flew open and suddenly Sergei appeared. I blinked and tried to reconcile the sight of him in my home.

His handsome face screwed up with concern, he scanned the scene in front of him before exhaling with what seemed to be relief. "Thank God. I thought someone was trying to attack you, *milaya moya.*"

"Not someone," I groaned my reply. "Just my shower."

Too tall to come through the door without ducking, Sergei also had to turn his shoulders because they were too broad to fit through the frame. He crouched down next to me and brushed his scarred knuckles along my cheek. "Are you all right? Do I need to take you to the emergency room? Did you hit your head?"

"No, only my pride is wounded."

Sergei gently grasped my upper arms and hauled me into a sitting position. The movement made me cringe with discomfort. "*Ow.* Okay. My bottom is probably bruised."

A mischievous smile curved that sinful mouth of his. "I'd be happy to take a look at it for you."

Reminded of my scandalously underdressed state, I tugged the shower curtain that was wrapped around my body a little higher, just to make sure my cleavage was totally covered. Ignoring Sergei's flirtatious offer, I pointed to the door. "Would you please grab my robe?"

"Later," he said softly and slid his arms under my body. Showing me just how strong he was, Sergei lifted me up off the floor and cradled me to his chest.

Eyes wide, I stiffened. "Put me down! You're going to break your back."

"Don't be silly." He actually smirked. Pivoting, he carried me out to the bedroom and carefully placed me on the bed. "Don't move."

Hugging the shower curtain around my naked body, I watched him return to the bathroom. He disappeared behind the door for a minute, probably to survey the damage in the shower, before returning with my fluffy robe and a folded towel. Chuckling, he held them out to me. "So I guess we've learned a valuable lesson about choosing the proper grout and preparing our surface before tiling."

Scowling at him, I grumbled, "In my defense, those DIY blogs make it seem so easy."

"That's their job." He crossed those massive arms of his. "I did warn you that this was too much work to be done alone."

Trying to forget how good it had felt to have those arms holding me tight, I concentrated on that January morning at my boutique when he had helped me pin the hem on Vivian's wedding gown. "No, you said it was man's work. In a very condescending tone," I added for good measure.

His smile faded. "That was wrong of me. I shouldn't have been condescending. I'm sorry."

I shrugged. "It's okay. I mean—I guess in a way you were right." Dropping my gaze with embarrassment, I gestured to my throbbing foot. "Maybe I am in over my head here."

Sergei stepped closer and knelt down in front of me. He cupped my foot in his big hand and my pulse sprinted. His fingertip traced the swollen splotch there. "You'll have to wear some sensible shoes for a few days, but you'll be fine."

Swallowing hard, I murmured, "You haven't seen my

closet. A sensible shoe cannot be found in there."

He snorted softly and gently lowered my foot. "I'm not surprised." His thumb drew a circle around my ankle. "But you do make those impractical shoes look so good."

His compliment took me by surprise. Mouth dry, I tried to think of something to say. Sergei didn't seem to notice how he had affected me. Rising up to his full height, he patted the shower curtain. "You should get into your robe now. Do you have a tool set?"

I nodded. "It's in the guest room across the hall."

After he lumbered out of my bedroom, I shook myself from the temporary stupor of being touched by him and quickly unwound the shower curtain. I was tying the robe's sash when he returned. The comical look on his face made me smile. "What?"

He held up a tool bag and the hot pink hammer. "Pink tools? Really?"

"They're designed for a woman's hand," I said rather defensively.

"They feel like toys in mine."

"Well, you're like a seven foot tall giant. All sorts of normal-sized things probably seem like toys to you."

Sergei's lips parted but he snuffed out the witty comeback burning the tip of his tongue. I couldn't help but wonder what it was that he hadn't said—and why.

He inclined his head toward the bathroom. "I'll get your shower fixed and then we'll talk."

"About?"

Sergei's burning gaze swept over me. "Us."

Not giving me a chance to pipe up with my usual rejection of the very thought of there being an *us*, he spun on his heel and disappeared into the bathroom. Feeling totally off-kilter with that big sexy beast of a Russian puttering around in my house, I dabbed at my wet skin with the towel. What did I do now?

There had to be an easy way to get him out the front door without making it too weird. As I rubbed on some lotion and tried to figure out what to say to him next, a terrible clatter erupted from the bathroom. Sergei swore roughly in Russian and English—and was that Spanish too?

Curious, I approached the door and caught him stripping out of his soaking wet shirt and toeing off his shoes. My breath arrested in my throat. My God—I had no idea a man could look *that* fine.

He was all lean, smooth muscle without even a hint of fat. I counted the rippling ridges of his abdomen and wondered what it would feel like to run my hands over his powerful body. Oh, I would definitely take my time tracing those tattoos he kept carefully hidden under his clothes. The small gold medallion dangling from a thin chain around his neck interested me.

Images of Sergei leaning over me in bed, my thighs wrapped around his waist as he thrust into my slick, womanly heat tormented me. The tempting sight of him melted the icy wall I had erected between us. Suddenly, I started to question why he was so wrong for me.

As if he felt my intense gaze, Sergei glanced at me. "Where is your water shutoff valve?"

"My what?" His mundane question threw me.

"The water shutoff," he repeated. "Have you been having problems turning your water on and off here at the shower faucet?"

"Oh. Well...yeah." I looked to the shower where a blast of hot water spewed from the broken pipe there. It seemed even stronger than earlier. No doubt that had been the cause of Sergei's cursing. "I bought a replacement faucet and the tools to fix it, but I wasn't sure how to start."

"You need to shut off the water and bleed the line first. There's no local shutoff here so we'll have to do it outside."

"Wait. Is that the funny little handle thing in that box outside?"

Sergei's mouth slanted to one side. "Yes, sweetheart, it's the funny little handle thing."

There was only warm amusement in his voice and no condescension to be found. I refused to allow myself to dwell on the way my belly quivered at the sound of him calling me sweetheart. Flicking my fingers, I turned away from him. "That shutoff is outside in between the rose bushes."

"Of course it is," he grumbled. "Wait. Here. I brought this for you."

Spinning to face him, I watched him retrieve my cell phone from the pocket of his tuxedo jacket. "How in the world—?"

"Vivian," he said. "She borrowed it from your purse."

"Borrowed, huh?" I rolled my eyes at her interfering. "I love that girl but she knows how to push my buttons."

Sergei chuckled. "Try guarding her. She's impossible to keep out of trouble."

"Sounds stressful." I shuddered to think what Nikolai would do if Vivian was ever hurt under Sergei's watch.

"You have no idea." He held out my phone. "I suppose we should thank her. If I hadn't been at your door when you fell—"

"Hey, wait a second." I held up my hand as another thought struck me. "How the hell did you get inside my house?"

"About that..." Sergei rubbed the back of his neck and made an apologetic face. "I know a guy who builds custom homes. He uses a lot of antique reproductions. I'll call him first thing in the morning to get you a new door."

"A new door?" Mouth agape, I left the bathroom, crossed my bedroom and strode out to the landing. Leaning against the handrail, I gazed down into the entryway of my home to see wooden shards and splinters scattered across the floor. The door hung lopsided on its hinges. A good breeze probably would have knocked it over. "Oh. My. God."

"I'm sorry."

Startled by the closeness of his voice, I glanced back at him in awe. He now stood less than two feet behind me in just his tuxedo pants. "How do you move so quietly?"

He shrugged those broad shoulders of his. "It's a useful skill."

I decided to not to ask him why he needed that particular skill. Looking back toward my destroyed door, I asked, "Did you use a sledgehammer?"

"No, my foot."

"Are you freaking serious?" I turned around and examined his huge feet. They were surprisingly nice with neatly trimmed nails. "You can tear down a door with your legs?"

He smiled. "I can do a lot of things with my body that would amaze you."

"Uh-huh." I didn't even try to stop the grin that tugged at my lips. "You never quit trying, do you?"

Sergei closed the distance between us and placed his big paws on either side of me on the handrail. Boxed in by his massive, half-naked body, I gulped. The amount of body heat pulsing off of him stunned me. He lowered his face until we were breathing each other's air. "Not when it comes to a woman as special as you."

Me? Special? For a moment, I considered this was part

of his game, but then I realized he was dead serious. He really thought I was something special.

My belly trembled as his mouth descended toward mine. Heart racing with anticipation, I held my breath and waited for the touch of his lips. At the last second, he diverted his landing and playfully pecked my cheek. Even though it wasn't the kiss I wanted, I still felt an electric jolt of contact.

He must have seen the slight disappointment in my eyes because he smiled sweetly and dragged his finger along my jaw. "I'm going to head outside and shut off your water. If you'll put a broom and dustpan near the door, I'll clean up that mess."

"I'll do it."

Sergei shook his head. "I made the mess. It's my responsibility."

He backed away from me. Immediately I missed his closeness and wanted him back. As I watched him head downstairs and out the door he had demolished with those tree trunk legs of his, I finally understood that Sergei was much more dangerous to me than I had ever imagined.

I'd finally gotten a taste of how sweet and gentle and protective he could be—and already I wanted more.

* * *

Grunting, Sergei reopened the water valve to the house and swiped his sweaty forehead with the back of his hand. The stifling, muggy May heat made the simple tasks he'd undertaken seem to last ten times as long. Wondering why he hadn't immigrated some place cool and dry, he replaced the heavy metal cover protecting the shutoff valve and trudged back to the porch.

He used the kitchen towel he'd draped over the railing to clean off the muck sticking to his toes and the soles of his feet before entering the house. Once inside Bianca's home, he surveyed the quick fix he'd done on her front door. He had found some extra lumber in one of the bedrooms she had turned into a workspace and had used it to patch up the splintered door. The lock was a lost cause so he nailed a board into place to keep the door shut for the night.

"All done?"

"Almost," Sergei replied and checked the board to make sure it would hold. When he turned to face her, a streak of heat raced through his stomach. His dick throbbed at the sexy vision before him. Clad in a silk robe, Bianca leaned against the doorway between the living area and the entryway. Her bare legs peeked out from beneath the modest hem to tease him. The thought of pushing her up against the closest wall and kissing his way from the very tips of her toes to the hidden vee between her thighs hit him hard.

She held out an ice cold beer. "I thought you could use this."

Surprised by the offer, Sergei accepted the chilled longneck and took a slow drink. The flavor of it pleased him and he glanced at the label. "This is good. It's not a brand I recognize."

"A friend of mine runs a microbrewery attached to his restaurant. I'm not normally a beer drinker but I'll sip one of his any day."

He hated that the mere mention of a male friend sent darts of irrational jealousy right through him. He had no right to feel that way. Bianca wasn't his. She was free to date any man she wanted, but that didn't make it easy to stomach the thought.

After another drink, he gestured upstairs. "I'm going to check the shower."

"Okay." She didn't make a move to follow him. Was she afraid to be close to him?

Heading back upstairs, he made a mental list of all the things he needed to pick up at the hardware store. He was relieved to find the shower turned on and off without issue. As he replaced the shower curtain and put the rod back into place, he studied the poorly done tile. It would all have to be ripped out. In fact, the tub and shower surround needed to go too.

Leaning back against the counter, he scanned the bathroom and started to mentally sketch some ideas for renovating the space. It was larger than most bathrooms in houses this old. A walk-in shower would go beautifully in the corner and a claw foot tub would fit perfectly in a spot right over there. He envisioned a crisp, clean honeycomb tile pattern on the floor, a new set of custom cabinets and marble countertops.

Sergei would jump at the chance to help Bianca restore her home to its former glory but would she allow him to work with her? He knew for a fact that she had been taking bids from other contractors for various projects around the place. Even if he came in with a rock-bottom bid, she'd probably laugh in his face and send him on his way.

Facing the mirror, he frowned at the dirt and grime marking his hands and chest. He'd smeared rust on his face while working. Mud and flecks of grass clung to his pants. Wanting to get cleaned up, he shucked his pants and boxer briefs and stepped into the shower. The tepid water blasting his skin made him move a new hot water heater to the top of his shopping list. He grimaced at the floral scent of her soap but lathered up with it anyway.

After drying off, he wrapped the damp towel around his waist and examined his tuxedo. There was no way he was getting back his deposit now. In fact, he'd be lucky if the rental place didn't come after him for damages. There was no way he was slipping back into the wet fabric tonight. He considered asking Bianca to run out to his SUV to grab the gym that held two changes of clothing. The sound of her moving around in her bedroom gave him another idea.

Her earlier reaction to the teasing kiss he'd placed on her cheek emboldened him now. What if he went for it? No more sweet and playful overtures that she could so easily shoot down. It was time to be brave and maybe even the slightest bit brash.

Wearing only the towel, he opened the bathroom door and stepped into the bedroom. She had her back to him as she arranged an outfit on the back of her closet door. He could tell by the modest cut of the pretty green dress that she planned to wear it to church. He hadn't been joking earlier when he'd said he wanted to hear her sing.

Judging by the look she'd given him, Bianca must have thought he was crazy. He'd long ago stopped caring what other people thought of him. When he wanted something, he went after it. The hell with other people's opinions.

"I guess the shower works?" She draped a wide belt over the hanger holding the dress.

"Yes."

"Great. I really wanted to thank you for..." Her words drifted off when she pivoted to face him. Her dark eyes flashed open, and she gestured wildly to his mostly naked state. "Where are your clothes?"

"They're wet and dirty." He didn't even bring up the jeans and T-shirt tucked into his gym bag outside. He wanted to see how far this would go.

"So put them on, go home and throw them in the dryer." Her voice had risen to a slightly higher pitch. What was she so afraid of? Was it his size or his criminal ties? Or was it something else? Was she afraid of how good they would be together and how hard it would be to push him back outside that fence she'd built around herself?

"I'm not going home tonight."

She blinked. "Excuse me?"

"I broke down your door." He gestured in that direction. "I'm not leaving you alone in a house that can't be properly secured, especially when you have a prowler bothering you." He tilted his head. "Unless you want to come home with me?"

"No!" She hastily shot down that option.

"Then I'm staying here." He took a step toward her bed and started to remove the plush, decorated pillows. She had the sort of bedroom that looked like it was straight out of a designer catalogue. Though why one woman needed nine pillows on her bed perplexed him!

She held up her hands. "What are you doing?"

He tossed a fringed pillow onto the floor behind him. "It's late. I'm tired. I'm getting in bed."

"Not in this bed," she retorted sharply. "You can go sleep in the guest room down the hall. Pick up those pillows and stack them neatly on that bench on your way out."

Gathering the fluffy, girly pillows in his arms, he carted them to the upholstered bench she had indicated. He carefully lined up the pillows as she had asked but didn't leave her bedroom. "There's no way I can fold myself into that daybed."

The irked expression on her face softened. With a sigh, she reached for one of the normal-sized pillows tucked inside ruby-red silk. "I'll go. You stay here."

"Is that really what you want?"

She gulped and hugged the pillow tighter. "Yes."

"You are a terrible liar, Bianca."

"I haven't had much practice."

Holding the pillow like a shield, she skirted the edge of the bed and headed for the door. In three quick, long strides, Sergei intercepted and blocked her. She gazed up at him, a mix of apprehension and the faintest flash of excitement brightening her dark eyes. He gripped the pillow and tugged it from her hands.

She licked her lips, betraying her nervousness. "What are you doing, Sergei?"

"No more, Bianca." He tossed the pillow onto the bed behind her. "We're done playing this game."

"What game?"

"The one you've perfected." He stepped closer, and her smaller hands flew to his chest. He could have easily overpowered her, but he immediately halted his forward motion. "Bianca, I would never use my size or strength against you."

"Sergei…"

"No." He placed a gentle finger to her mouth, silencing her rejection. "One kiss, Bianca. You let me kiss you properly one time. If you don't feel anything—if you really don't want me—I'll go downstairs and sleep on the couch. After I fix your door in the morning, I'll never bother you again."

Her perfect white teeth dug into her lower lip. Finally, she nodded. "Okay. One kiss."

Grinning triumphantly, he slid his hand along the nape

of her neck and dragged her against him. He was determined to make this a kiss they would never forget. If he only had one chance, he was going to make it count!

CHAPTER THREE

What the hell are you doing?

I silently chastised myself while warily watching Sergei. Towering over me, he seemed so much more dangerous—and delicious.

"Come here. I'm too tall to do this comfortably while standing. It will be better if I'm sitting." He grasped my hand and tugged me back toward the low, wide club chair and ottoman in the corner of my bedroom. Sinking down onto the soft, worn leather, Sergei pulled me between his knees. The towel wrapped around his waist had climbed up rather scandalously, but I didn't dare let my gaze linger on his lap.

When his huge hands glided along my thighs and cupped my hips, I swallowed hard. "What are you doing?"

"What does it feel like I'm doing?" Sergei nuzzled my neck, his hot breath wafting across my skin.

"Everything but kissing me." Delightful shivers coursed through me, rushing through my belly and into my chest.

"I'm getting there," he promised.

I had the distinct feeling I had been hoodwinked by agreeing to let him have one kiss. Something told me that I would soon be agreeing to much more with him.

His hands slipped under my robe and the short nightgown underneath. He had the roughest palms I'd ever felt. After dating only professional types, it was something of a novelty to have such incredibly manly hands gliding over my curves. He whispered something in Russian that I didn't understand. As if remembering we didn't share that common language, he repeated, "You're so damn soft, Bianca."

I gasped when he grabbed my bottom in his big hands and gave it an appreciative squeeze. A short laugh escaped his throat as he ran his palms over my panties. Bending low his dark head, Sergei gripped the loosely tied belt of my robe between his teeth and gave it a tug. The sides of my dressing gown fell open, and he let the belt fall from his mouth. Dragging his lips side to side along my collarbone, he whispered, "Take off the robe."

"I really shouldn't."

He smiled at my quavering voice. "Then I'll do it for you."

Abandoning my backside, Sergei pushed the robe down my arms. The silky fabric fluttered around my feet. Even sitting, he was so damn tall that we were eye-to-eye while I stood. His heated gaze burned me as it roamed my body.

Without the robe covering me, I felt incredibly exposed in the thin, too short nightgown. Though I projected confidence and was normally comfortable in my skin, I suddenly experienced a wave of insecurity. All I could think about were the imperfections marring my body. Was he comparing me to all the other women he'd dated? I feared I wouldn't measure up well.

Cupping my chin, Sergei peered into my eyes. "You're even prettier than I'd imagined."

His compliment took me by surprise. "You've been imagining me like this?"

Sergei's mouth quirked to the side. "Well...I've been imagining you in much less." He fingered the spaghetti strap of my nightgown and started to slide it down my arm. "Much, much less."

"Wait." Breathless, I put my hands on his shoulders. "We need to slow down."

"Five months, Bianca." He reminded me of how long we'd been doing this will-we-won't-we dance. "That's slow enough."

Conceding he had a point, I pressed my forehead to his. "So stop messing around and kiss me."

He laughed and wound those massive, tattooed arms of his around me. Relishing the heat and power of him, I closed my eyes and waited for the first touch of his lips. His long fingers sifted through my hair just as his mouth brushed mine. His other hand rode the curve of my spine to settle on my lower back.

With a low groan, Sergei kissed me. It was the sweetest, most chaste of kisses, but there was something incredibly erotic about it. Perhaps it was the knowledge that so much more awaited us. It was the teasing, easy beginning to a night that promised to be among the best of my life.

The tip of his tongue flicked the seam of my lips. Dropping all pretenses of not wanting him, I surrendered to his seeking kiss. Our tongues touched timidly at first and then with more confidence as we grew accustomed to the taste and heat of each other. Cradling the back of my head, Sergei deepened the mating of our mouths until my knees were wobbling. I clutched his shoulders for support and whimpered under his sensual assault.

Proving he was an attentive lover, Sergei clasped the backs of my thighs and hefted me off the floor before my lust-weakened legs gave way and I crumpled to the floor. I gasped against his lips and started to protest the caveman move but he silenced me with another amazingly perfect kiss. Straddling his lap, I was glad I had picked such a wide, comfy chair for reading.

The caress of his hands left me aching with such incredible sexual hunger. He made me feel so alive with anticipation and excitement. All those neatly collected reasons to keep him at arm's length were slowly being wiped away from the list I'd jotted down in my head. This was bad. This was so, so bad.

Except—oh my God. It just felt so, so good.

His hands sneaked under my nightgown, and I giggled at the ticklish swipe of his fingertips. He chuckled against my lips but continued his exploration. Palming my breast, he brushed his thumb over my nipple, and I moaned as my throbbing flesh tightened to a peak. He lightly pinched it, and I rocked against him. "Sergei."

"I want to see you naked." He buried his face against the curve of my neck and nipped at the sensitive skin there. "I want to see all of you."

I started to say that we needed to turn down the lights but stopped myself. Sergei didn't seem to mind the extra weight I carried. There was no faking the attraction and desire reflected in his eyes and carried in his admiring touch. He wanted me—just the way I was.

Embracing my inner sex kitten, I reached for the towel between us and gave it a playful tug. "Only if you get naked first."

"As if you have to ask!" Sergei nibbled my lower lip. "I'm going to make love to you tonight."

I hastily applied the brakes. "No."

He leveled a look my way. "Don't make me beg, Bianca." Massaging my breast, he murmured, "I want you, and I've waited so long."

Something in his voice piqued my interest. "When was the last time you went out on a date, Sergei?"

He held my gaze. "I haven't been with another woman since a week before I met you."

My lips parted with shock. "Are you serious?"

He brushed his knuckles down my cheek. "After I saw you that first time in December, I knew no other woman would ever come close. It seemed pointless to waste my time with others when all I wanted was you."

His sincerity stunned me. Guilt rocked me. "Are you mad at me?"

His brow creased. "For what, *milaya moya*?"

"Dating other guys while you were sitting on the sidelines," I explained nervously.

He wrapped a few strands of my hair around his finger. "I won't sit here and lie to you. I didn't like seeing you with those other men." He hesitated. "I was relieved you didn't bring anyone tonight—but that doesn't mean I'm mad at you. Annoyed, maybe," he said with a smile. "But never mad."

I captured his mouth in a lingering kiss. "For what it's worth, I haven't been intimate with anyone since Vivian's wedding." Deciding to be totally honest, I admitted, "No other man has made me feel even a tenth of what you've made me feel so far tonight."

"It's early yet, Bianca." He teased his mouth against mine. "I have so much more to show you."

Tapping my finger to his nose, I shook my head. "You still can't make love to me."

"But—"

"I don't have any protection in the house. Unless you have something tucked away in your tuxedo pants…"

"I don't." Then, with a careless shrug, he said, "What I really want to do to you doesn't require protection."

My core clenched with anticipation. "And what's that?"

"You'll see. Now—you decide. Here on the ottoman or on the bed?"

"I guess that depends on what you have in mind."

"First, I'm going to tear this off you." He gripped the front of my nightgown. "Then I'm going to use my mouth to trace every last inch of you." His hand slipped between my thighs so he could cup my sex. "I'm going to spend most of the night with my tongue right here."

Oh. Sweet. Jesus.

A wicked flare scorched me when I imagined everything he had described. Shaking inside and dry-mouthed, I managed a whispered response. "We should probably move this to the bed."

"Good choice. But first…" Fisting the front of my nightgown, he jerked hard on the delicate fabric, shredding the lace and silk blend in his fearsome hands. His alpha display of strength left me momentarily speechless.

When I recovered from the shock of having my clothes ripped off of me, I sputtered, "Sergei, you can't just tear my clothes!"

"I'll buy you some more." He said it as if that was the only issue at play here and brushed the ruined gown back from my body to see my bare breasts. His hands moved to my panties but I clasped his wrists to stop him.

"Don't even think about it."

"Then stand up and strip for me." He was dead serious. "Now."

I started to tell him off...but there was something incredibly arousing about the idea of it. On limbs as shaky as a newborn colt, I slipped off his lap and stood in front of him.

"On the ottoman," he ordered and leaned back in the chair.

No man had ever had the stones to give me an order. Even as a younger woman, I'd always been the bossy, intimidating and totally in control girl. Sergei seemed to be attracted to those qualities in me, but I suspected that here, in the bedroom, he wanted to be the one giving orders and driving the action.

My courage bolstered by the lust flashing in his eyes, I stepped onto the ottoman. Standing up here, I had a clear view of the impossibly huge hard-on tenting the towel. Holy. Hell. From what I could tell, his cock looked like it ran half the length of his thigh. Apparently he was really big *all* over.

He ran his hand along the outline of his erection. "Show me, Bianca."

My belly flip-flopped, but I did as he instructed and peeled the torn gown from my body, baring my plus-size curves to him. The burning glint of desire that crossed his face told me that Sergei liked what he saw. Just as some people preferred vanilla ice cream to the more complicated flavors, this outrageously sexy Russian seemed to enjoy big girls.

And I wanted to fall to my knees and thank the heavens for my stroke of luck.

He murmured something in his native tongue while his hungry gaze roamed my naked body. I wasn't sure if that was another direction. "Um...what?"

He glanced at me and made an apologetic face. "Sorry. I'm used to being able to slip in and out of

Russian."

"Vivian has tried to teach me how to speak it, but I only know how to say a few things. Greetings and things like that," I explained. "I didn't understand anything you just said."

"You look magnificent."

My eyebrows arched at his compliment. "Magnificent, huh?"

"Sexy," he added. "Perfect."

"Well, I don't know about that."

"I do." He spoke with authority. "Someday I want you to dance for me."

"Are you crazy?"

He laughed. "About you? Yes."

Butterflies swarmed in my belly. The idea of dancing and stripping for any man had never been one I'd relished but I found myself unable to tell Sergei no. "Maybe someday."

He didn't push. Instead, he made a spinning gesture. "Turn around and take off your panties."

Tummy aflutter, I spun away from him, brought my shaky fingers to the waistband of my undies and dragged them down my hips. When I reached my thighs, Sergei gruffly ordered, "Bend over, Bianca. I want to see all of you."

Face aflame, I spread my feet a little farther and wiggled my hips while drawing my panties down toward my feet. I dropped them on the floor to the sound of Sergei pushing out of the chair, the leather creaking as his large frame left the cushioned comfort. A second later, his big hands grasped my waist. He pulled me upright, my back against his hot, hard chest. Brushing aside my hair, he started a long trail of ticklish kisses that followed the curve of my spine and ended on my left buttock. Without warning, his massive paw smacked my plump cheek.

"Sergei!" I gasped and tried to slide away from him but he held tight.

"This ass of yours has been tempting me for months. The least you deserve is that single spanking."

Something primal ignited within me. "Do you...I mean...is that something you like to do?"

"Not in the way you're probably thinking," he said and sucked hard on my neck. I prayed he wouldn't leave a love bite but decided that I wasn't going to stop him from marking me. "But when I fuck you from behind, I'm going to make sure I leave my handprint right here."

I shivered with need when he patted my bottom and gave it a loving squeeze. I understood that his style of lovemaking would be rougher and more intense than anything I had ever experienced—and I couldn't wait to get started.

Apparently, Sergei shared my desire. He swept me up into his arms and shot me a look that warned me not to protest. Showing him that I liked the way he carried me, I wrapped my arms around his shoulders and brushed my lips against his cheek.

"*Potzluy menya*. Kiss me."

His deep voice did crazy things to me. I pressed my mouth to his as he placed his knee on the bed and took me down to the mattress. Our tongues tangled wildly. He crawled over me on the bed and planted his hands on either side of my head. Wanting to feel his skin on mine, I jerked free the towel and reached between our bodies. The moment my fingers touched his cock, Sergei cursed in Russian and smashed his mouth to mine, stabbing his tongue deep and groaning so loudly the vibrations rattled down my throat.

Marveling at the size of him, I realized I couldn't even

wrap my fingers around his shaft. I stroked down the length of his erection. His cock just kept going and going and going. My pussy throbbed at the very idea of having all of this buried inside me. It wouldn't happen tonight, not without a single condom available, but soon I hoped.

Careful. A small voice in my head warned me not to start making plans too far into the future with him. I had already decided to have him tonight but I couldn't—wouldn't—let myself think of having him any other night. This had to a one-time thing, a momentary indulgence, and nothing more.

Caressing me, Sergei worked his way down my body. He suckled my breast, pulling my nipple between his lips and laving it with his tongue. He released my flesh with a noisy pop before biting down gently and making me yelp at the quicksilver flash that pierced me. Soothing the tiny hurt with his tongue, he tweaked my other nipple, and I moaned at the wicked sensations rocking me.

Eyes closed, I ran my hands over his muscled shoulders and upper arms while he licked and nibbled me. No man had ever awakened these kinds of feelings within me. I felt so alive, the electric currents of arousal and desire vacillating through me. He touched me as if I were some incredibly precious thing. His fingers glided over my body and paused to enjoy interesting spots he discovered, the places that made me sigh and rock my hips.

When he slid to the floor next to the bed, I knew the moment he had earlier described to me had finally arrived. I struggled to drag a full breath into my lungs. Clutching my waist, Sergei dragged me right down to the edge of the mattress. He clasped my ankles and placed my feet into the position he wanted, spreading my legs wide open and swiping his palms up and down my inner thighs.

"Bianca." He breathed my name with a touch of awe and ran his thumb along the seam of my pussy. Showing me how gentle he could be, Sergei carefully parted my labia with those long, thick fingers so he could gaze upon the dewy center of me. He growled something in Russian that sounded suspiciously naughty, but I didn't have the courage to ask him to translate. He ran his fingers through my slick folds and held them up to show me the glistening evidence of my arousal. "Look at how wet you are for me, baby."

The low, rumbling way he pronounced baby made my pussy clench. Lightheaded, I shivered with anticipation as his dark head lowered toward that secret part of me. I didn't know what to expect but I had a feeling Sergei wasn't going to show me a few half-hearted flicks of his tongue before abandoning me to resentment and frustration.

He licked me right from the soaking entrance toward my throbbing clit and repeated the motion twice more. Drawing a moan from my throat, he fluttered his tongue over my clitoris. I gripped the covers under me and reveled in the wondrous way he explored my pussy. With leisurely licks, he painted me with the tip of his tongue and gave me time to acclimate to his intimate touch.

By slow degrees, he increased the tempo of his fluttering and flicking. He zeroed in on the rhythm and pressure that drove me wild. Running his hands along my sides, Sergei used that incredibly talented mouth of his to push me right over the edge. The intense, deliberate circles he drew around my clit made me dig my toes into the mattress.

When those first shuddery bursts started to rock my core, I clapped my hand over my mouth to stifle the loud cry I feared would soon erupt. Without missing a beat, Sergei reached up and tugged my hand away from my mouth. Our gazes clashed as he ate my pussy—and I came apart right in front of him

"Sergei!"

He groaned hungrily, the noise so excited, and began to feast on my pulsing flesh. As he attacked my pussy with that skillful tongue, I rolled my hips and rode the wondrous waves of my orgasm. The joyful explosions rocked me, making me shout his name again and again.

Shaking and breathing hard, I tried to come down from the euphoric high he'd induced, but Sergei wasn't done with me. Using his fingers, he parted the slick lips of my pussy and exposed my clit, drawing it out from beneath the hood to tease the super-sensitive bud with his tongue. I cried out and tried to wiggle free from him but Sergei put a hand on my breast and caught my gaze. "No."

"Please," I begged pitifully.

He shook his head. "No."

And then he fastened his lips around the pink pearl peeking out there and sucked hard. I nearly died, my heart stuttering in my chest and the air rushing out of my lungs. Sergei tongued me like some sort of human vibrator. It was unbelievable, and I found myself pressing my pussy against him in a desperate search for more.

"Ah!" My hips shot off the bed as my second climax slammed right into me. Sergei's big hands slid under me, gripping my ass while he went wild between my thighs. I came so damn hard I started to see spots dancing before my eyes. "Oh! Oh! *Oh*!"

Growling like a bear, Sergei finally showed me some mercy but he didn't abandon my pussy yet. No, he stabbed his tongue inside my channel to taste me in the wickedest way. Mouth agape, I tried not to pass out as he did unimaginably wanton things to me.

Limp and overwhelmed, I exhaled loudly when he finally dragged his mouth away from me. He replaced his tongue with two fingers, working first one and then the other into my slick passage, and thrusting them into me at a torturously slow pace.

Crawling over me, Sergei trapped me between his thighs, putting his knees on either side of me, and captured my mouth. I knew he felt my reaction to the sinful kiss we shared because he groaned against my lips when my inner walls clenched his invading fingers. He made love to my mouth while penetrating me with those long digits of his.

All along I had suspected there was this kind of passion locked up inside me but I never suspected it would take this outrageously sexy beast of a man to release it. Sergei read me like an open book. It was as if the instructions to showing me extreme pleasure were written on my skin in ink only he could see.

My thighs fell wide open when he shifted his position over me, putting his knee between both of mine for better access to my body. He latched onto my nipple and thrust into me faster and harder. His fingers curved inside my pussy, and my hands flew to his shoulders. Holding on for dear life, I howled like a banshee as he forced another powerful orgasm from me. "Sergei!"

He captured my mouth and swallowed my cries of passion. I surrendered to his wonderful kisses and the intense feelings he'd aroused within me. After coming so hard, so many times, I couldn't even form coherent thoughts. Deflated and aching, I gazed up at him in such wonder.

He grinned wolfishly and stunned me with the erotic

vision of him sucking my glistening nectar from his fingers. "You taste so fucking good, Bianca."

My face burned with such embarrassment at his frank comment. "The things you say!"

"They're true." He nuzzled me lovingly and kissed my neck. Hovering above me, Sergei smiled and traced my cheek with his finger. "You look so pretty after you come."

I reached up to caress his proud, strong face and felt myself falling hard for this impossibly complicated man. My brain screamed for me to put on the brakes but my heart? Oh, God. My heart was already entangled, and I didn't know if I had the strength to cut away from him.

Or if I even wanted to anymore.

"What are you thinking about, *milaya moya?*"

Refusing to get caught up in troubling thoughts, I pushed on his shoulders and pressed him onto his back. Up on my knees, I leaned forward and teased my mouth against his. "I'm thinking it's your turn now."

CHAPTER FOUR

Finally!

Head pounding and heart racing, Sergei watched Bianca crawl over him. She brushed her mouth to his and nipped at his lower lip before flicking their tongues together. His cock throbbed in time with his pulse as he wondered what she had in mind for him. Looking at those plump lips of hers, he prayed she planned to wrap them around his dick very soon.

Grabbing a pillow, he tucked it behind his head so he had a perfect view of her luscious body and gorgeous face. The taste of her sweet cunt still teased him. Those whimpering sighs and her high-pitched cries as she came against his tongue echoed in his head. He was already thinking of all the ways he could make Bianca scream his name when he was finally able to make love to her.

Her heavy, full breasts rubbed against his chest. Wanting to feel their weight, he cupped them. The dark discs of her nipples enticed him. He lightly pinched her flesh, drawing the points to puckered peaks. She sighed with such pleasure. Straddling his thigh, she rocked atop him and her wet pussy dragged against his leg. He battled the primitive urge to haul Bianca up a little higher and thrust up into the slick, feminine heat of her.

Buying the biggest box of condoms available jumped to the top of his to-do list. He'd always been very careful with the women he slept with, never trusting birth control to protect against a pregnancy or relying on anything less than that latex barrier to prevent an STD. The underground fighting club where he competed required the fighters to be tested regularly because the matches usually left the floors so bloody. He trusted the results provided by the club doctor but he would never ask Bianca to rely on them. He'd never put her at risk like that. He'd have to get proof so she would believe he took her safety seriously.

"Relax." Bianca placed her smaller hands on his chest and swept them across his pecs and down his biceps. "It's my turn to make you feel good."

He groaned as her hand glided down his abdomen. "You already are."

She sifted her fingers through the nest of curls there before grasping the base of his dick. "Look at how big you are, Sergei."

His cock had always been a point of fascination for women. He suspected it was one of the reasons so many of them threw themselves at him—and used him to satisfy their curiosity. Hearing Bianca remark on his impressive length and thickness touched on a weakness in his emotional armor. He didn't want to think she was like that but...

Eyes narrowed with concern, Bianca touched his jaw. "What's wrong? Did I—?"

Framing her face between his hands, he sat up and peered into the dark orbs that had ensnared him those many months ago. "Why are you letting me have you tonight?"

Her expression sharpened to one of annoyance. "What kind of question is that?"

"I want to know if you're letting this happen because you actually want me or if I'm a box you want to tick off some list."

"Did it ever occur to you that I'm wondering the same thing?"

He was taken aback by her question. "Why would you—?"

"Have you looked at us?" she interrupted. "You're, like, this ridiculously sexy Adonis of a man, and I'm this short, fat—"

Refusing to listen to Bianca cut herself down, he corrected gruffly, "Beautiful, smart, talented, successful businesswoman." He shook his head. "You could have any man you want. I'm the one who had to chase after you, remember?"

She studied his face. "Why, Sergei? Why me?"

"If you have to ask that question, I haven't done this right. Maybe I need to take another turn right down—"

"No." Smiling, she grasped his wrist and stopped his hand from slipping between her thighs. "I think I got the message."

Sergei laced their fingers together. Even though he typically despised any signs of weakness, he allowed that hard mask he'd worn since his teenage years to slip momentarily. "Do you like me at all, Bianca?"

She caressed his cheek but didn't answer immediately. Eventually, she admitted, "I've tried not to like you. I really have....but I can't stop what I'm feeling. I'm here with you right now in my bed and not in the guest room or downstairs on the couch because I want to be here with you. Because *I* want *you*."

Bianca kissed him then, her mouth so soft and sweet against his. She trailed her fingertips down his face, the pressure as light as a feather, and deepened their kiss. The erotic tangle of their tongues made his stomach clench and his balls ache. With a little shove, she pressed him back to the mattress and began peppering kisses down his chest. Her lips danced around his navel before traveling over the indentations at his hips.

The tease refused to put her lips where he really wanted them. She wiggled down the bed, positioning herself between his spread legs, and stroked his cock. She palmed his sac and kissed all around his shaft but didn't touch it.

Groaning, he pumped up into her hand and begged, "Use your mouth."

Bianca didn't make him plead again. When she sucked him between her lips, he bit off a curse and clawed at the bedding. Her hot mouth enveloped him, the suction just perfect. Her velvety tongue sent shivers through him. She moaned around his cock, and Sergei knew he wasn't going to last nearly as long as he wanted.

Using her hands to torment him, Bianca bobbed up and down on his shaft, her pliable lips gliding over the head of his cock. She massaged his balls while taking his dick deeper into her mouth and using that wonderful tongue of hers to stimulate him. Gripping the comforter under him, Sergei tried to maintain control. He didn't want to scare or hurt her by thrusting up into her mouth, even if every male impulse within him demanded it.

"Turn toward me," he said, his voice husky and breathless. "Let me touch you, Bianca."

She licked her lips and stared at him for a few seconds before doing as he'd asked. Though he would have loved the chance to sixty-nine her, he understood the differences in their height made that position an unlikely one for them. Instead, she moved to the side of him, putting her knees next to his right hip and presenting that unbelievably gorgeous ass of hers right where he wanted it.

After wetting his fingers with his tongue, Sergei began to probe her silky depths while she resumed her incredible blowjob. Her tight pussy squeezed his digits as he slowly fucked her with them. When he rubbed his thumb against her clit, her cunt fluttered around his fingers, telling him that she really liked that.

Mesmerized by her pussy, Sergei decided to surrender to the intense sensations she caused with her mouth and hands. All that sucking and stroking and fondling was making his balls draw up against his body. The soles of his feet began to buzz, and the muscles in his legs tightened.

"That feels so good, Bianca." He used his other hand to lovingly pet her plump bottom. "Don't stop, baby."

She whimpered around his cock and pressed back against the fingers buried in her pussy. Smiling, he gave her what she wanted, thrusting into her cunt a little faster and harder. She rewarded him by eagerly sliding her mouth up and down his shaft and sucking him with such enthusiasm.

Whispering her name, he flexed his feet and tried to stave off his impending orgasm. When she took him even deeper into her mouth and moaned, the erotic vibrations hurtled him over the edge. At the last second, he wondered if she would be angry with him for spilling his seed in her mouth. Trying to give her warning, in case she wanted to pull off, he hurriedly grunted, "Bianca! I'm co—"

He didn't get the rest of it out. Her soft lips tightened around his cock and she sucked him hard while rubbing her tongue right there against the crown of him. The dam built around those months of pent-up sexual frustration detonated then and he let go. Growling her name, he came like a fucking freight train, his hips rocking and his legs shaking as she milked every last drop of cum right out of him and swallowed.

Shuddering and panting, Sergei groaned while she licked him clean. When she pushed up onto her knees and shifted to face him, he kept his fingers buried in her pussy. Her eyebrows arched questioningly but he didn't take his hand away. Her mouth fell open when he started to thrust into her and strum her clit. "Sergei..."

"Come for me, baby. One more time and then I'll let you sleep."

Clutching his forearm, she let him have what he wanted. He reached up to palm her breast and gave it a squeeze while his other hand drove her crazy. Wetter than any woman he'd ever been with, Bianca bucked against his fingers, swiveling her hips and grinding her pussy on him. He couldn't wait to get his mouth on that juicy slit of hers again, to pull her swollen clit between his lips and circle it with his tongue.

As he made her lose control, Sergei enjoyed the sight of her climaxing. He couldn't believe this was actually happening. He expected to wake up any minute now, alone in his bed and feeling so empty.

But it wasn't a dream. This was real. Tonight, Bianca was his.

When she fell onto the bed next to him, Sergei trapped her in place with his leg and took his time loving her mouth and stroking her body. He wanted Bianca to know this wasn't just a one-night stand to him. He needed her to know that he wanted something long-term with her.

Eventually, he found the strength to disentangle their bodies. She darted into the bathroom, tossing the still-damp tuxedo pants he'd requested at him. He slipped into them and went downstairs to check the house one last time. Using the side entrance to her house, he walked out to his SUV, grabbed his gym bag and gun, and locked the vehicle. He didn't expect trouble, but with a prowler on the loose, he couldn't be too careful, especially where Bianca was concerned.

Satisfied the house was secure, he climbed upstairs and found Bianca already in bed. He paused in the doorway to appreciate the scene. She was curled on her side with her hand resting on the empty space she'd left for him. His chest constricted at the image she presented and the teasing glimpse of a life he'd always wanted, of a woman of his own and a nice home.

Of a future that seemed somehow always just beyond his reach.

Feeling a bit shaken up by the thoughts invading his mind, Sergei dropped his gym bag on the ottoman and crossed the room. He stripped out of the tuxedo pants, switched off the lamp and slid into bed next to Bianca. The moment he opened his arms to her, she cuddled up against him and pecked his jaw. "Good night, Sergei."

His lips curved in a pleased smile at the gentle moment they were sharing. "Good night, Bianca."

She hooked her leg across his and rested her cheek on his chest. Once she had settled into a comfortable spot, he pressed a tender kiss to her forehead. Despite the exhaustion gripping him, he found it impossible to drift off to sleep. Content to stroke her hair, Sergei stared up at the dark ceiling and considered all the ways he could convince Bianca that she could trust him and that he was worth breaking her rule.

He'd chased after her for five months without so much as looking at another woman. If she wasn't impressed by his dogged determination to win her, then he would simply have to try harder.

Sergei had finally tasted his personal heaven—and he wasn't giving her up without a fight.

* * *

When I came downstairs the next morning, I hesitated just outside the entrance to my kitchen. Feeling a bit nervous, I touched my hair and the front of my robe. Sergei had already slipped out of bed and out of sight by the time I finally dragged my groggy backside into the bathroom to go through my morning primping routine. I had no idea how he could wake up so dang early, especially after that torrid night we'd shared.

My face burned with the memories of all the dirty things we'd done together. I couldn't remember ever behaving so wantonly. I sure as hell had never gone all the way on a first date. Not that we'd even had a real date. I cringed at the realization I had fallen into bed with him so easily. What in the world must he think of me?

Hoping he wouldn't mistake my embarrassment for shame, I schooled my features and stepped into the kitchen. Wearing a gray T-shirt and black shorts, Sergei stood with his back to me while he tended something on the stove and listened to a Russian language radio station. I hadn't known that channel existed so the sound of it took me by surprise.

Judging by the scents filling the kitchen and the ingredients on the big island behind him, Sergei had fixed pancakes. Impressed by his sweet gesture, I decided to show him something equally as sweet. I tried to remember exactly how to pronounce good morning in his native tongue. Vivian's voice echoed in my head. I wasn't sure if I could get it out correctly but I was going to try.

"Um...*dobroye utro.*"

Spatula in hand, Sergei spun toward me. He looked amused as he repeated the greeting. Then, with a teasing slant to that sexy mouth of his, he added, "I'll be sure to tell Vivian to give you high marks on your next report card."

I rolled my eyes and headed for the coffee pot on the counter. "Very funny."

Sergei stepped close to me, wound his arm around my waist and hauled me against him. Stooping down, he claimed my lips in a sinful kiss. "I hope you like blueberry pancakes."

My insides quaking from the possessive swipe of his mouth. "I do."

He released me and gave my bottom a pat before returning to his post at the stove. "I hope you don't mind me using the blueberries in the fridge. After I'd dumped them into the bowl, it occurred to me you might be saving them for something special."

"I normally just toss them into my yogurt in the mornings." Pouring coffee into a cup, I said, "Cooking breakfast for me is pretty special, Sergei."

He shrugged. "I was hungry and thought you would be too."

I didn't miss the way he wouldn't meet my curious gaze. He said it with the faintest hint of defensiveness. Was he feeling as emotionally exposed as me this morning? Was he questioning where this thing between us was going or if I'd simply used him in the way I had a feeling a lot of other women had?

Remembering last night's glimpse at the chink in his emotional armor, I abandoned my cup of coffee and wrapped my arms around his waist. He glanced down at me, his gaze almost wary. "I'm really glad you're here this morning."

Sergei visibly relaxed and dropped a kiss on the top of my head. "I'm glad you let me stay."

He turned back to the pancakes and I finished fixing my cup of coffee. At the round table near the bay window overlooking the backyard, I discovered the newspaper and two place settings. He carried over a plate piled high with steaming hot pancakes as well as a butter dish and the organic syrup I preferred. After turning the radio to an English-language news program, he ducked into the refrigerator to find some juice before rejoining me. Soon, we were eating breakfast and trading sections of the newspaper. To say it was a surreal experience was an understatement.

"What is that, sweetheart?"

Secretly loving all the little pet names he used for me, I looked in the direction he was pointing with his fork. "Oh. That's my design board. It's the spot where I collect all the pieces that inspire me for redoing the house."

"It's nice." He splashed more orange juice into his glass. "What time do you leave for church?"

I patted my mouth with a napkin. "Ten. It's not that far from here but I have to pick Mama up first and that takes a while these days."

"How is your mother doing? Is rehab helping her?" He must have seen the surprise on my face because he quickly added, "Vivian told me about the stroke your mother had last year."

"Oh. Well, rehab is going well. It's a lifelong process, I

guess."

He hesitated before asking, "They took her leg, yes?"

"It was the diabetes and high blood pressure that caused the stroke in the first place. Then, when she was in the ICU recovering from the stroke, she developed a blood clot in her leg that caused some problems with her feet." I shook my head sadly. "Basically, those first four months after her stroke were a nightmare. Every time they would solve one problem, another would pop right up. They took her right leg when they couldn't get the infection under control, and she had another mini-stroke while in surgery."

Sergei swore softly and reached for my hand. "I'm sorry, Bianca. That must have been difficult to go through alone."

"I wasn't totally alone. I had my extended family and the church and the boutique employees and Vivian. She used to go right from her morning classes to the boutique to run the registers and help with brides all afternoon and then she'd go straight to Samovar to wait tables until ten at night. Sometimes, she'd let herself into my mama's house—where I was staying at the time—to do my laundry or clean the place."

"I'm not surprised. Vivian doesn't do anything by half-measures." He pulled another stack of pancakes onto his plate. "Your mother has live-in help now?"

"No. She's in an assisted-living community."

The knife he'd stabbed into the butter stopped midway to his plate. "You put your mother in a nursing home?"

Taken aback by his tone, I bristled defensively. "It's not a nursing home, and I didn't put her there. She chose to go there."

"I find it hard to believe that any person would choose to go into a place like that." He gestured around the kitchen with the knife. "Your mother should be here with you."

I started to tell him off but then it occurred to me that maybe this wasn't about me at all. Leaning back in my chair, I asked, "Where does your mother live, Sergei?"

His jaw tightened, and he smashed the butter onto the pancakes in front of him. Finally, he growled, "I had to leave her behind."

The pain etched into his handsome face slashed at me. "Why?"

He glanced away from me and fixed his gaze on the opposite wall. "Something very bad happened back in Russia, and I had to get out—fast. There wasn't time to make arrangements for my mother or my brother—"

"You have a brother?"

He dragged his gaze back to me. "I had two brothers. Now, I...I only have one."

"Why do I get the feeling we have more in common than I'd ever suspected?"

"Because we do," Sergei said with a sigh. "But it's much too early to get into all of that ugliness."

"Yeah, you're probably right." I didn't feel like digging into the painful memories of my past either. "So your mother and brother are back in Moscow?"

"Yes."

"And...you haven't tried to bring them over?"

His expression turned dark. "I've been trying for two years. It's a complicated and very expensive process."

Another thought suddenly struck. "Um...are you legal?"

Sergei snorted and sliced his fork through his pancakes. "Yes. I have a green card. I'm a permanent resident."

"Oh. Okay."

"Why? Would you not date me if I wasn't?" He popped a triangle of pancakes into his mouth.

"I would be hesitant to get involved with someone who could be deported at any moment." I fiddled with my fork and poked at the sliver of pancakes left on my plate. "Is that what we're doing? Dating, I mean."

He swallowed his mouthful. "I thought we were going to start. After last night, I'm not going back to the way it was between us. We either begin to date and give things between us a try, or it ends here with breakfast."

Despite my reservations, I couldn't bear the thought of sending him away. The connection between us was too real to deny. "I'd like to try dating."

"Good." He ate another bite while I sipped my coffee. Sighing again, he reached out and touched my knee. "I shouldn't have snapped at you about your mother. That's…that's *my* baggage and *my* bullshit. I'm sure that your mother is very happy where she is now."

"It's a nice place. Really," I added upon seeing the skepticism that flashed in his eyes. "She has her own apartment and round-the-clock access to skilled nursing and on-site rehab. There's a chef and housekeeping and an amazing recreation center where she gets together with other residents. She even plays video games now!"

Sergei laughed. "Are you serious?"

I giggled. "Yeah. It's part of developing her motor skills, I guess."

"Maybe I'll have to challenge her to a game."

I tried to imagine Sergei and my mother playing virtual tennis. The image was just too comical. "She'd probably like that."

"I want to meet her."

I swallowed hard. "We'll see."

He smiled knowingly but didn't push the issue. We

finished breakfast, and I started to clear away the table. When I began to load the dishwasher, he called out to stop me. "I'll do that after you're gone. Come here, Bianca."

Wondering what he was playing at, I nevertheless returned to the table. He clasped my hands and dragged me between his wide open thighs. The heat of his caressing hands seared right through the silky fabric of my robe and the thin cotton nightshirt I'd donned earlier. He captured my mouth in a slow, easy kiss. The taste of blueberries and the sugary sweetness of syrup teased me.

When his hand glided along my thigh and slid toward my panties, I gasped and pulled away from his mouth. "Sergei, what are you doing?"

"Sh." He gently hushed me while slipping his fingers under the cotton guarding my pussy. "Let me."

Even though I could think of a dozen reasons why we should stop, I slid my feet apart and welcomed his sensual touch. Sergei nibbled my earlobe while probing my folds. When he cupped my breast, I arched into him and groaned, encouraging his exploration.

With a needy growl, Sergei lifted me right up and placed me on the table. He swept the newspaper onto the floor and shoved aside the remaining dishes and breakfast items. A man on a mission, he opened my robe, pushed up my nightgown and jerked my panties down my thighs, throwing them over his shoulder and letting them land heaven only knew were. Before I recovered from the shock of being so hastily undressed, Sergei freed that massive cock of his and stroked it from the base to the tip and back down again.

Breathless, I reminded him of our lack of protection. "Sergei, we can't—"

"We aren't," he assured me. Leaning over me, the big,

sexy Russian kissed me until I was dizzy. "I'm not going to make love to you on a table." His mouth curved impishly. "Well—not our first time, at least."

Still wondering what he had in mind, I gasped when he dragged the blunt crown of his fat cock between my labia. He gathered some of the wetness at my entrance and used it to ease the friction between our bodies. When he circled my throbbing clit with the head of his penis, I finally got it.

"Ah!" Falling back against the table, I brought my feet up to rest against the wooden edge. Sergei's free hand slid under my nightgown to torment and tease me. He continued to rub his cock between the petals of my sex and made sure to bump against my clit with every stroke.

I couldn't believe how good it felt. Unlike the pressure and firmness of his fingers, the tip of his cock was softer and yielding but so hot and smooth. The width of his thick shaft stimulated so much more of me. Wanting him closer, I hooked my feet against his backside and hauled him in a little tighter. He grinned down at me and sped up the pace of his thrusting cock.

Clutching his forearm, I was shocked by how close I was to coming. Somehow Sergei had figured out the combination to my orgasm lock. He swirled the head of his dick around my clit, and I came with a loud cry. The intense waves of pleasure rolled through me while he rubbed against me faster and harder.

Still shaking with joyful bursts, I wrapped my hand around his cock and started to caress him. Sergei gripped my thighs in those big hands of his and pumped against my palm. Sucking in air, he thrust toward me and climaxed. The first splash of his seed hit my lower belly, followed quickly by another and another.

Sergei slumped over me on the table and crashed his

mouth to mine. Gathering me in his arms, he dropped down into the chair and hauled me onto his lap. He smoothed back my hair and whispered sweetly to me in between his erotic kisses, telling me I was beautiful and sexy. I could feel the pearly beads of his cum cooling on my skin and reached down to wipe them away with the hem of my nightgown.

"Don't," he chided softly. "I like the look of my cum on your skin."

I should have been offended by the remark but the possessive glint in his eyes made me quiver. With a quirked tilt to my mouth, I asked, "What? Are you marking your territory?"

"As pretty as you are, I probably need to," he replied with a husky laugh.

"That goes both ways," I murmured, thinking of how damn sexy he was and how many other women would kill to have him.

"You think I'm pretty?"

I rolled my eyes and pinched his arm. "You know what I meant."

"I do." Chuckling, he brushed our mouths together. "Even though I want to take you to bed, I know I have to let you go. You need to get moving if you're going to get to church on time."

"Considering the sinful things we've been doing, I definitely need my dose of the gospel this morning."

Sergei gestured toward the ceiling. "I hear he's rather forgiving."

Sliding off his lap, I pecked his cheek. "For our sakes, let's hope so."

Laughing, he popped my bottom before I moved out of reach. "I'll have that door fixed in a few hours."

"I won't be home until the early evening. Mama and I

go out for a nice lunch after church and then she likes to go over to the shop for a few hours."

"I'll take care of dinner."

My heart raced at the idea of spending another night with him. Was I ready for that? We had agreed to try dating but this didn't feel exactly like dating. We were charting new territory for me. I'd never allowed a man to stay over at my place, and this breakfast thing was a first, too. Now he wanted to make me dinner?

"Unless you'd rather I give you some space tonight?" he asked carefully.

"No." The word was out of my mouth before I had a chance to overthink the situation. I decided to go with my instincts on this one—and my instincts urged me to keep him close. "I'd like to spend time with you tonight."

Still seated, he grasped my hand and tugged me back to his side. Cupping my nape, he peered into my eyes. "You're afraid."

I swallowed and nodded. "I blew off all that talk of my prowler during the reception but honestly? It scared me to hear something—someone—walking around my yard in the dark. I liked having you here with me last night. It made me feel secure."

As if making a vow, he pressed his lips to my bared neck. "I'll keep you safe, Bianca."

Embracing him, I inhaled his masculine scent and relished his heat. "I know you will."

CHAPTER FIVE

"Well, what do you think?" George wiped his hands on a rag and gestured to the beautiful wooden door they had just finished installing.

Sergei stepped back to admire the stained glass inset in the polished and richly stained wood. "It's perfect. She's going to love it."

"It's damn close to the picture you brought down to my warehouse."

Eerily so, Sergei thought to himself. He had gone to see George hoping the master carpenter would have something left over from one of those multi-million dollar builds that might fit Bianca's house. He had been fully prepared to walk away empty handed and in need of a temporary door from a hardware store. The second George had taken a look at the photo Sergei had borrowed from Bianca's inspiration board, the older man had simply laughed and beckoned Sergei to join him in that massive workshop of his.

"You know," George leaned his shoulder against the house, "I actually put in a job bid here a few months ago."

"For what?"

"Full bathroom and kitchen remodel and the carriage house out back. I got the feeling she wasn't expecting numbers that high. She was really sweet about it but declined to hire us. It's a shame." George ran an appreciative hand along the side of the house. "It's a beautiful old place. I still can't believe she got it for a song at that tax sale."

Sergei suppressed the annoyance that flared within him at the discovery that Bianca had probably gone to every single contractor in the damned city except him for help. "Do you still have a copy of that bid?"

"Sure. You want it?"

"Yes."

George's brow lifted. "You thinking of taking on the work? I thought your guys only did retail."

"They do. It wouldn't be my guys. It would be me alone on some projects and hiring out for others."

After settling up with George for the cost of the door, he tidied up the front porch and entryway before washing his hands. The lukewarm water pouring over his hands reminded him that he needed to get a plumber out here to look into replacing that water heater. There were certain jobs Sergei didn't mind tackling on his own but plumbing wasn't one of them.

His phone began to ring so he dug it out of his pocket and glanced at the screen. The number he recognized as Kostya's made his chest tighten. A call from the cleaner on a Sunday? That was never a good thing. "Yes?"

"Meet me at Sugar's. We have a problem."

The call ended just as abruptly as it began. The very last place he wanted to visit on a Sunday afternoon was one of Kostya's strip clubs, but he didn't question the order. With a tired sigh, Sergei pocketed his phone and left Bianca's house. It wasn't until he'd been driving for nearly ten minutes that he remembered the new keys to the front door were both in his pocket. Thankfully, Bianca could still get in the side or back entrances. He hoped to beat her home because he wanted to see her face when she first noticed the new door.

By the time he made it to the strip club, Sergei had the emotionless mask that he wore at work firmly in place. Whatever Kostya had called him here to see was probably going to be terrible. After his amazing night and morning with Bianca, Sergei began to understand how difficult it was for Nikolai to separate the two halves of his life—and why their boss wanted to move the family into cleaner, easier earning.

Parking his SUV in the rear of the joint, he made sure to lock the doors. Unlike some of the higher-end clubs Kostya partly owned, Sugar's was in a seedier area and served a low-rent clientele. At the back door, he banged twice on the dented metal with his balled-up fist and waited for an answer. A scrawny kid who looked to be maybe twenty opened the door and waved him inside.

Sergei stepped by the kid and headed down the narrow hallway. The heavy hip-hop beats from the stage area and main floor reverberated through the thin walls of the backstage section of the building. A couple of women in bikinis two sizes too small strutted by him, their bodies dusted with glitter and their faces covered in a thick layer of makeup. Here, in close quarters, he was able to see what the makeup and onstage lighting camouflaged—the tired lines around their mouths and eyes, the subtle signs of aging and the deadness in their gazes.

Hugging the wall, he gave them a wide berth but smiled kindly. He understood only too well what it was like to be stuck in a job that seemed to suck the life right out of you. Until Nikolai had transitioned him to Vivian's keeper, Sergei had basically spent the last few years hurting or intimidating anyone who stepped out of line or threatened the family. It wore on him, tearing at his conscience and worse. In the end, his loyalty had been rewarded with a stake in the construction business and the cushier job protecting the boss' most precious possession—but he remained firmly under Nikolai's thumb.

Stripping for fat, groping fucks with handfuls of wrinkled dollar bills on a Sunday afternoon wasn't a dream job for these women. They weren't shaking their asses and rubbing their tits in the faces of men that soured their stomachs because they enjoyed it. No, they wanted to keep a roof over their heads or food in their children's bellies or buy medicine for their sick parents.

The blonde closest to him playfully rubbed his stomach as she passed. He didn't bat away her hand, though the urge was strong. In a world where flirtation went hand-in-hand with a paycheck, he couldn't blame her for trying, but his entire body rebelled at the alien sensation of another woman touching him. With her kisses and gentle caresses, Bianca had branded him as hers. As if already mated, it was only her scent and heat that he craved.

The women continued on their way, and Sergei's nose twitched at the smell of their cheap clashing perfumes. His brain conjured the pleasant scents that swirled around Bianca. Everything she chose, from her soap to her perfume and hair products, complemented one another so nicely. She just smelled so damned good.

Kostya stepped out of a door. The grim look on the man's face didn't bode well. Sergei joined the cleaner, glanced through the open doorway behind him and was surprised to find Nikolai crouched in front of a black couch where a couple of women were sobbing softly into their hands. The sight of his boss in a strip club knocked Sergei for a loop. As long as he had known the boss, he had never once seen him in a place like this.

Upon closer inspection of the women, he realized they had been beaten—or worse—overnight. After years of fighting for money, Sergei had come to recognize the color shifts in bruises that formed after a bout of violence. The maroon splotches and purple streaks marking their arms told him the oldest blows had happened sometime last night. Some of the newer, fresher marks on their necks and bellies were only a few hours old. Fury bubbled in the pit of his stomach when he began to count up the bruises.

Movement in the corner of the room caught Sergei's eye. He spotted Besian, the recently promoted head of the local Albanian outfit, leaning against the wall and looking murderous. Glancing back at the women, Sergei tried to figure out what the hell was happening here. He couldn't make the connection between Kostya's piece of action in Sugar's, the two strippers and the two bosses until Nikolai addressed one of the women in Russian, telling her that he was going to take care of everything. It occurred to him that the woman was one of them, part of their tight-knit community of immigrants and ex-pats. Whatever terrible thing had happened to her, Nikolai had taken it as a personal affront.

Rising tall, the boss glanced at him. The briefest hint of sadness flashed across the other man's face. Was he thinking of how nice and easy it was last night at Ivan's wedding and how messy things were probably going to turn? Did Nikolai feel some guilt at whatever he was going to ask of Sergei?

Besian stepped forward, laid a gentle hand on the other woman's shoulder and spoke to her in Albanian. The sound of ice rattling against plastic caught Sergei's attention. He leaned back for a better view of the hall and discovered the scrawny kid bringing a bucket of ice from the bar and a handful of plastic bags and towels.

With the women occupied nursing their injuries, Nikolai gestured to the hallway. Sergei fell into step behind the two bosses who followed Kostya to an office. When Besian dropped into the chair behind the desk and looked instantly comfortable, Sergei realized the Albanian owned part of the club. It wasn't the first time Kostya had crossed party lines to make a business deal, and Nikolai obviously didn't mind. Still, Sergei doubted their boss would have let anyone else in their crew get away with so bold a move.

Closing the door, Sergei took up a sentry's position inside the office, automatically putting his body between Nikolai and any danger that might come through the portal. After settling into a chair across from the desk, the boss rubbed his face between his tattooed hands and exhaled roughly. He'd seemed tenser lately and short-tempered. Sergei hadn't asked what was bothering Nikolai because questions like that were none of his business, but that didn't stop him from worrying about the man who had saved his life not so long ago.

"Last night, those women were picked up a by a couple of guys who turned out to be recruits for *nochniye volki*." Nikolai said the words with a disgusted sneer.

Night Wolves. It was the name of the local skinhead gang. They weren't major players in the Houston underworld, especially not after backing Grisha in his failed coup against Nikolai. Most of their gang had been rounded up on charges of murder and human trafficking. The men who had avoided the legal entanglements seemed to be on a recruiting drive for racist assholes, something that Houston sadly seemed to have in abundance these days.

"Apparently, the girls thought they were working a private bachelor party, but as you can see, it turned out to be anything but that. Those two got away and hid at a friend's house until this afternoon. There was another one who wasn't so lucky." Nikolai shook his head as he continued the gruesome tale. "This morning, they found her body behind Besian's social club."

Sergei inwardly winced but didn't allow a single change to his cool, collected façade. His gut roiled. What had those two women in the other room survived? What about the one who hadn't been able to get away? What had she endured? No doubt those racist bastards had been exceedingly cruel.

The boss spun his wedding ring around his finger. Was Nikolai thinking of the horrific ordeal Vivian had survived when she had been kidnapped and prepared for trafficking? Or was he thinking about the young girls—most of them underage—who had been held captive with Vivian and later rescued from the clutches of the Night Wolves gang that was selling them?

"I've got the police so far up my ass I can taste donuts." Frustration filled Besian's voice. "They know the woman worked here so they're convinced I had her taken out. It's so stupid. Shawntelle was one of my best earners! Why would I hurt her?"

Nikolai's irritated gaze slid to Kostya. "This is exactly why I keep us out of this line of work." He gestured around the office. "You sit here in this nice room and rake in all the money while other people have to degrade themselves." He let that cold, terrifying stare of his land on the two business partners. "I hope the thousand dollars they paid you upfront for that bachelor party was worth it."

Kostya visibly flinched but didn't utter a word in his defense. Even Besian squirmed a bit uncomfortably. Thinking about the women in the other room, Sergei decided to break the silence. "What are we going to do about the girls?"

Nikolai glanced at him. "Danny is on his way. Take them to see the doctor. I would have preferred for them to go the official route, through the emergency room and the police, but they're refusing so this is the best we can do for them."

Sergei didn't like the idea of covering this up, but the women couldn't be forced. They likely thought they would be safer relying on street justice for protection than the police or district attorney. Sergei wished their instincts were wrong—but he conceded they were probably right. Knowing what they had been through, he would be extra gentle with them. "I'll take care of them."

"I know you will." Clearly, Nikolai had handpicked him out of every man at his disposal for a reason. This was a task that required some sensitivity. "When they've been treated, take them to the apartment complex we just renovated. They had their wallets stolen so they're afraid trouble will follow them home. The manager is expecting them at the complex, and Danny will handle whatever moving arrangements need to be made."

Sergei had a feeling both women would both be given better jobs to go with their new homes, probably at Besian's expense. Not that new jobs and more money made up for the beatings they had taken. "And when I'm done with them?"

Nikolai's shoulders lifted in a careless, easy shrug. "Go home. It's your day off."

The direction surprised Sergei. He'd come here expecting to put his skills to use and now the boss was assigning him glorified babysitting duties. "Aren't we going after them?"

Nikolai's brow lifted with some surprise at his question. "On my terms, yes."

His statement put an end to the discussion. A heartbeat later, a knock sounded at the door. Danny's voice carried through the wood, and Sergei was dismissed to handle the tasks he had been assigned. Getting the women medical treatment and taking them to the apartment complex took up the next two hours.

While Danny got them situated in their new housing, Sergei drove to the nearest big-box store and picked up some basics. Pushing the cart down each aisle, he couldn't shake thoughts of Bianca. In his mind, the images of those bruised women melded with her sweet face. His stomach churned at the very idea of her being touched by such violence. He had never killed a man—but he wouldn't even blink at the idea of doing something so brutal in defense of Bianca.

Back at the complex, he separated the groceries, toiletries and household items and carted them to the apartments the women had been given. He spotted a handful of Besian's men loitering in the parking lot and deduced they had taken on the task of guarding the women.

Nikolai's remark about settling this on his own terms circled round and round in Sergei's head. Was he thinking of inviting Darren Blake, the leader of the Night Wolves, to a sit-down? When the Hermanos, a Latin street gang, and the Albanians had been at each other's throats earlier in the year, Nikolai had brokered a peace by offering them some of the illegal action he'd wanted to shed in lieu of safer earning avenues. It had been an elegant solution that had yielded surprising results, especially when Grisha had pulled his shit and murdered anyone who got in his way of usurping Nikolai's position. Both outfits had stood side-by-side with Nikolai and provided a tremendous amount of help.

Sergei suspected the two bosses wanted to find a way to avoid an all-out war with the skinheads. Bloodshed and violence weren't good for business, and nowadays Nikolai and Besian were businessmen first. Whether the skinheads were smart enough to take a deal remained to be seen. They were new enough on the block that they might think showing their strength was an easy way to build their reputation as men who shouldn't be crossed.

And they couldn't be more wrong.

"How much do I owe you for this?" The woman called Katya poked through the bags he had placed on the small dining table that came with the sparsely furnished unit.

"Nothing."

She shot a dubious look his way and hugged her oversized shirt tighter to her body. He didn't miss the way she raked her appraising gaze up and down his body and took the smallest step backward. The realization that something about him—his size, his demeanor or simply his connections with the underworld—frightened her left him feeling hollow and pained. It was a stark reminder of the reasons Bianca wanted to keep him at arm's length and how many obstacles he still had to surmount to convince the woman he wanted to let him stay in her life.

With a tired, resigned voice, she said, "I can't pay you back today. It…it wouldn't be any good for you. Come back later this week, and I'll make it worth your while."

Aghast that she thought he wanted to trade sex for food and shelter, Sergei slashed his hand through the air. "*No.* When I said nothing, I meant *nothing.* You don't have to trade favors for anything that you've been given today. Do you understand? If any man bothers you, come to see me or the boss. They won't bother you again. This is all free. No strings."

She seemed skeptical but nodded. "All right."

Glad to have that out of the way, he bid her farewell and left the apartment. Hard and brutal as he was, Sergei's skin still crawled at the idea of forcing some woman to blow him for the promise of protection. His stomach clenched as he considered the way he had maneuvered his way into Bianca's bed last night. He had definitely overstepped the line when he'd come out of her bedroom in a towel and when he had cajoled her into letting him have one kiss.

But he hadn't forced Bianca. He had flirted outrageously and won his chance fair and square. This morning, she had come to him of her own accord, hugging him and kissing him and enjoying their sensual play together. She was an incredibly strong woman and wouldn't have allowed him to take any liberties with her. Over the last five months, she had proven that she had no qualms about shutting him down.

Sergei noticed Nikolai's car rolling into the parking lot. Sure his boss would want a word, he leaned back against the door of his SUV and waited. Kostya climbed out of the driver's seat of the outrageously expensive sports car but headed straight for the apartments instead of making the detour to Sergei's vehicle with Nikolai.

"You got them situated?" His lucky lighter clamped in his hand, Nikolai fiddled with the souvenir he had carried since his teenage years. As far as Sergei knew, the boss hadn't had a smoke since January, but an unopened pack of cigarettes still sat in his desk at Samovar. No matter how strong the urge must have been to light up and give in to a lifelong addiction, Nikolai seemed to be beating it.

"I did. The doctor patched them up but they didn't have any serious injuries. It's all bruises."

His boss hesitated before asking, "Were they *hurt*?"

Sergei understood he meant raped and shook his head. "No. They seem to have escaped the worst of it."

"A small mercy, I suppose." Nikolai tucked his lighter back into his pocket. "Are you going to ask me or not?"

Sergei considered the invitation. "What are we doing? Why aren't we going after them right now?"

"We're waiting for the perfect opening. This isn't the right time to rise to provocation."

"Because they're only strippers?"

Nikolai's eyes narrowed to slits, and Sergei realized he had overstepped. "Last night, it was two dancers. Tomorrow, it might be one of our wives...or a girlfriend," he added pointedly. "These men aren't playing by the rules."

"I understand."

Nikolai tilted his head. "Do you know why I didn't send you to beat the shit out of those skinheads today?"

Sergei took a moment to study all the angles. Finally, he said, "Because I'm fighting in less than three weeks and I could hurt my hands."

"That's part of it," the boss agreed. "Before he left on his honeymoon, Ivan made me promise I would keep you out of trouble before this tournament. He worries about you because he knows what it's like to be inside that cage. I need you healthy if we're going to win."

His mouth slanted with amusement at the way Nikolai

said *we*. The last time Sergei had checked, he was the only one taking hit after hit and kick after kick inside that cage. Sure, the money he earned was nice, and Nikolai made sure to pay him a fat bonus after every match, but the punishment his body had taken over the years was beginning to show its toll.

After studying the way Ivan and Alexei Sarnov, another notorious underground fighter, had used their skills and winnings to escape the clutch of the mob, Sergei had made his own exit plans. It wouldn't be easy and it would probably cost him some friendships he held very dear, but he couldn't do this forever. He had to get out before he ended up in prison—or dead.

Now that Bianca had let him into her life, he was going to fight for the chance to stay in it permanently, to build something new and *clean* with her.

"How did it go last night?"

Nikolai's question surprised Sergei. The man never pried into his private life. "Fine."

The boss didn't miss a beat. "I'll have to tell Vee her ploy worked."

"Not the way she had planned," he replied gruffly.

"Do I even want to know?"

Sergei glanced away and admitted, "I kicked down her door."

The other man's eyes widened fractionally, betraying his shock. "Since you didn't call me to bail you out of jail last night, I assume you had a good reason for it."

"I thought she was being attacked, but she had fallen out of her shower."

"I see."

Sergei shrugged. "It was an interesting night."

Nikolai's mouth twitched with a hint of a smile. "I'm sure it was." He paused. "You like this girl very much."

He wasn't asking but Sergei confirmed it with a nod. "That's why I didn't send you today."

Now it was Sergei's turn to frown with confusion. "What does that mean?"

"It means that you're more sensitive to that white supremacist bullshit than the others. I was concerned you might take that more personally and react in ways I couldn't anticipate, especially once you realized the woman they killed last night was black."

Sergei started to protest but clamped his lips together. Nikolai was right, of course.

"But it's more than that, Sergei. We like to pretend that our world is just like the world that Vee and Bianca live in, but it's not. This thing with *nochniye volki*? It's not going to end quickly or peacefully. It's going to be messy. I'm trying to mitigate the collateral damage, but I make no promises." Nikolai's cold stare sent a chill through him. "You understand what I'm trying to tell you?"

"*Da.*" Sergei got the message. It was only a matter of time until the skinheads learned that a member of the boss' inner circle was dating a black woman. After that, all bets were off. Bianca would become the perfect target for striking at their family—and it was entirely his fault for pursuing her and putting her in that precarious position.

"When you consider Bianca's history with these assholes—"

Sergei held up his hand. "What history?"

Surprised, Nikolai gestured toward him. "Vee told me that she explained to you about Bianca's brother."

"She said he was killed in a robbery at a convenience store. She said it was a bunch of gang punks."

"Yes—a white supremacist gang. The leader of the Wolves, Darren Blake, is the older brother of the guy who killed Bianca's brother. They were attacking a store owned by some immigrants. Pakistani, I think."

Reeling from that revelation, Sergei began to grasp how incredibly dangerous this situation was. He wiped his hand down his face and exhaled roughly. Seeking advice from a man who had seen and survived it all, he asked, "What do I do?"

Nikolai didn't hesitate. "Walk away from her."

An invisible band constricted his chest. He'd never had a heart attack but the thought of walking away from Bianca made him *hurt*. "I can't."

"I know." The boss sounded sad about that. "I tried with Vee for years but..." His hand brushed chest, right above his heart, and he shook his head. "If you can't leave her alone, you have to keep her close."

"At night, that's not a problem, but during the day, I'm watching Vivian."

"So hire it out," Nikolai suggested.

He thought of the younger guys who were slowly working their way into Nikolai's crew. A handful of them trained at Ivan's warehouse. They were strong, smart and hungry for more opportunities to earn. It was a good compromise, but he would have to be careful. Bianca would hate being guarded so he would have to give clear instructions to stay out of her sight. The last thing he wanted was to upset or terrify her.

Nikolai clapped his shoulder and turned toward the apartment complex. "Go home, Sergei. Enjoy your woman." He glanced back and added, "Vee wanted me to remind you that she's running in the morning. She wants to do the full 10K."

The boss didn't seem happy about that. Last week, Sergei had overheard Vivian arguing with her husband about her morning runs and the charity half marathon she planned to complete in June. He had smartly stayed out of it, but it had left him wondering about the state of things between the couple.

For reasons Sergei couldn't fathom, Nikolai seemed to be tightening his hold on his wife. He was afraid of something happening to her but what? Sergei didn't think it was the skinheads. It seemed somehow more personal, but Sergei wasn't bold enough to ask for details. He trusted that the boss or Vivian would tell him when the time was right. Until then? He was keeping his head down and minding his own business.

Sergei acknowledged the order with a wave of his hand and slipped behind the wheel of his SUV. He'd barely gotten out of the parking lot before his phone started to ring. Vivian had broken him of his bad habit of juggling his cell phone while driving by insisting he learn how to sync his phone with the entertainment system mounted in the dash.

"Hello?"

"Seryozha?"

Hearing his mother's voice made him smile. He'd forgotten that it was time for her weekly call. "Ma!"

She immediately launched into her usual rundown of the prior week, telling him what his brother had been up to and what was happening around her block of flats. He listened intently as she told him stories of people he hadn't seen in years or in some cases ever even met. Some of the snippets of gossip she shared made him chuckle.

"But, Sergei, you're so quiet today," she commented knowingly. "What's wrong?"

The strongest sensation of relief spread through him. If anyone could be trusted with the problems burdening him, it was his mother. She would give him the advice he needed, not the advice he wanted.

Certain she would want the whole story, he sighed and

started at the very beginning. "I met this girl…"

CHAPTER SIX

"What do you think of this one, Mama?" I handed her a sketch from my pile of new designs. It was a strapless A-line gown with an asymmetrical waist and ruching. "I designed it with a plus-sized bride in mind, but I think it would look great on a smaller woman too."

While I had been forced to set aside my dream of having my very own bridal design label to take over the family business, I hadn't stopped sketching. I had managed to design and produce a handful of gowns that had been incredibly well-received in the local press and even a few of the nationally circulated bridal magazines. I figured my goal of a bridal design empire might take a few more years to attain now that I was running Bradshaw's, but I wasn't giving up on it.

She grasped the paper in her right hand, the one with the failing grip, but didn't drop it. Every day, she pushed herself harder and harder in hopes of regaining as much of her physical abilities as possible. Her fight toward recovery never ceased to amaze me. Yet again, she'd shown me just how deep that well of inner strength was and made me so incredibly proud of having her as my mother.

After a minute of deliberate study, she finally gave her opinion. I had gotten so used to her slow, drawn out way of pronunciation that I hardly even noticed it these days. "You'll be using silk?"

"Yes."

"And the train?"

"I was thinking chapel."

"It's a nice balance," she agreed. Brushing her fingers over the design, she remarked, "It's very beautiful."

"But?"

She hesitated. Whether it was her speech delay from the stroke or a mother trying to carefully choose her constructive criticism, I couldn't tell. "This is a dress for a girl with curves. Do you think she needs to show off all this?" Her shaky hand gestured to her bosom. "This neckline? Too much of a plunge for a church!"

I fought the urge to roll my eyes at her old-fashioned ideas. "Mama, not all brides get married in a church. Some of them are proud of all this." I motioned toward my own generous bust. "What's wrong with putting the girls up on display?"

She clicked her teeth. "Really, Bianca!"

I laughed. "Come on, Mama. Not every bride wants lace from neck to toes."

"I'm just saying that *some* girls might like to keep a little mystery. Show a little modesty," she added. "Draw a second bust option. Something with the same clean lines but higher. Give the brides a choice."

Trusting her instinct, I took the sketch back and placed it in a different pile on my desk. "Yes, ma'am."

She pointed to the magazines stacked on the corner. "Bridesmaids catalogues?"

I shook my head. "No, they're actually *quinceañera* gowns."

My mother's eyebrows arched toward her hairline. "I see."

"Mama," I said carefully. "I don't know if you've noticed, but the neighborhood around here is changing. The Latino population is booming, and their fifteenth birthday celebrations are a big deal. We already carry four racks of Sweet Sixteen and prom dresses. Why not add a rack or two of gowns that would work for a *quinceañera*?"

Always a businesswoman, she asked, "Have you run the numbers?"

"Most of our vendors already have lines specifically for this so we're guaranteed some fantastic discounts and wholesale prices. If the sales volume is high enough, I might seek out some different designers to offer a wider selection."

"What about marketing? Promotions?"

"You know my friend Benny? The one who runs that Mexican bakery a few blocks over?"

"Yes."

"She's offered to let me put promo materials in her shop and the consultation room there. She's already put me in touch with some event planners who do lots of these parties."

"And the advertising?"

"I'm thinking girls in Cinderella dresses with big poufy skirts and gorgeous tiaras. I've already chatted with the photographer we used for the last promo shoot about putting together a print package and a commercial for the local networks. She's done plenty of *quinceañeras* so she knows the market well and has a huge list of contacts for me to use." I squeezed Mama's hand. "This will be great for the business."

She smiled at me and gave my hand a pat. "I trust your instincts. You practically grew up in this boutique. You know the business inside and out." Her gaze turned wistful as she glanced around the office. "Do you remember when we started and were in that tiny, cramped shop space on the corner?"

"Not really," I admitted. The business had come so far since then and now occupied an entire row of prime shopping real estate in a three-story building where we did everything—from design to creation to alteration—on site.

"Well…you were only four but my goodness! You were into everything." She chuckled softly. "I'll never forget the day Perry zipped you up in that garment bag after you cut up his baseball jersey to make a dress for your doll."

"Now *that* I do remember. I was six?"

She nodded. "That sounds about right. We'd just brought in Maggie as a seamstress, I think."

Reminiscing about happier times made my chest ache. Mama must have sensed my sadness because she rubbed my arm. "I don't know why they say it gets easier because it doesn't."

I placed my hand over hers and tried to imagine what it must have been like to lose her husband and son, one to drunk driving and the other to a senseless act of hatred and violence. To think she'd overcome all of that grief only to be hit with a stroke that nearly killed her! Life was just so unfair sometimes.

"It's ten years next month."

The slight warble to her quiet voice brought tears to my eyes. I glanced away and quickly blinked to clear the stinging wetness that threatened to spill onto my cheeks. Thinking of that awful afternoon when that monster had shot my brother in the chest brought back the worst memories. I refused to let them resurface and ruin our afternoon.

Clearing my throat, I asked, "Did you want to do something special?"

"The reverend mentioned the possibility of a memorial service. I thought we might see if some of Perry's friends might like to come. You've kept in touch with Kevan, haven't you?"

I shot her a look. "You know we've dated on and off for a while."

"I thought you two were off since February?"

"We are."

"So who gave you that love bite?"

My face flamed as I reached up to touch the spot I had thought was well hidden by the collar of my dress and the double strands of pearls. "Well! This is embarrassing."

Mama grinned slyly. "So, what's his name?"

"Sergei."

She looked surprised. "That Russian boy you told me about?"

I laughed at the notion of Sergei being called a boy. "He's quite a bit bigger than your average boy, Mama."

"And more dangerous?"

I sighed and rubbed the side of my face. "I don't know. I thought I knew who he was but now?" I shook my head. "I'm not so sure."

"It sounds like you might be more focused on *what* he is instead of *who* he is."

"Maybe."

"You like him?"

There was no point in denying what she could see. "Yes."

"Maybe it's a little more than just liking him?"

"Maybe." I wasn't ready to commit to anything else. "He's…tenacious. I'm honestly surprised he's kept after me for so long. I thought for sure he'd find someone better or—"

"Better?" Mama puffed right up. "And who in the world is better than my baby girl?"

"You know what I mean, Mama."

"No, I don't. You're pretty, smart, successful and talented. Show me another woman who can design dresses, run a business, belt out gospel music and take care of her mother like you do."

"Well…"

"There's no *well* to it, honey. There's a reason this boy has been tenacious. He knows a woman worth catching when he sees one."

I ran my finger along the edge of the desk. "How do I know if I'm ready to be caught?"

She sat forward and held my gaze. "Is that what all this is? Is that why you never get serious with any of these nice boys? Are you afraid of commitment?"

"It's not commitment that scares me. I want what you and Daddy had."

"But you're afraid of being left behind," she guessed.

As usual, she had hit the nail right on the head. Every man I had ever loved had been taken from me. The idea of giving my heart to any man scared the daylights out of me. "I watched what it did to you after Daddy was killed by that drunk."

Mama released a long, slow exhale. "Losing your father was terrible. The pain was indescribable." She grasped my hand. "But everything before that? Oh, honey, you don't want to miss out on all that love and happiness. If my life has taught me anything, it's that I have to live every day to the fullest." She touched my cheek. "No regrets, baby girl."

She had never steered me wrong with her advice, but I didn't know if I was ready to take it yet.

"This boy Sergei?"

"Yes?"

"He's a gangster?"

"He seems to have some legitimate business interests, and I guess as far as his possible criminal ties go, he's mostly above board but..."

"Is that all he wants out of life?"

I shrugged. "I don't know. I get the feeling he wants something else, something more."

"Then I suppose you have to make a decision about whether you're willing to wait for him to make the changes you need."

She was right. After last night, though, it wasn't going to be easy to break it off with him. That wasn't simply the afterglow from all the fantastic sex we'd had talking either. I recognized that the two of us shared a connection that was impossible to ignore. There was so much possibility in our fledgling relationship if I was brave enough to give it a chance and practical enough to accept who and what he was *right now* and not what he might be in a year or two or three.

The urge to call Vivian was strong. If anyone could help me sort out my conflicted feelings toward Sergei it was her, but the Russian behemoth who had ensnared me in his love trap was always guarding her. How in the world could I finagle some privacy with Vivian?

Perplexed by that little quandary, I took my mother back to her apartment and made sure she had everything she needed for the evening. I waited for her nurse to come by to check in with her before leaving. Even though I knew she was in extremely capable hands and happy in her current living situation, it still saddened me to walk away from her.

Earlier that morning, Sergei had shaken my belief that this was best for her. In truth, I had shared his distaste for the arrangement when it began, but Mama had convinced me that this was what she wanted. I had been so skeptical those first few weeks, but then I had noticed that she seemed more relaxed and at ease with a professional staff at her beck and call. I had finally understood that she needed and wanted that safety net.

I decided to give Sergei a good whack the next time I saw him for making me feel guilty about Mama's living arrangement. Even as I considered where to thump him, I couldn't shake my sympathy for his situation. He had been less than forthcoming about the reason he'd had to leave Russia in a hurry, but I didn't need all the details to see how badly he missed his mother and brother.

But what had happened over there? Was it something really bad? It must have been, right? Why else would he have left his homeland in a rush? And what was all that business about having only one brother now?

I wanted answers. It would have been only too easy to call Vivian. She would have told me anything I wanted to know, but I wanted to hear the story from Sergei. I needed to sit across from him and stare into his eyes as he came clean about his past. I didn't think he would lie to me, but I had to concede that I didn't really know him well enough to make that call.

But that wasn't exactly true, was it? Maybe I didn't know every single minute detail of his life but I *knew* him. It was almost a sixth sense that allowed me to read him in the same ways he seemed to be able to read me. Were we on the same wavelength because we had both survived something dark and terrible?

Years ago, before anything even remotely romantic had occurred between them, Vivian had tried to explain the connection she shared with Nikolai. I hadn't understood their intense bond then any more than I truly understood it now. That they loved each other was plain enough to anyone who saw them, but they seemed to be bonded on a nearly soulful level.

Even though I worked in the wedding industry, I had always scoffed at the idea of soul mates and considered the idea fantastic and fanciful. Watching Nikolai and Vivian together had cured me of those doubts. Some people were just meant to be together. Some couples simply couldn't be broken apart, no matter what the world threw at them.

I didn't dare hope that something so incredibly wonderful awaited me. After the long line of ho-hum dates and relationships that fizzled after a few months, I wasn't exactly a prime candidate for an epic love story. I had all but given up on the prospect of meeting a man who made me ache with desire or throb with need.

Until Sergei...

That night at Faze, when he'd stood watching me from the corner of the VIP section with those outrageously strong arms of his crossed in front of his broad chest, I had tingled with the most deliciously sinful awareness of him. No man had ever looked at me like that. He looked at me as if he wanted to just strip me naked and worship every last inch of my body.

And he had done exactly that last night, hadn't he? Sergei didn't need to make elaborate speeches to tell me what he felt about me. He had shown me his feelings in a way that had left me shuddering with ecstasy and feeling beautiful and special.

Okay. So, kicking down my door was a bit over the

top, but I understood why he had done it. Realizing he was *that* protective of me had thrown me for a loop. He had been willing to do anything to get to me when he thought I was in trouble. After so many years of being independent and on my own, there was something awfully enticing about having such a strong, protective man in my life. Without a shadow of a doubt, I knew I could count on Sergei for anything.

I was still thinking about the possibilities when I turned down the narrow alley that provided access to the rear of my property. The gate noisily creaked open, reminding me I probably needed to have someone out here to service it, and I pulled onto the half-moon gravel drive. Eventually, I hoped to be able to use the carriage house as a garage but the dilapidated structure needed a lot of work.

"When was the last time the slide chain on that gate was greased?"

Sergei's deep voice startled me as I stepped out of my car. Jumping, I spun around and found him standing next to the ramshackle carriage house. Hand on my chest, I grouched at him. "You almost gave me a heart attack!"

He offered an apologetic smile. "*Prostite.* Sorry," he added quickly. "I didn't mean to scare you."

I closed my car door with a bump of my hip and listened for the locks to engage. "What are you doing out here anyway?"

"I was taking a look at this structure. It's in terrible shape, Bianca."

"I know. I had a couple of contractors who do historical renovations come out here to take a look at it, but most of them suggested I salvage whatever I can and then tear it down. Only one guy had a plan for fixing it up, but his bid was so low I had doubts he could finish the job on budget."

Sergei made that low, grunting noise that seemed to accompany anything he found distasteful. "He was probably trying to cheat you. He'd have gotten halfway done, made your life miserable and then asked for more money than even your highest bidder."

"I don't know about that." He shot me a dubious look. "No, really. Marcus—the contractor—said he grew up around here and wanted to see this place restored to the way it was when he was a kid."

"That sounds like a bullshit story to soften you up and make you sign a contract with him so he could rip you off."

"Wow!" I said with an exaggerated huff. "Aren't you just grizzly this evening?"

Sergei winced and rubbed the back of his neck. The movement stretched his black T-shirt tight across his broad chest. The flexing of the crazy huge muscles in his arms made me feel a bit woozy. "I'm sorry, Bianca."

Sensing something was wrong, I closed the distance between us and reached for his hand. I interlaced our fingers and stared up at my big, sexy giant. "What's up with you?"

"It's been a long day for me. I had to take care of something ugly."

I swallowed. "Are we ever going to talk about what you do? About what you are?"

His fingers tightened around mine. "I think you know what I am and what I do."

"I don't know specifics."

"And you won't," he warned. "I will not involve in you in that part of my life."

"Don't you think I deserve to know what I'm getting into if—"

"If?" He seized on the word. "Am I still on probation with you?"

"I don't know, Sergei. You can't stand here and tell me that you had to do something ugly today and then refuse to give me details. What I'm imagining is probably a thousand times worse."

"What are you imagining?" When I didn't answer, he prompted me with that rumbling voice of his. "Bianca, what do you think I do all day?"

"I know that you guard Vivian." After some hesitation, I added, "I've heard that you fight for money."

"I do."

"And that you maybe, you know, beat people up sometimes."

"There's no maybe to it, Bianca. When someone steps out of line, I'm the one who persuades them to get back into formation."

"By hitting them?"

"I don't have to hit them that often."

Sizing him up, I figured that was probably true. If Sergei walked through my door and I was on the bad side of his boss, I'd toe the company line pretty damned quick. "Do you like doing that?"

He visibly flinched, his cheeks tightening and his lips pursing. "Do you really believe that I enjoy hurting people?"

I shook my head. "But why do it?"

His wide shoulders bounced. "What the hell else could I do? When I came here, I had very few choices, Bianca. I worked at the Samovar as a dishwasher until Nikolai saw me fighting. He sent me to Ivan to be trained, and eventually I was brought in as his enforcer. This wasn't the life I wanted, but there was no other choice for me."

"I don't believe that. There are always choices."

His jaw tensed as he rubbed his thumb across my knuckles. "You're right. I could have taken a different path, but I didn't. This is where I am right now, Bianca. If you want to be with me, this is where we start our journey."

"Where are we headed?"

He gulped, his Adam's apple sliding up and down as he carefully chose his words. "I have a destination in mind...and it takes us far away from this point to some place much better. To a place where you could be as proud of me as I am of you."

His sweet compliment touched me. The promise of what we might have if I just had a little faith in him tempted me a great deal. I wanted to believe that Sergei could find a way to deftly extract himself from the mobbed-up life he led.

My thoughts turned to Erin and Ivan. From what Vivian had told me, Ivan had been in a spot almost identical to Sergei's once. He had gotten out and made something of himself, becoming hugely successful and wealthy. If it had been done before, perhaps Sergei could follow in Ivan's footsteps.

Grasping the front of Sergei's shirt, just above his belt, I dragged him down for a kiss. Before our lips met, I caught a whiff of cheap, nasty perfume. It was the sort of alcohol-tinged, too heavy on the musk drugstore concoction that the girls I went to high school with used to wear. I had an idea of what sort of women might still wear it, and I wasn't pleased.

Recoiling from the stink of it, I stepped back and let go of his shirt. That's when I noticed the glitter dusting the front of his shirt and now stuck to my palm. Holding up my hand, I demanded angrily, "What the hell is this, Sergei?"

"Look, it's not what you think, Bianca."

"It had better not be," I warned. "Because you look and smell like you've been hanging out at a strip club!"

"Okay," he said carefully. "I was at a strip club this afternoon. But," he cut in quickly, thwarting my outraged outburst, "I wasn't there for pleasure. It was business."

"Business?"

He wavered before confessing, "A couple of dancers were beaten up at a private party. The club is partly owned by a friend of mine, and he needed some help. I took the dancers to see a doctor and then got them situated in a safe place. That's it, Bianca. That's all that happened."

I studied his handsome, sincere face. He was telling the truth, but I sensed there was way more backstory to the situation. "I believe that nothing happened with the strippers."

He seemed relieved. Sliding his hand along my nape, he peered into my eyes. "I don't want any woman but you, Bianca. Sometimes I have to go places that aren't very nice to conduct business, but I'm not interested in anything those women have to offer."

Gripping the front of his shirt again, I hauled him down with a sharp tug. "Convince me."

And he did. With a kiss so erotically sensual that my panties grew damp, Sergei staked his claim on me and proved that he wanted me and only me. His tongue fluttered against mine before dipping deeper. He sucked my lower lip and gave it a light nibble, making me rise up on my toes and clutch at his brawny arms.

Though I wanted the kiss to go on forever, he ended it gently and let his hand glide down my spine to rest on my bottom. He gave my backside a pat and grinned boyishly. "I want to show you something."

"Okay."

Holding my hand, he led me down the sidewalk that curved through the backyard and along one side of the house. Out front, I spotted his SUV pulled up against the curb. "You can park out back, if you'd like. There's plenty of space behind my car."

He smiled at me. "Is that your way of inviting me to stay the night?"

Glancing away from him, I felt suddenly shy. "Well, I mean, if you want to stay..."

He curved his arm around my shoulders. "I'm staying."

I had a sneaking suspicion he meant for much longer than one night.

When we rounded the side of the house and turned toward the front porch, I immediately spotted the new door. My lips parted with shock. "The door! You found *my* door!"

Sergei chuckled happily and brushed his fingertips along the side of my neck. "I took the picture from your inspiration board. My friend had a door that looked almost exactly like the one you wanted."

"This is one is so much better!" I hurried up the steps for a closer look. Unable to help myself, I ran my hands along the highly polished wood and traced the gorgeous panes of stained glass. "It's so beautiful, Sergei."

His warm hands settled on my shoulders. A moment later, he pressed a ticklish kiss to the side of my neck. "I'm glad you like it." Another kiss made me shiver with anticipation. "Come inside. Dinner is waiting."

I let him lead me inside the house, all the while wondering what this night held in store for me.

CHAPTER SEVEN

Later that evening, I flicked through my closet in search of the perfect outfit for the morning. The bathroom door across the bedroom was cracked just enough for me to keep tabs on Sergei's shower. I had managed to evade most of his amorous advances, including his attempts to climb into the shower with me earlier, but my defenses were quickly failing. Once he came out of that shower, I was giving in and letting myself have exactly what we both wanted.

Bumping hips as we plated a simple dinner had been the beginning of our flirtation. He had caressed my hand while we sipped wine on the couch after dinner and talked about my plans and dreams for the house. I had slipped away to take my evening shower while he moved his SUV around back and peeked at my water heater.

Craving Sergei's heat and touch like crazy, I settled on my favorite wrap dress. The top sported a bold giraffe print that complemented the deep rust-colored skirt. I liked the way it hugged my hips and nipped in my waist. But which shoes? I pulled out a pair of gold strappy heeled sandals and nude pumps.

"The gold ones," Sergei said, coming into the bedroom. "They're prettier."

Glancing at him, I fought the urge to lick my lips as I ogled his nearly naked body. He had a towel slung low around his hips, but the loosely tucked end threatened to fall free at any moment. Soon, I hoped.

Lifting the gold sandals, I said, "Prettier, yes, but not as comfortable. Mondays are always busy around the shop, especially in May."

He shrugged. "So wear the pumps."

I held the pumps up against the skirt and compared them to the sandals. They looked fine, but they didn't pop. "No, I think I'll go with pretty."

"Good choice." He came toward me and bent down to peck my cheek. "Your legs look amazing when you wear those."

My brows knitted together. "You've seen me in these shoes before?"

He nodded and strode across the room toward the gym bag he had dropped onto the ottoman earlier. "You wore them a few weeks ago when you and Vivian went to that art show for that Brazilian painter. You had on a purple dress and big hoop earrings—but your legs?" He practically growled. "They looked so fucking sexy."

I turned my gaze toward my legs. "Really?"

"Yes." He touched his ear. "You should wear those earrings again. I liked the way they looked on you."

Taken aback by his recollection of my outfit, I nevertheless smiled at him. "Okay. I will."

"You can wear them on Friday."

"What's Friday?"

"We're going out on a proper date."

"Is that so?"

"Yes." He started digging through his bag, totally oblivious to my frustration with him.

"Don't you think you should ask me first?"

He glanced at me. "Do you want to go out on Friday?"

"Yes, but—"

"So what's the problem? I want to go out. You want to go out. I made plans. It's done."

I rolled my eyes. "It's not just *done*, Sergei. I don't know how you did things with other women, but I'm not the kind of girl who likes to be told what to do."

"You seemed to like it last night." His gaze darted to the chair where he had sat last night and ordered me to strip for him.

My face flamed with embarrassment. "That was different."

"But you liked it," Sergei countered. "You were soaking wet for me by the time I got you into bed. You liked being told what to do, didn't you?"

He wasn't going to stop until I admitted that he was right. Even now, as he described how wet I had been, I could feel my nipples growing hard. "Yes, I liked it very much."

"But you don't like it when I take control outside of the bedroom?"

I fidgeted with the cuff of my silk dressing robe. "I don't know. I'm used to doing things my way. I like your way of doing things in here, but I'm not sure I'll ever be the type of woman who just nods her head whenever her man makes a decision."

Sergei studied me for a few unnerving seconds. "Okay."

I blinked. "What? Just like that? You're okay with it?"

"I'm not an ogre, Bianca, but I am a man and I like being in control."

"But?"

"But one of the things that attracted me to you is your confidence and the way you run your life," he explained. "You're perfectly capable of taking care of yourself."

"Yes, I am. I don't need a man."

"No, you don't." He stared expectantly my way, as if waiting for me to say something.

I swallowed nervously and decided to be honest with him. "I would like a man I could count on in my life. Someone who wants to take care of me, I mean."

"I want to take care of you, Bianca. I want to be the man you count on for everything and anything you need."

"I know you do," I said quietly.

"And?"

Holding his gaze, I murmured, "I know I can count on you."

"Anything you want, I'll give you."

He wasn't talking expensive trinkets either. He meant *anything*. He was offering me everything I had ever wanted but had been too afraid to seek out. All I had to do was ask.

"I know." Turning away from him, I finished picking out the accessories for my outfit while he draped running clothes across the arm of my reading chair. When I closed the closet door, I caught him retrieving the biggest freaking box of condoms I had ever seen. Unable to help myself, I busted out laughing. "Oh my God! Are you serious?"

"What?" Sergei carelessly tossed the box onto the bed. "I wanted to be prepared."

"For what? Six months?"

He snorted and started to prowl toward me. "Six months? Bianca, we'll be lucky if that lasts the week."

My jaw dropped. "You're out of your mind."

Sergei held up five fingers as he walked toward me. "Count them, Bianca. For five months, I've gone without sex." He stopped right in front of me and peered down into my eyes. "For five months, I've waited for you to let me into your bedroom." He slid an arm around my waist and dragged me tight to his hot, hard body. "I intend to make up for all that lost time."

Trembling inside, I ran my hands along his muscular arms and across his impressive chest. I fingered the gold medallion dangling from his neck. "What is this?"

"Hmm?" He nuzzled my neck and nipped at my skin. "It's Saint Sergius, my namesake. My mother gave it to me when I was younger."

"For protection?"

"I suppose."

I let the medallion drop from my fingers. "Are you religious?"

"Not particularly," he replied. "Nothing like Vivian." He traced the vein in my neck where my pulse beat wildly. "Bianca, you're stalling."

I glanced up at him from beneath fluttering eyelashes. "Am I?"

"Yes." He tugged on the belt of my robe and dragged the garment from my arms. He let it fall to the floor and shoved it aside with his bare foot. His finger followed the lacy shells adorning the bodice of my chemise. "Do you always sleep in things like this or are you choosing them for me?"

"I like sexy, pretty things, but I dug this one out of my drawer just for you."

"I appreciate the thoughtfulness." Grasping the bottom of my flimsy chemise, he pulled it up and over my head. "Do you approve of this removal method?"

Smiling at the memory of him ripping my nightgown, I

patted his chest. "It's nice to know you're not a total caveman."

He chuckled against my lips. "You might want to see what I have planned for you before you sing my praises." Putting those big hands on my shoulders, he pressed gently. "Kneel."

Like last night, my entire body vibrated at his gruffly spoken word. I wasn't sure how he wielded such power over me or even why I liked it so much, but I chose not to question it. I embraced this new, sensual awareness and slowly lowered myself to the floor.

Licking my lips, I gazed up at him, taking in his wonderfully sculpted frame. He peered down at me and caressed my cheek. Taking off his towel, he tossed it aside and gestured to his half-erect cock. "Get me hard, Bianca."

With shaky fingers, I stroked the length of him, all the while marveling at his size. I almost wanted to run across the hall to grab a tape measure from my tool kit to satisfy my curiosity. Even with both hands wrapped around his thick shaft, I still needed at least one more hand to cover all of him. My pussy pulsed at the prospect of having his huge dick buried inside me.

Lavishing his cock with my tongue, I relished the low groans he made. I sucked the blunt tip of him into my mouth and hummed with appreciation. He growled something in Russian before threading his fingers through my hair and shifting his feet wider apart. "Suck me, Bianca."

White-hot frissons of excitement quivered through me at the rough demand. Bobbing up and down on his shaft, I took him deeper with every down stroke and hoped I pleased him. Giving head had never been a sex act I enjoyed, but the way Sergei encouraged and complimented me was so exciting. Relaxing my jaw, I put my hands on his thighs and silently asked him to take my mouth by pulling him into me.

Breathing hard, Sergei slid forward only an inch or two. My lips stretched wide to accept his girth, but he didn't try to take it too far. Instead, he tapped my nose and ordered, "Look at up at me."

With his cock in my mouth, I gazed up at Sergei. The utter adoration etched into his face took me by surprise. "You're so fucking beautiful." He pulled free from my mouth and bent down to capture my lips in a passionate, rough kiss. "So. Fucking. Beautiful."

And then he swept me right up off the floor and tossed me onto the bed. Bouncing on the mattress, I squealed with shock but then giggled as Sergei crawled over me, pinning me to the bed and kissing me into submission. Closing my eyes, I reveled in the wicked sensations he evoked with his masterful hands and mouth. He nibbled and kissed and licked all the wonderfully sensitive spots on my body until I was panting and clutching at him.

Sitting back on his heels, Sergei reached for the box of condoms and ripped into them. He grabbed a strip, tore one package free and split open the foil wrapper. "Open your legs."

Swallowing hard, I did as instructed, parting my thighs for him and letting him gaze upon the dewy, womanly center of me. His massive cock stood at attention, the ruddy tip point right at me. He ran his hands over his shaft and cupped his sac before rolling on the condom. Scooting between my legs, he put his hands on my inner thighs and pushed them even farther apart. "Show me where you want my cock, Bianca."

Embarrassed, I hissed, "Sergei!"

"Show me where you want my cock—or else I'll choose and you might not like it as much."

Gulping at the idea of his thick penis intruding into the one spot I had never let any man touch, I hurriedly reached down to touch my pussy. "I want you here."

"Let me see. Open yourself to me."

Lightheaded with desire, I separated the slick, hot petals of my sex to show him exactly where I wanted that big dick of his. "Here. Sergei, I want you right here."

Gripping the base of his shaft, my Russian lover pulled the fat crown of his cock between my labia. Flashbacks of our naughty play on the table this morning popped before my eyes. I wondered if I would ever be able to have a bowl of cereal there without thinking of the dirty things this unbelievably passionate man had done to me.

"*Unnhhh.*" I moaned loudly when Sergei finally thrust into me. My pussy had never taken anything so big, and it protested the sudden invasion of his monster-sized shaft. My hands flew to his chest as he bore down on me. "Wait! Oh! *Wait!*"

Sergei went still. Concern darkened his face. "Am I hurting you?"

I shook my head and bit my lower lip. Sliding my hands to his shoulders, I pulled him down for a kiss. "Easy," I pleaded. "Just go easy."

"Anything you want," he whispered and claimed a loving kiss. Rocking slowly, he thrust deeper, then retreated and thrust into me again. He took his time, increasing his pace and force gradually.

Our foreheads touched, and he let loose a needful groan. "Baby, you're so fucking tight. It's killing me." His tongue tangled with mine. "So good."

I didn't think I would ever get tired of hearing Sergei call me his baby. Clutching his shoulders, I wrapped my thighs around him and held on tight for the ride of my life. He snapped those trim hips of his and ran his hands over my breasts. When he pinched my nipple, I cried out and arched up against him. "Oh!"

He buried in his face in the curve of my neck and whispered my name. His hand traveled down to my belly to the spot where our bodies were joined. He framed my clit between two fingers and stimulated the throbbing nub until I shattered beneath him. Head thrown back, I howled and shuddered with utter ecstasy. "Sergei!"

His lips dragged along my neck and across my cheek before settling against mine. Still thrusting into me, he fucked my mouth with his tongue, mimicking the way our bodies undulated together atop the bed. Just as I started to come down from my orgasmic high, he tore away from my mouth and began to rub my clit faster. "Again, Bianca. Come for me again."

I tried to brush away his hand. I was so sensitive, and his swirling fingers made me tremble and gasp. "I can't."

"You can." He nibbled my lower lip. "Come, Bianca. Squeeze me with your pussy and come."

Staring into his dark eyes, I realized how completely he controlled me. Here, in my bedroom, I seemed to be totally at his mercy. There was nothing I wouldn't do for him, especially not when he commanded me in that baritone voice of his.

God, everything he did to me just felt so good. My body hummed beneath his. Those swirling fingertips pushed me right over the edge again. My thighs tensed as he pounded into me. His cock stretched and filled me and brought me to a mind-blowing climax. "*Sergei!*"

He rocked into me until I sagged against the bed, limp and boneless and unable to move—but he wasn't done with me yet. Withdrawing from me, Sergei fell onto his back, reached over and hauled me right on top of him. I gasped when he gripped my hips and pushed me into the position he wanted.

Suddenly anxious about my weight, I shook my head. "No, I'm too heavy. This isn't a good—"

He popped my backside with both hands, his flattened palms cracking my bottom. "Hush."

"Ow!"

He soothed the sting with his loving hands. "I'm a big man, Bianca. I can take everything you give me." He thrust up into my slick, wet heat. "Woman, you were made for a man like me."

Heart racing, I gazed into his sincere face and realized he meant every word of it. He grasped my ass in both hands, pulled me forward and then pushed me back on his lap. "Fuck me, Bianca. It's your turn to make me come."

Without any experience in this position, I moved awkwardly at first. Sergei seemed to sense that I needed some help so he guided my movements with his strong hands. It didn't take me long to figure out what he liked. I grew more confident in my abilities and rode his cock like a damned cowgirl.

Beneath me, Sergei groaned and massaged my bottom. When his finger drifted between my cheeks, I tensed, my pussy clutching at his cock as he brushed a part of me that had never been breached.

"Haven't you ever—?"

"No!" I interrupted him before he could even finish that thought. "And don't get any dirty ideas, Sergei. You are not putting your—"

"Cock?"

"Yes."

"In this perfect, tight ass?"

"No!"

He shot me one of those sinfully mischievous smiles. "We'll see."

"No, we won't."

"Later," he said and sat up to kiss me. "Right now, I'm more interested in coming inside this sweet pink cunt of yours."

"Sergei!" I couldn't believe the way he said the word with such ease. Yet I couldn't deny how freaking hot it sounded and how much I loved the things he did to me.

"Give my mouth something else to do, and I'll stop using these dirty words that make you blush." He hugged me tight and flicked his tongue to mine. With his cock fully sheathed in my channel, we traded erotically charged kisses until we were both panting and shaking.

Sergei fell back to the bed and thrust up into me again. Planting his feet on the mattress, he cradled my bottom with his bent legs and started to jackhammer my pussy. Mouth agape, I cried out again and again as he showed me exactly what his magnificently toned body could do.

I hadn't expected to climax again, but Sergei ripped a shockingly unanticipated orgasm from me just seconds before he thrust up into me so hard it nearly bucked me off his lap. With those steely arms encircling me, he growled my name and jerked beneath me while he enjoyed his release.

Sweating and huffing, we collapsed together in the center of my bed. Sergei brushed the damp strands of hair from my face and kissed me sweetly. We smiled at each other and enjoyed a few moments of afterglow. When he pulled away from me and headed for the bathroom, I rolled onto my side and enjoyed the view of his fine, taut ass. Giggling like a fool, I tried to convince myself that this wasn't a dream and that he actually belonged to me.

He picked up the destroyed box of condoms, switched off the lamps and rejoined me in bed a few minutes later. I hadn't missed the way he had taken the side of the bed between me and the door. The old school action of placing his body between mine and any danger assured me he had probably checked every door and window in the house while I showered. It seemed he meant every word about protecting me and keeping me safe.

Despite having just made love to me, Sergei didn't seem satisfied with merely cuddling until we fell asleep. In the darkness, he caressed my body and kissed me until I vibrated with desire. His cock didn't remain sated long. The blazing hot length of it nudged my belly and rubbed against my thigh.

When I heard him slapping around on the bedside table for the strip of condoms he had placed there, I couldn't help but laugh. "Sergei! We just had sex. You can't seriously want to go again."

"You'll be lucky if I let you get four hours of sleep tonight."

"I thought you were going running with Vivian in the morning. Don't you need to rest?"

The crinkly tear of the wrapper echoed in the stillness of my bedroom. "I'd rather be buried deep in your pussy than get an extra hour of sleep. Now come here."

"No!" I playfully tried to evade his clutching paws, but Sergei easily won the mock battle. Giggling, I pushed against his chest, but it was impossible to move his solid frame. He swooped down for a kiss, his face highlighted by the moonlight streaming through my wooden blinds, but I turned my face at the last second, denying his prize. "No way! I'm tired."

"Hush."

Thinking he was trying to shush my half-hearted

protests, I turned back toward him. I fully expected him to kiss me now, but instead I found him staring at my open bedroom door. His entire body had gone rigid. "What is—?"

I didn't get the rest of my question out. He placed his fingertips against my mouth, gently silencing me as he listened for something. Holding my breath, I strained to hear whatever it was that had killed his amorous mood.

A long, whining creak pierced the night. My heart leapt into my throat as the unmistakable tap of footsteps met my ears. Someone was walking across back porch directly beneath my bedroom!

In a flash of movement so fast it startled me, Sergei moved off the bed. He hefted me up off the mattress and hurriedly pushed me toward the bathroom. After dropping a quick kiss on the top of my head, he shoved me inside the room. "Lock the door."

It clicked shut softly behind him as he disappeared. Stunned by the way he had switched from lover to protector in the blink of an eye, I stared at the closed door. A few seconds later, I shook myself from the stupor and wondered what I was supposed to do now.

Locking the door and waiting for Sergei's return was probably the safest course of action…but what if he got hurt? What if the creep prowling around my house was armed? The thought of Sergei being shot or stabbed made me sick.

Disobeying Sergei's direct order, I left the bathroom and scurried across my bedroom in search of my phone. Slipping back into my chemise and robe, I dialed 9-1-1 and prayed the police would get here before anything bad happened.

CHAPTER EIGHT

Out for blood, Sergei slowly unlocked the front door and slipped onto the porch. The newly installed door opened with barely a whisper of noise, permitting him to leave the house without alerting the asshole creeping around Bianca's property. Sticking to the shadows, he edged the front of the house and carefully rounded the corner of the wraparound porch.

As he crept along the right side of her home, he listened carefully for any indication that the prowler was walking toward him. Hearing nothing, he wondered if the man had gone off into the grass or if he'd already made his way to the left side of the house. Over the soundtrack of crickets and cicadas, Sergei detected a low, creaking groan as weight settled on an old wooden step. A second later, wood crunched and splintered and a grunt of pain filled the air.

Got you!

Earlier, when coming back from parking his SUV, Sergei had noticed the step along the back needed to be ripped out and replaced. He had actually been surprised it bore his weight without snapping. Apparently, the prowler hadn't been so lucky.

Running around the porch, Sergei spotted the lumpy shadow of a man crouched on the ground. "Hey!"

The prowler's head popped up, but it was too dark in the backyard for Sergei to get a good look at him. He seemed to be a medium-sized man. The bastard had quick reflexes and leapt to his feet, dashing around the side of the house and disappearing.

As Sergei made chase, he realized the man knew the neighborhood well because he had taken a shortcut from Bianca's yard that spit him out on the side street. Irritated that he had lost the man, Sergei relied on his instincts and took a hard left.

Wearing only his running shorts and sneakers, he silently scolded himself for not grabbing something to defend himself. He had left his gun tucked away in his vehicle because he had been more interested in getting inside the shower with Bianca. If Nikolai could see him now, he would surely make a quip about thinking with his little head instead of the bigger one.

Coming to a corner, Sergei slowed his pace. He followed the curve cautiously and spotted an alley up ahead. The dark roadway between tall privacy fences was too shadowy for him to scout properly. The man he was chasing had probably taken up a position there to ambush him and inflict an injury.

The sound of running footsteps ricocheted off the privacy fences. The sound grew louder and sharper, telling Sergei the man was headed right for him. Hugging the closest fence, Sergei prepared to attack the man when he burst out of the protective shadows. Hands clenched, he lifted his arms high and counted down the seconds until he struck. The footsteps drew nearer, and Sergei swung his arms toward the oncoming man, fully intending to clothesline the creep.

But when the man burst out of the alley, Sergei's eyes widened with shock. It wasn't a prowler. It was a police officer on a foot pursuit!

He stopped the downward motion of his arms before it was too late, reacting with lightning speed to avoid hitting a man who could make his life very miserable. The officer spotted him and jumped back, drawing his weapon and pointing it right at Sergei's chest. "Hands in the air!"

Shit.

Complying instantly, Sergei threw up his hands. "I thought you were the prowler bothering my girlfriend. I wasn't trying to hurt you."

The officer didn't lower his gun even a fraction of a centimeter. With the business end trained on Sergei's heart, the officer stepped forward into the light. He was close to Sergei's age and had skin the same shade as Bianca's. Not one to fuck around, the man barked an order. "Turn around. Hands on the back of your head. Spread your feet."

Irritated with the bullshit pat-down, Sergei nevertheless did as commanded. He had always managed to stay on the right side of the law and wasn't about to risk that tonight. The officer roughly frisked Sergei but found no weapon. "Face me again."

Staring down at the cop, Sergei kept his hands on his head. "Did you see the man I was chasing?"

"I did. Funny thing. He looked sort of like you."

"No." Sergei's internal alarms clanged. It would be a cold day in hell before he let the police pin this on him. "If I was a prowler, would I be dressed like this? No! The guy I was chasing was shorter than me and not as big. I followed him out of my girlfriend's yard and out this way."

"Right." The officer wasn't buying Sergei's story. "I'm supposed to believe a mobbed-up son of a bitch like you has a girlfriend who lives in this neighborhood? I thought you guys all dated strippers from Sugar's and waitresses from Samovar?"

Sergei's eyes narrowed. Not bothering to deny or argue with the man, he continued to play nice, but it was obvious the cop had his number. The fact that a beat cop recognized him on sight made him slightly nervous. This was something Nikolai would want to know. Was there some new legal trouble brewing?

"Take me back to my girlfriend's house. She'll tell you the truth."

"Yeah? And just who is this girlfriend of yours?"

"Bianca Bradshaw. She lives at—"

"I know where Bibi lives," the police officer interjected sharply. "And I know that she doesn't have anything to do with lowlifes like you." Stepping toward him, his gun still drawn, the cop growled, "Were you trying to rob her? Rape her? Maybe you're trying to strong-arm her into selling her business because you Russian mob pricks want her building?"

Bibi? Jealous that this cop had a nickname for *his* woman and that the prick would even insinuate that he would do anything so cruel to her, Sergei snarled, "You're crazy. She's my girlfriend. I was trying to protect her."

"We'll see about that." The police officer pulled his cuffs free from his belt and gestured for Sergei to lower his hands. "I'm sure you know the drill."

Clenching his teeth, Sergei turned around and presented his wrists to be cuffed. The cop made sure to tighten them a notch too far. Pushing Sergei's thumbs into a stress position that sent pain shooting up his arms, the officer perp-walked him back down the alley to an idling cruiser. He shoved Sergei into the cramped backseat and made radio contact with his dispatch center.

"I don't suppose you've got your license tucked into your shorts?"

With his knees shoved up toward his chest and his shoulders hunched, Sergei glared at the police officer's reflection in the rearview mirror and rattled off his name, address, birth date and driver's license number. The cop showed surprise when the dispatcher relayed that Sergei had no outstanding warrants. Checking the computer screen mounted just above the console, the officer voiced his doubt when he saw that Sergei had never even had a parking ticket.

Keeping his mouth shut, Sergei stared out the window as the cop drove him back to Bianca's house. Whoever this guy was, he seemed intent on embarrassing Sergei. He was going to have to do a lot worse than this. Not that Sergei relished the idea of showing up on Bianca's doorstep in handcuffs. After trying to show her that he was better than his criminal ties, this episode wasn't going to help his case.

The cruiser rolled to a stop at the curb outside her house. The lights in the master bedroom, living room and entryway were on which meant she had gone against his order and left that bathroom. He had put her there for a reason. He had needed to know she was safely tucked away in case he crossed paths with the prowler inside the house. If he'd struck out blindly at a shadowy figure, he would have been confident that it wasn't Bianca getting caught in the crossfire.

The cop dragged him out of the backseat and marched him up the sidewalk. They hadn't even reached the top step before the front door jerked open and Bianca appeared in a whirl of blush pink silk. She had a phone to her ear and hurriedly ended the call. Stepping onto the porch, she cast shocked eyes on him. "Sergei!"

Before he could explain his cuffed state, the police officer stepped into the light beside him. Bianca's sharp intake of breath warned Sergei he was about to hear something he didn't like.

"Kevan!"

The name spurred a memory. *Of course.* Hadn't she mentioned the ex-boyfriend she had gone to for help when the prowler first started bothering her? Now the perfect-for-her ex had him cuffed. *Great. Just. Fucking. Great.*

"Hey, Bibi." Kevan was all charm now. "Sorry to bother you so late."

"It's fine." Wringing her hands, she asked, "Is there a reason Sergei is cuffed?"

"I was the closest guy to your house when the 9-1-1 report of a prowler came across the radio. I saw the suspect duck into an alley so I chased him and this guy jumped out of the shadows and tried to punch me."

Mouth agape, Bianca stared at Sergei. His chest tightened as he waited for her to jump to the wrong conclusion. "No, that doesn't sound like Sergei at all. He wouldn't hit a police officer."

The corners of Sergei's mouth lifted with a pleased smile. Once he had discovered she had history with the cop, Sergei had been sure she would take the officer's word over his. It wasn't often that he was proven wrong, but he relished the unnatural feeling this time.

"Do you know who this guy is?" Kevan didn't sound very happy. "He's trouble, Bibi."

"I'm not twelve years old, Kevan. I don't need a

lecture."

The police officer stepped forward, moving close enough to Bianca that Sergei's alpha instincts screamed for him to react. Shoving them down, he refused to take the bait. Instead, he glared murderously at the cop's back as the man whispered to Bianca.

"Perry was my best friend, and I know he'd want me to look out for you."

Bianca reached out to touch Kevan, softly rubbing his upper arm in a kind, all too familiar gesture that made Sergei's stomach lurch. "I appreciate you keeping an eye out for me, but I'm a big girl, Kevan." Lowering her voice, she added quickly, "We've talked about this before, remember?"

The officer went ramrod straight, his reaction similar to a man who had just been slapped. Sergei wondered at the interplay between the two acquaintances. Why, exactly, had Bianca cut things off with her brother's friend? From what Sergei could tell, the guy was basically her dream man. Kevan fit into her life much more neatly than he ever would.

Stepping back beside Sergei, Kevan dug out his keys. "Since you're in my territory, I've been adding extra passes by your place when I'm on shift. I'll make sure the others guys on this beat do the same thing. We'll catch this guy, Bibi."

"Thank you, Kevan."

"It's no problem, Bibi. I'm always here for you. All you have to do is call, and I'll come running."

"I know. I appreciate that."

Kevan unlatched the too-tight cuffs and removed them. As he tucked the manacles into the holster on his belt, he turned to Bianca and offered a sly smile. "I'm glad I finally got to see you in that pink silk. I knew it would be beautiful on you."

The knowledge that Bianca was wearing lingerie this man had bought for her hit Sergei like a fist to the gut. She refused to meet his gaze but smiled timidly at Kevan. "Um...thanks."

"Your birthday is coming up. Maybe I'll have to get you something in red."

Sergei's nostrils flared as the man blatantly came on to Bianca. If he hadn't been wearing a uniform, the smug little bastard would have found himself on the receiving end of Sergei's fist. The guy had crossed the line too many times. Presenting him at Bianca's door in handcuffs had been bad enough but to stand there and flirt with her? It was too much.

As if sensing that Sergei hovered on the edge, Bianca grasped his hand and tugged him toward her. She shot him a pleading look, and he exhaled the pent-up breath puffing out his chest. Sliding his arm around her smaller shoulders, he publicly staked his claim on her. She put a gentle hand to his bare stomach and petted him in slow circles.

Holding Kevan's irritated gaze, Sergei reminded the man who Bianca wanted now. "Come on, Bianca. Let's go back to bed."

"Okay." Smiling at the police officer, she bid him farewell. "Night, Kevan."

"Good night, Bianca. I hope I'll see you at Lulu and Corey's wedding. If you need a ride or anything—"

"She's got a ride and a date." Sergei stepped in front of Bianca, blocking her from Kevan's view. "Good night, Officer. I'm sure you have criminals to chase."

"Yep." Kevan backed away from the house. "In fact, I've got my eye on one right now."

Sergei watched the police officer return to his cruiser

and drive away from the curb before turning toward Bianca. Gripping her robe in her hands, she looked up at him with apprehension—and fear. Exhaling with exasperation, he asked, "Are you really afraid of me?"

She closely examined his face. Whatever she saw calmed her nerves. Her shoulders relaxed, and she released the tight grasp on her robe. "No."

"I would never hurt you. *Never.*" Sweeping the long, black curls from her face and tucking them behind her ear, he added, "Especially not after the way you defended me."

"You're too smart to hit a police officer and much too careful to swing blindly." She tugged on his hand. "Come inside."

He followed her inside the house and locked the door. Facing her, he leaned back against it and decided to just get it all out there on the table. "So this cop Kevan?"

To her credit, she didn't drop her gaze or avoid looking at him. "He and my brother were best friends. After Perry was murdered, he stepped into that older brother role for me. Eventually, our relationship changed, and we tried dating."

"But?"

She shrugged. "He's a great guy but he's not right for me."

"Because?"

"I don't know. It didn't feel right." She paused and then gestured between her body and his. "It never felt anything like what we have."

His irritation with Kevan fled. "What we have is better?"

She nodded. "Stronger. Deeper. *Real.*"

Trying not to break out into a goofy grin at her admission, he glanced away briefly. His gaze settled on the fully illuminated living room. "Why did you disobey me?"

"I'm sorry. Are you my father now?"

He met her aggravated gaze head-on. "No, but I was trying to keep you safe."

"Well, I was trying to keep you safe. You went running out of the house without any shoes or a shirt or a weapon. You could have been shot or stabbed!"

Sergei's heart swelled upon hearing her say that she had wanted to protect him. Even so, she needed to be more cautious. "We'll get a cheap burner phone for your bathroom and keep it plugged in there. That way you'll always have a phone to call 9-1-1, even if you're hiding behind a locked door."

"Seriously?"

"Yes." Upon further consideration, he said, "Actually, we should probably look into converting that master bedroom closet into a panic room. We could put in a reinforced door and—"

"Sergei, this is Houston, not war-torn Somalia! I don't need a panic room in my house."

"Every home needs a safe place," he countered.

"Sergei…"

He slashed his hand through the air. "It's late. We'll discuss it tomorrow."

She rolled her eyes but didn't argue with him. "Fine. Let's go to bed."

"Not yet," he said and pushed off the door. Touching the pink silk robe, he experienced a fresh wave of jealousy. "Take this off."

Her dark eyes flashed with surprise—and excitement. "Are you serious?"

"Now, Bianca."

She gulped and did as he ordered. Peeling out of the

robe, she handed it over to him. Without having to be asked, she removed the pretty chemise too. When she placed it on his hand, she didn't immediately let go. He wondered if she was having second thoughts about his possessive reaction, but she seemed curious.

"Did you mean it, Sergei?"

"Mean what, *milaya moya*?"

"That you're taking me to Lulu and Corey's wedding?"

"We're together now, aren't we?"

"Yes."

"So we go to weddings together," he answered simply. "Of course, I should probably ask who these people are."

She smiled. "Lulu is my cousin, and Corey is one of Perry's friends." Her mouth settled into a nervous line. "Kevan will be there. He's one of Corey's groomsmen so if this is going to be a problem..."

"It won't be a problem. I'll be on my best behavior." He drew a cross over his heart. "Promise."

"I'm holding you to that." She released the chemise into his hand. "So now what? Are you going to tear that up and burn it?"

"No." He paused to reconsider her question. "Well— I'm definitely not going to burn it."

She laughed softly. "You're something else, you know that? It's just a nightgown. It doesn't mean anything."

"It meant something to Kevan when he picked it out for you." Even saying the words gave him heartburn. "Was it a special gift?"

"He gave it to me before Valentine's Day, right before we broke up. I...uh...wasn't ready for *that* step with him and getting the box with the pretty nightgown sealed the deal for me. I knew it was time to put an end to our relationship."

Learning that she hadn't slept with Kevan soothed his

raw nerves. It was a completely primitive reaction, but he couldn't help it. He liked knowing that she had trusted him more than the cop.

Stepping forward, Bianca caressed his chest. "I really didn't mean to hurt your feelings, Sergei. It was just a pretty chemise in the bottom of my drawer. That's it. I honestly didn't even think about Kevan when I picked it. I just thought it might look pretty on me."

"It did." He leaned down and captured her mouth. "From now on, I buy all of your sexy, pretty things, okay? If there's anything else in your closet or drawers, get rid of it."

She drew a shape on his pec. "I should be really annoyed by this possessive streak of yours."

"But?"

"I sort of like it."

"Sort of?"

"Okay. I really like it."

"Good." Kissing her again, he swatted her plump ass. She jumped and pressed those luscious tits of hers against him. When he massaged her bottom, she mewled like a kitten. Breaking away from her mouth, he grinned and brushed their noses together. "Go upstairs and wait for me. I'm going to give you a head start while I turn off the lights down here."

"Why do I need a head start?" she breathlessly asked.

"So you can think of a way to make this," he gave the clothes a little shake, "up to me."

With a squeal of excitement, Bianca dashed upstairs. Still amped up with adrenaline and so easily aroused by her, Sergei groaned at the sight of her voluptuous body streaking toward her bedroom. Chuckling at how much fun they were having together, Sergei switched off the lights and checked the windows and doors again.

Pausing in the sunroom, he looked out over the dark backyard. His gaze settled on the dilapidated carriage house that somehow seemed so ominous. That prowler was still out there. What he wanted with Bianca was any man's guess—but Sergei would be damned before he let that freak get anywhere near her.

The daytime detail he had planned to put on her starting tomorrow no longer seemed enough. It wasn't just those racist assholes who posed a threat to Bianca. It was this nameless, faceless being who skulked in the night.

Sergei couldn't decide who was more dangerous.

* * *

Putting one foot in front of the other, Sergei trailed Vivian along her morning jogging route. Not far behind, Danila Cherevin, one of the Nikolai's trusted men, followed in a black sedan. Sergei thought the escort was overkill. They had never encountered any problems while running, but the boss had very specific orders when it came to guarding his wife. Rather than risk his wrath—or Vivian's life—they worked in pairs and made sure she was closely watched.

Although he had assured Bianca he would rather make love than sleep, Sergei was feeling the effects of that choice this morning. Not that he would have changed anything. Even now, he daydreamed about getting balls-deep in her silky wet heat again. Though their evening had started off with her shy and unsure participation, it had ended with Bianca unleashing the confident sex goddess he had always suspected lurked within her.

Pushing aside those lusty thoughts, he concentrated on

Vivian's bouncing ponytail. Typically, she was whipping his ass by this point in the run. Although Ivan required him to jog as part of his training regimen, Sergei had always been better at short sprints than long distance. That's where Vivian excelled. Lithe and spry, she had been running cross-country and marathons since her teenage years

But today she seemed to be losing steam much earlier than he had ever seen her. He thought back to their last run. Her pace had been bad enough that he'd caught up with her by the time they reached their usual cool down point. Worried about her, Sergei kicked up his speed.

As he drew near, Vivian stunned him by bolting off the path and racing toward the nearest trashcan in the park. Gripping the sides of the bin, she made a terrible sound and began to vomit. Sergei cringed and put his hand on her upper back, rubbing between her shoulder blades as her stomach emptied. Just as she neared the end of the eruption, she began to dry heave violently. The sound made him wince with sympathy. Whatever she had eaten for breakfast must have been bad.

Unless...

He hastily pieced together the signs. Her sickness, the way she hadn't been ordering a glass of wine with lunch, her early bedtimes, Nikolai's overprotectiveness—they all fit together to form one very clear result.

"Hey! Is she okay?" Danny ran across the green grass to join them at the trashcan near the bench and tree. In his hands, he held a bottle of water and a package of wet wipes. "Here. I thought she might need these."

Sergei twisted open the cap on the water and pressed it into her hand. "Here, sweetheart. Take this."

She accepted the bottle and rinsed her mouth before taking a few slow sips. Danny handed him a couple of wet wipes that Sergei used to swipe her face and the back of her neck.

"The car is right over there." Danny gestured to the spot where he had illegally parked. "We should get her home."

Drinking some more water, she wagged a finger. "I need to cool down and walk or else I'll start to cramp."

"I don't think that's a good idea. You're sick. You need to go home."

She frowned at Danny. "I'm not sick. I'll be fine."

Sergei pursed his lips as Vivian shoved by them and headed for the path. He tapped Danny's shoulder. "Take the car three blocks and wait for us."

"If she says no?"

"I'll pick her up and throw her in the backseat myself." Pushing away from Danny, Sergei jogged toward Vivian and finally caught up with her. She had her hands resting on her head as she walked. He noticed her pallor and the drawn lines around her mouth. "You should get in the car and rest. You don't have to prove anything, Vivian."

She glanced up at him. "You sound like Kolya."

"He's right. If you're pregnant, you should be careful."

Vivian stopped dead in her tracks and narrowed her bright blue eyes at him. "Did he tell you?"

Sergei shook his head. "I put together the clues." Curious, he asked, "Why the secrecy?"

She started walking again so he matched her pace. "I just wanted something that was *ours* and only ours for a little while. No offense," she glanced at him, "but with you and Danny following me everywhere, I never get to keep anything to myself. I wanted this to be for us and only us for a few weeks."

"I get it," he assured her.

"And then, you know, Erin and Ivan were about to get

married, and Benny and Dimitri are still waiting for their baby girl to be born," she continued. "I didn't want us to announce our happy news and take anything away from them. They deserve to have their special moments in our group of friends without having to compete with news of another baby."

Sergei wasn't surprised that she was thinking of Erin and Benny's feelings. Sometimes he worried that she thought about other people too much. Considering some of the discussions he had overhead between Nikolai and his wife, the boss thought the same thing.

"Also…." She drew out the word and seemed to be wavering between completing her thought and keeping it to herself.

"Also?" He prompted carefully, certain she needed to get whatever was bothering her off her chest. They had developed a close enough friendship that he could read her that easily nowadays.

She finally answered him. "I think Nikolai is trying to shore up defenses to make sure I'm protected while pregnant. I get the feeling he's uneasy about blowback from that mess in January. I want to keep this quiet as long as possible so he has time to do whatever it is he needs to do."

Sergei wasn't fully apprised of the arrangement between the married couple when it came to the boss' private business, but he assumed Nikolai wasn't telling her *everything*. Vivian was smart enough to fill in most of the blanks. With a father like Romero Valero, one of the most infamous and violent men of the underworld, she had learned about the darkness in the world the hard way.

How much did she know about the Night Wolves problems heating up right now? After the way the skinheads had beat up the two dancers, it was clear the

Night Wolves knew Besian and Nikolai had been behind framing them for the murders Grisha had committed. Did they also suspect Vivian had been the one to hand over the incriminating evidence that caused the Feds to raid them and free those trafficked girls?

Suddenly, Nikolai's behavior over the last couple of weeks made sense. Sergei couldn't even imagine how much stress the man had been under trying to make sure his wife and unborn child were safe. After the upheaval during the winter, Nikolai could no longer pretend that the people he loved were untouchable. Grisha had shattered the old rules. Everyone feared it might soon be open season on the families of the men mired in Houston's seedy underbelly.

An unexpected vision of a pregnant Bianca danced before him. Before that moment, considering any woman pregnant with his child had sent him into a panic. He had always been extremely careful in his dalliances to avoid exactly that outcome…but he couldn't deny that there wasn't something oddly intriguing about sharing such a connection with Bianca.

He could just imagine her sweet, smiling face and round, high belly. Enjoying the daydream, he pictured the two of them kicked back on that big, comfortable couch in front of the den fireplace. She would have her head resting in his lap while he caressed the curve of her belly and they talked about decorating a nursery or picking baby names.

Another thought, this one more horrifying, struck him cold. A man with a shaved head and dark tattoos attacked Bianca outside her bridal boutique. Pregnant, she would be too clumsy and slow to escape. His eyes closed briefly, and he swallowed hard, forcing down the bile threatening to erupt from his throat.

God! No wonder Nikolai had been on edge. Sergei wasn't even close to reaching a point where the good parts of his daydream could become a reality—but Nikolai was living it. Nikolai loved Vivian so deeply. No doubt he loved that baby growing inside her just as much. The boss must have been consumed by the need to keep them both very safe.

"I won't say a word to anyone. This secret stays here."

She smiled gratefully. "What about Danila?"

"We'll tell him it was something you had for breakfast. He won't question it. Even if he does guess, he knows better than to say a single word."

She nodded. "I trust him."

"We'll take care of you, Vivi. You don't need to worry. Just concentrate on the baby and we'll do the rest."

Vivian slid an arm around his waist and hugged his side. "Listen to you! You big, soft Russian marshmallow!"

He snorted and pulled her ponytail. "Marshmallow, huh? If I'm so soft, you better tell your husband to pull the money he'll be betting on me in a couple of weeks."

Her arm fell from his waist. "Does Bianca know?"

His jaw tensed. "No. I haven't told her yet. I had the weekend off from training, but I start this evening. She'll wonder what I'm up to."

"You need to tell her, like, tonight."

"She won't approve."

"No, she won't," Vivian agreed, "but she really likes you. If you're honest with her now, she can process her feelings before the tournament. She'll want to be there for you."

"Like hell!" Sergei shook his head. "I don't want her anywhere near that place."

"Okay, so, maybe not *physically* there, but she'll want to support you, especially considering the reasons you fight."

She must have caught the way he shifted uncomfortably. "Sergei, you did tell her about your mom and brother, right?"

"I mentioned them, yes, but I didn't go into details." Before Vivian could push him on the issue, he reminded her, "You didn't tell me that Bianca's brother was killed by a guy with ties to *nochniye volki*!"

She rolled her eyes. "You didn't ask for specifics. If you want all those gruesome details, you need to talk to the girl who was actually there when it happened."

Sergei didn't enjoy the thought of baring his secrets to Bianca or asking her to come clean about hers, but it needed to be done. They were early enough in their relationship that the foundations needed to be built on solid ground, not on a bed of shaky, shifting lies. "I'll tell her tonight."

"Good." They walked in silence for a few minutes. "So it's going well between the two of you?"

He laughed. "As if you haven't been calling and texting her fifty times a day to ask?"

She thumped his arm. "I have not! I decided to stay out of it—"

"By asking me how it's going right now?"

"Forgive me for being curious about two of my favorite people."

"Okay," he said with a chuckle. "It's going well. We're making it work."

"I'm really happy to hear that. You two look good together."

"I like to think so."

Danny's idling car came into view, but he tapped Vivian's shoulder to stop her before they got any closer. She glanced up at him expectantly. "Yeah?"

He nervously rubbed the back of his neck and finally

worked up the courage to ask her something a bit awkward. "Where would I go to buy some really nice, like extremely classy, lingerie for Bianca?"

An amused smile stretched Vivian's mouth. "*Oooh!* This sounds exciting!"

He groaned. "Come on, Vivian. Don't make fun of me."

"I'm not." She patted his arm. "I'll take you to my favorite shop after we shower and change. I've gone there with Bianca so I know they have her measurements on file. It's a very high-end place. You'll find plenty of beautiful things for her."

Considering Nikolai only allowed Vivian to buy the very best, Sergei was assured of the finest quality for Bianca. He had no doubt it was going to be outrageously expensive, but she was worth it. Besides, he had promised to replace the nightgown he'd torn from her body that first night. After that mess with Kevan, he never again wanted to think of any other man when he peeled away the frilly, silky things she liked to wear. He wanted to know that it was something he picked especially for Bianca that she wore for him.

While he guided Vivian across the street to Danny's idling car, he wondered at the overwhelming possessiveness he felt toward Bianca. He'd had plenty of girlfriends before her and never once had he experienced such a surge of greediness. It surprised him considering he had shared women in bed—sometimes with other women and sometimes with other men—on at least half a dozen occasions. He hadn't experienced the slightest bit of jealousy during those encounters.

The idea of letting another person touch Bianca the way he enjoyed touching her made his heart seize. His fingers curled into tight fists. Hell. Fucking. No.

He remembered Ivan once telling him about the moment Erin had walked into his life. His trainer and mentor had confessed that Erin ensnared him with one simple, easy smile. Ivan swore he had known the moment he brushed tears from her face that she would be his—always and forever.

But Sergei's intense reaction toward Bianca perplexed him. From his very first date as a young, innocent teenager to now, he had only ever felt this level of possession with Bianca. He had dated some beautiful, sweet, lovely women over the years, but only Bianca made him feel this way.

Deep down inside, he suspected the answer was simple enough. In fact, it was a four-letter word that he'd never uttered to anyone except his family. Instead of gripping him with dread or panic, the realization settled upon him like a warm embrace.

Fairly certain that Bianca needed much more time, Sergei decided to keep this discovery to himself. He didn't dare confess the depth of his affection just yet. She was still so skittish and might reject him outright.

Things like this couldn't be rushed. After waiting five months for her to let him into her life, he could find the patience to wait a little while longer. The last few days had proven that Bianca was well worth the wait.

CHAPTER NINE

Checking my rearview mirror, I switched off the ignition and slid out of my car. I glanced around the quiet, upscale and incredibly private neighborhood where Vivian lived. I expected to see the maroon sedan or the slate blue truck I swore had been following me all day, but the street was clear. Deciding that the visit from my prowler had put me on edge, I chalked it up to paranoia, headed up the sidewalk and rang the doorbell.

When the ornately carved door swung open to reveal Nikolai, I smiled nervously. Although he had never been anything but kind to me, he had an intimidating air about him. The sleeves of his crisp dove gray shirt were rolled up to his elbows, revealing a swath of tattoos I had never before seen. A couple of them were similar to the marks decorating Sergei's skin, but I suspected Nikolai had dozens more than the Russian heating up my sheets.

Doing my best not to stare at his arms, I met his inviting gaze. "Hi, Nikolai."

"Hello, Bianca." He stepped aside and gestured toward the entryway. "Please come inside. Vee is in her studio.

She's waiting for you."

"Great." I walked by him but didn't go any farther than a few feet behind him. He probably wouldn't have minded if I had headed straight back to the recently converted home studio space, but I wouldn't have felt comfortable getting too casual in his home.

After he locked the door, Nikolai motioned for me to walk with him. "How is business?"

"Wedding season is in full swing so it's pretty wild around the shop."

"We're fully booked at Samovar with rehearsal dinners and catering orders. I can imagine what your schedule must look like."

"I'd rather be working my tail off than begging for business, you know?"

"Oh, I know."

The faint thump of electronic music filtered through the closed French doors sealing off the studio. He reached for the handle but didn't immediately open it. Instead, he glanced at me and asked, "How long have you had this problem with the prowler?"

Surprised by his interest, I replied, "Um, you know, just a few weeks. Why?"

His shoulders bounced nonchalantly. "You're one of Vee's best friends. She cares about you, and it's important to me that the people she cares for are safe."

"Oh. Well…thanks."

He tilted his head in acknowledgment and rapped his knuckles against a glass pane before opening the door. "Vee? Bianca is here."

She appeared with paint-stained fingers and a smock smudged with old, dried paint. Twirling a palette knife, she waved me inside. "Hey! I'm just finishing up. You want to help me clean brushes?"

I issued a little laugh. "Sure."

"Vee," Nikolai cut in carefully, "I'll take care of that for you later." He gestured around the studio. "The fumes, *solnyshko moyo*."

So he was worried about the fumes from paint thinner? I ticked another box on my running list of pregnancy symptoms. Now I was all but certain Vivi had a little Nikolai bun in that oven of hers.

Vivian placed her paint-splattered hand atop her husband's on the door knob in a loving gesture. "All right, Kolya. I'll leave the brushes for you."

He bent down, kissed her cheek and then brushed his lips along the curve of her throat in a sensual, intimate way. Smiling at us, Nikolai backed away from the door. "Bianca, will you be staying for dinner?"

"Oh, I wouldn't want to intrude."

"You're not," he assured me. "I'll set a third place for dinner."

"What about Sergei?" Vivian asked. "Is he free tonight?"

"No, he's staying late at the gym. He told me he was going to grab a bite with some of the guys from the warehouse."

"Would you like a glass of wine, Bianca? I'd be happy to bring one to you," Nikolai offered.

"No, but I'll have one with dinner." I held up a finger. "It's my one glass limit when I'm driving."

"Smart girl," he said and left us.

Vivian looped her arm through mine and brought me into the studio. "I'm trying to finish up a few new pieces for my London show."

"Oh! Right!" After her spectacularly successful show in January, Vivi had networked her little backside off and snagged a major benefactor in the international art world.

Niels Mikkelsen, the Danish billionaire art collector and magnate, had fallen in love with her art and had massaged his contacts abroad to get her an invitation to show her pieces in one of London's best galleries. It was a huge accomplishment for her, and I couldn't be prouder.

"Are you going to come?"

"To London?"

"Yes."

"Um…"

"Come on! You know you want to go."

"Well…"

"You and Sergei could make it a romantic getaway." She suggestively waggled her eyebrows. "You both need a vacation."

The idea tempted me enough that I didn't immediately shoot it down. "We'll see."

Smirking triumphantly, she dropped her dirty paint brushes into a plastic bin and put the lids back onto the tubes of opened paint. I examined the canvases propped up on easels. Upon closer inspection, I realized she was reviving old techniques I hadn't seen her use since high school. "You're doing mixed media with this collection?"

"I'm building off the tattoo histories for this collection and doing my interpretation of all this." She whirled a palette knife around her head. "You know, this bizarre life of mine and the juxtaposition of *nice* Houston with, well, the *darker* side of the city. It felt right to go back to something grittier, more textured." She studied her works. "Layers, you know? In art and life."

"I get it. I like it."

"I knew you would." She smiled at me. "So…tell me about Sergei."

I leaned against her worktable and fiddled with a paper towel. "It's really good."

"I hear he kicked in your door." She started to giggle. "I would have loved to have seen your face when you saw that door hanging off its hinges."

I couldn't help but laugh with her. "He made it all right by replacing the door."

"And running off your prowler last night?"

"Yes. Did he tell you about getting sort of arrested?"

"No! What happened?" She peeled out of her smock. "Should I be worried?"

"No. It was a stupid thing with Kevan. Sergei was chasing the prowler, and I called 9-1-1. Kevan was the closest police officer so they ran into each other. Kevan didn't buy his story so he cuffed Sergei and drove him to my house to prove that he was a liar. Honestly, I think he probably recognized Sergei as one of Nikolai's, um, employees. Kevan knows that I'm friends with you so I think he was trying to make a point about Sergei being the wrong type of guy."

She gave me a look. "Well that's awkward."

"You have no idea." I decided not to tell her about Sergei stripping me of the gifted clothing and making love to me until I thought I was going to pass out. I figured she wouldn't appreciate the details of Sergei's skills as a lover, especially since she considered him almost a brother. "Whatever Kevan was trying to do, it didn't work on me."

Vivian came to me and took my hand. She didn't say anything at first and seemed to be choosing her words carefully. "I know it's really hard for you to break your rule. I understand, and I respect your reasons for it."

Wondering where this was coming from, I frowned. "I know you do."

"So I'm not going to stand here and tell you that Nikolai's men are different than the men who took your brother away from you. I'm just going to say that Sergei is hands-down one of the finest men I've ever known." She held up her hand. "Okay. Yes, so he sort of crosses the line every now and then, but I know that he's never crossed *those* lines."

"But he's done so many illegal things." I voiced my fears. "How do I overlook that?"

She swallowed hard. "I accept Nikolai for what he is— and what he isn't. I love him, and I'm willing to take this walk with him, wherever it leads us."

"You sound like Sergei," I said softly. "He says we have to start our journey here, where we are now."

"And where is the journey going?"

"I don't know, Vivi."

"That's okay." She squeezed my shoulder. "You're still feeling out the parameters. It's a very new relationship."

"Is it?" I spoke aloud a thought I had been having all day. "Sergei and I have been dancing around this for months. Let's be real here. I've been in lust with that man since the first moment I saw him. What I feel for him now? It scares me. It's *that* strong."

"You say that like it's a bad thing."

"It's unsettling for me."

"So talk to Sergei," she suggested. "He's a good listener. I chat his ear off all day long. He always gives good advice when I need it."

"Really?"

"Yep." She squeezed my hand. "I know Sergei looks tough and scary, but he's a gentle soul. If you want him, let him know that you need some time. He'll wait for you."

"I already made him wait five months for a single kiss, Vivi."

"And he was happy to do it," she insisted. "Listen to

me. Guys like Sergei and Nikolai? You know what they want? They just want a strong, sexy, smart woman they can love, spoil and pamper. If you think that's something you might want..."

"It is. Just...not yet."

"So tell him."

"I will."

Nikolai knocked at the door and popped his head inside the sunroom-slash-studio. "Dinner is ready."

Sitting down with the couple for dinner was a pleasant experience. I had no idea Nikolai cooked so well. Perhaps I should have suspected as much considering he owned one of the finest and most popular restaurants in the city. I noticed the way he poured a half glass of wine for Vivian and the way she didn't touch it. I so wanted to indulge my curiosity but held my tongue and comment on their ruse.

While enjoying my dessert and a cup of coffee, I caught her yawning and wound up my visit. They both walked me to the door, but Nikolai actually came out onto the sidewalk, almost as if he wanted to make sure I got to my car all right. I found it slightly strange but chalked it up to his overprotective streak.

When I got to my car, I glanced up and down the street—and saw that damned maroon car sitting farther down the street. Frustration welled inside me. *What the hell?*

Hiking my purse higher on my shoulder, I abandoned my car and marched across the street. I had had just about enough of weirdos trying to scare me this week. Whoever this creep was, he was about to get an earful from me.

"Bianca!" Nikolai called out my name. "Stop! Come back!"

But I was already at the passenger side door. Pissed off, I knocked hard on the darkly tinted glass. "Hey! Jackass! Lower this window right now!"

Instead of lowering the window, the driver's side door opened, and the very last person in the world I had ever expected stepped out. It was Eric Santos, Vivian's cousin and a detective who specialized in Houston's gangs.

"Eric?" I sputtered his name with surprise.

He offered a boyish, lighthearted grin. "I prefer that to jackass."

Thrown for a loop by his appearance, I asked, "What are you doing here?"

Eric's gaze slid to Nikolai who had finally reached us. "I'm on business."

I glanced at Nikolai and immediately recognized that taut expression. There was some very old, very complicated history between these two, and I really didn't want to step in the middle of it.

"Santos."

"Nikolai."

With an aggravated sigh, Nikolai said, "Santos, I've made it abundantly clear that you are welcome in my home."

"Your home, huh?"

Nikolai's mouth settled into a tight line. "Our home."

"Uh-huh."

"You don't have to skulk on my street every time you want to visit Vee."

"Your street?" Eric looked up and down the road. "I was under the impression these streets belong to the city of Houston."

Nikolai didn't touch that one. Instead, he said, "Vee would like to see you. It's been a few weeks since the two of you have had lunch. You should come in and say hello."

Eric looked like he wanted to say yes, but he shook his head. "I can't. I'm on the clock."

"Outside my house?"

"No. I'm not sitting on your house."

If he wasn't sitting on Nikolai's house that meant...

Nikolai's gaze snapped to me, and a cold chill crept up my neck. Mouth dry, I asked the obvious question of Eric. "Why are you following me?"

Eric seemed to be weighing his words very carefully. "I have some concerns about your safety."

My stomach dropped. "What do you mean?"

"You've had multiple prowler reports in the last few weeks. The ten year anniversary of your brother's death is coming up very quickly. After Adam Blake's attack—"

Hearing the name of my brother's killer sent icy shivers down my spine. "What attack?"

Now it was Eric who looked shocked. "Kevan didn't tell you? I thought for sure—"

"He didn't say anything." Betrayal twisted in my chest. Why hadn't Kevan mentioned something like this to me? It was important, and I needed to know!

"Adam Blake was attacked in a prison yard fight. They got to him with a shiv that nearly gutted him. He's in bad shape. They're saying he won't walk again, and he's going to be attached to a colostomy bag for the rest of his miserable life."

If it had been anyone else, I might have felt some sympathy. Instead I felt the oddest sensation of justice. Maybe it was vengeance. Either way, it felt good to imagine that monster suffering for what he had done to my brother and what he had taken from my family. Deep down inside, I knew it was wrong to feel that way, that I should show some mercy and forgiveness, but I just couldn't do it.

"So what? You think some of his friends are trying to scare me?" It didn't make sense to me. Narrowing my eyes with suspicion, I pushed for more information. "What aren't you telling me, Eric?"

His pointed gaze fixed on Nikolai. "The prisoner they fingered as the main attacker is tied in with the Albanian crew."

"So? I don't know any of those people."

"No, you don't, but the man spending time in your bed sure as hell does."

My teeth instantly clenched as Eric's nasty insinuation. "Are you seriously going to stand there and accuse me of hiring a hitman?"

"Adam Blake shot your brother in cold blood right in front of you when you were fourteen years old, Bianca. People have arranged prison hits for a hell of a lot less."

A righteous anger burned through me. "Eric, you better be glad there's a friggin' car between us. Otherwise, I'd be knocking you upside the head with my purse for saying something so ugly to me."

A glimmer of regret crossed his face. "For what it's worth, I don't think you had anything to do with it, but the Night Wolves? They won't be so forgiving." He glanced at Nikolai again before focusing fully on me. "You probably don't want my advice, but I'm going to give it anyway. Get yourself a big ass dog, a really big gun and a security system. Hell, spring for a bodyguard if you can afford it. But most importantly, Bianca? Stay away from Sergei Sakharov."

"You're right, Eric. I don't want your advice." Pivoting on my heel and still pissed off at him for accusing me of arranging a murder, I snarled over my shoulder, "And stop wasting taxpayer dollars following me around. Go look for some real criminals."

"Like the one walking you back to your car?"

I couldn't believe he had the balls to lob that parting shot. To his credit, Nikolai didn't take the bait. He matched my steps and kept his gaze fixed forward. When we reached my car, I unlocked the door but didn't slide onto the driver's seat. Hand on the door, I turned to my best friend's husband and tried to get a read on him. He was impossible to decipher.

"Did you know?"

"About the attack on Adam Blake? Yes."

"Why didn't you tell me?"

"I assumed your lawyer or that ex-boyfriend cop of yours would tell you. It seemed unlikely that you wouldn't hear about it through your own personal network."

"Well, I didn't."

"I am sorry, Bianca. I can tell how shaken you are."

He seemed sincerely upset for me. "Is that why you asked me how long I'd had the prowler?"

"Yes. I was concerned that *nochniye volki*—sorry—the Night Wolves would try to hurt you."

"And Sergei? Did he know about Adam Blake?" The thought of Sergei keeping something like that from me made my stomach knot.

"No. In fact, he didn't even know you had ties with that skinhead crew until yesterday. He was very surprised and troubled by it."

The knot in my stomach loosened a bit. At least Sergei wasn't lying to me. "Troubled? Why?"

Nikolai drummed his fingers on the roof of my car. "It's a complicated situation, Bianca, and one that, frankly, I'm uncomfortable explaining in detail with you. All I will say is that it ties back into Vee's kidnapping last year. They're making things difficult for some of my business partners—"

"You mean those dancers that Sergei had to help?"

Nikolai didn't look pleased by my interruption. "In a way, yes."

I was pushing my luck asking for more information, but I decided to throw caution to the wind and be nosy. "What about the Albanians? Were they really behind Adam's attack?"

"No." There was an air of finality to his answer. Shifting his upper body, Nikolai lifted his hand. On cue, a pair of headlights popped on in the direction he faced. I gasped as I recognized the shape of the vehicle as the grayish blue truck that had been following me.

"Yes," he said gently. "Sergei worried that the skinheads would learn that one of my most trusted men was dating a girl like you."

"Like me? Oh." I motioned toward my face. "You mean a nice brown-skinned girl, huh?"

A twitch in his cheek told me I had hit the nail right on the head. "That sort of thing doesn't matter to anyone in my family, you understand? That's *those* people. Not us. But, yes, your race makes this a tricky situation. You're the perfect target for retaliation because of your skin color *and* because of your history with Adam Blake."

I glanced at the bright headlights. "So what? Sergei put a tail on me?"

"You mean everything to him, Bianca. He wants to protect you and ensure your safety. He can't be with you during the day because he's taking care of the most precious thing in the world to me so he chose men he trusted to look after you."

I didn't know whether to be touched that he was so concerned for my welfare or pissed off that he hadn't said anything to me about any of this. "He should have told me. I spotted them following me. Both vehicles," I added and looked back toward Santos' sedan. "It freaked me out."

"It's better to be freaked out than hurt, Bianca."

"I guess you have a point."

"After what I went through almost losing Vee?" He vehemently shook his head. "I'd rather my men risk the wrath of their women than leave them vulnerable."

Thinking of what Vivian had survived and what my brother had not, I grudgingly admitted to myself that Nikolai was right.

"Listen, Nikolai, um, let's not tell Vivian about this, okay?" Glancing back toward the house, I said, "I have a feeling she didn't see me running across the street like a crazy lady. If she had, I'm sure she would have come out here to investigate."

"Why don't you want me to tell Vee about this?"

"I don't want her worrying about me, especially in her condition."

His eyes widened slightly. "Her condition? Did she tell you?"

"No. I guessed. After she asked me to let out her bridesmaid dress, I had my suspicions." Daring to touch his arm, I promised, "I won't tell anyone. I figure you two have a reason for keeping it quiet."

"We do. I appreciate your discretion, Bianca."

I made a zipping motion across my lips. Then, with a teasing grin, I added, "I'll even practice my surprised face for when you two make your announcement."

"I'm sure you will." He gave my shoulder a squeeze. "Thank you, Bianca. You should get home. Be safe, please."

"I will."

Nikolai walked around my car and stepped onto the

sidewalk where he stood until I turned the corner and he disappeared from my rearview mirror. The truck driven by my babysitter followed close behind me. No doubt Santos inched along behind the truck.

My brain worked overtime to untangle the mess I had created for myself. The retaliation from Adam Blake's family and the racist Night Wolves gang couldn't be prevented but Sergei? Oh, that was all my own doing.

If I wanted to keep Sergei in my life, these types of episodes would probably be more frequent. Could I deal with that? Did I want to accept it? Those were the real questions I needed to answer.

One thing I knew for sure. Sergei had a hell of a lot of explaining to do.

CHAPTER TEN

Legs heavy and tired, Sergei slid out of his SUV and stretched his arms high overhead. He grimaced at the slight pull in his back and silently conceded that maybe his trainer Paco was right about laying off the bedroom antics until after the tournament. Not that he was going to listen, of course. Until Ivan returned from his honeymoon and put Sergei on dick-lockdown before the fights, he fully intended to enjoy every single minute he had with Bianca.

He retrieved the boutique bags filled with flirty, sexy lingerie and the suitcase he had packed before locking up his SUV for the night. After checking the gate, he started up the path to the house, his sneakers squelching against the brick pavers. When he'd driven down Bianca's street, Sergei had waved off the two guys he had hired to watch her. He hadn't heard a peep out of them all day so he assumed their babysitting shift had gone well.

Of course, when he entered the kitchen to the sound of Bianca slamming drawers, Sergei had second thoughts about that assumption.

Hovering just out of her sight, Sergei studied Bianca. With her hair in a messy bun, she wore tiny cotton shorts and a loose T-shirt. It was the very first time he had ever seen her looking even the slightest bit casual. She was stunning in her curve-hugging dresses and feminine nightgowns, but there was something oddly beguiling about this almost rumpled side of her.

When she bent over to pick up a spoon she'd dropped, Sergei had to bite back a groan. Those tight-fitting shorts rode up just enough to give him a peek at her bottom. He decided that tonight he was going to have her exactly like that, bent over with that sweet ass pressed against his thighs while he fucked her long and hard.

Ignoring the hard-on pressing against the front of his shorts, Sergei stepped into the kitchen and instantly drew her ire. Frowning at him, she said, "Oh, you're here."

Surprised by her cold greeting, he didn't come any closer. Obviously, he had missed something huge. "What's wrong?"

"That's a good question, Sergei." She tossed the spoon she had dropped into the sink where it landed with a noisy clatter and retrieved a clean one from the drawer. Without sparing another glance his way, she wrenched open the freezer and grabbed a pint of ice cream.

His chest tight and body tense, Sergei set down his suitcase and the lingerie bags. He crossed the space between them and took the ice cream and spoon from her hands, placing them on the granite island. Putting his hands on her shoulders, he gazed down into those chocolate-colored irises and asked simply, "What did I do to hurt you?"

She gripped the front of his T-shirt and stared up at him with a wounded expression that slashed at his heart. "Why didn't you tell me that you were having me followed? Why didn't you tell me about the problems you're having with the Night Wolves?"

Her question shocked him. "How did—?"

"Eric Santos," she cut him off. "Vivi's cousin the detective, you know?"

"Yes, I know Detective Santos." Memories of the storage locker and the man Nikolai and Kostya had interrogated for information on Vivian's disappearance flashed before him. It was the only time he had ever seen the detective cross the line.

"Eric thought I needed to know that Adam Blake had been shanked inside the prison yard and that his white power buddies think I'm the one who paid for that attempted hit."

"*What?*" Sergei's outraged shout made her snap back. Guilt-ridden, he gently stroked her arm. "I'm sorry. I didn't mean to scare you."

She ignored his outburst and poked him in the chest with the spoon. "You should have told me that you were having problems with those racist whackjobs! I had to go online to find out about the dancer who was killed. Didn't you think I needed to know about that?"

"I told you that I'm not going to involve you in that side of my life, Bianca. I didn't think you needed to know the gruesome details of that woman's death." Hand to his chest, he swore, "I did not know about Adam Blake's attack. I just knew that the Night Wolves were coming after us as payback, and I was worried about you. I put two men on you out of an abundance of caution."

"Yeah, well, they need to practice their stealth approaches. I noticed I was being followed by two different vehicles today. A truck and a car," she clarified. "When I came out of Vivi's house tonight, I spotted that car and marched across the street to investigate. That's when Eric popped out and decided to fill me in on all this craziness."

"You did what?" Outraged that she would risk her life, he cupped her face. "Don't ever do anything like that again! Do you understand me? What if it hadn't been the detective? What if it had been one of those racist assholes with a gun aimed at your chest?"

"Well, I didn't know I was supposed to be on the lookout for them, did I?" She snapped back at him and slapped his chest with the spoon. "I thought it was the creepy stalker prowler guy."

"Even if it was your prowler, you shouldn't have tried to confront him, Bianca. It wasn't safe."

"Nikolai was right behind me. He wouldn't let anything happen to me."

"As much as I would wish him to be, Nikolai is not infallible. You seem to be forgetting that I was there the night Nikolai and Vivian were attacked. Even with a gun to defend himself and all of his enforcers nearby, Nikolai still lost Vivian. I had to watch those monsters throw Vivian in an SUV, knowing there was nothing I could do to help her."

She must have heard the guilt in his voice because her anger seemed to subside. She trailed her soft fingertips along his jaw. Seeking her heat and comfort, he lowered his face and nuzzled her cheek. "That wasn't your fault, Sergei."

"He trusted me to protect him and to protect Vivian. I failed them that night. I won't fail again." He threaded his fingers through her thick, black hair and tilted her head back just enough to tease his mouth to hers. "I will not allow you to be harmed. Whatever it takes, Bianca, I will keep you safe."

She melted into him and allowed him to have the kiss

he wanted. When it ended, she patted his chest and sighed. "I think we need to talk."

The words struck fear right into his heart. Was this it? Was this the moment he had been dreading? Had today's experience helped her remember all those reasons she had refused to have anything to do with him?

An invisible ball formed in his throat and threatened to choke him. He tried to swallow but couldn't. Mouth dry and heart racing, he decided to be brave and take it right on the fucking chin. "No, Bianca. If this is it—if you're ready to break up with me—just do it. Don't try to spare my feelings."

She didn't say anything at first. No, she simply gazed up at him with the strangest expression on his face. "Breaking up with you is probably the smartest, safest thing for me to do."

His stomach swooped, and he clenched his teeth together. She was right. He couldn't argue with her on that point.

"But I'm not going to do that."

His heartbeat sprinted as her words hit him. Finally able to swallow, he cleared his throat. "No?"

"No." She smiled up at him and tapped his chest with the spoon again. "Let's have ice cream and talk."

"I can't." At her frown, he hastily explained, "I can't have ice cream. I have to eat as cleanly as possible until the fights."

"Fights?"

Nodding, he grabbed the pint of vanilla ice cream in one hand and grasped her fingers in the other. "You said we need to talk so let's talk."

He led her over to the sturdy wooden table and patted the surface. "Sit here."

She shot him a look of consternation. "Sergei, we're

not doing *that* right now."

He snorted with amusement and swatted her bottom. "That's not what I want right now. Later? We'll do whatever I want."

"Whatever you want, huh?" She pursed her lips with annoyance but there was no way she could hide that glimmer of excitement in her eyes.

Certain she loved being bossed around by him, he pointed to the table. "Sit. Now."

Following his order, she wiggled that plump ass of hers and slid onto the table. He dragged out a chair and placed it in front of her. Those dainty feet of hers, the toenails painted the brightest shade of orange, rested on his thighs. He peeled the lid off the vanilla ice cream and took the spoon from her hand. The delicious scent tempted him, but he planned to eat something even tastier in a little while.

Dipping the spoon into the creamy, vanilla bean flecked dessert, he gathered a small bite and lifted it to her mouth. "Open up."

One of her delicately arched eyebrows lifted with surprise. "Are you seriously going to feed me?"

"Yes, I seriously am."

She laughed and leaned forward to take the bite he offered. After she swallowed, she licked her lips, seemingly unaware of all the tantalizing images she spurred with that simple action. "You're just full of surprises, aren't you?"

He shrugged and scraped the spoon across the ice cream again. "What can I say? I'm a complicated man."

"Yes, you are."

He fed her another bite before exhaling with resignation. "Almost six years ago, my older brother, Vitali, became entangled with some government corruption. He always had big dreams, you know? Money, success, power—he wanted it all, but he didn't want to work for it. So he took the easy way and ended up working as a middleman for a mob crew and some government officials who wanted to clean up dirty money."

"Um...your mob crew?" she asked in a quiet voice.

"No." It was the first time he had openly confirmed his ties to the mob to her. Not that she hadn't always known, of course. "A rival crew that ran with people our government back home considered terrorists."

"Jesus," she hissed. "That sounds dangerous."

"It was." Shaking his head, he lifted another spoonful of ice cream to her pouty lips. "Vitya," he used his brother's nickname, "got in too deep. After a hostage situation that went badly, the government cracked down hard—and the officials he had been helping launder money got snapped up in a dragnet."

"Oh no."

"The gang decided he was a loose end that needed to be tied up so they went to his flat to deal with the problem, but he wasn't there."

Her worried gaze pierced his. "Who was?"

"His wife and my two nieces."

She put a hand to her mouth. "No."

At the muffled word, he nodded and gritted his teeth together. Shoving down the painful feelings that threatened to bring tears to his eyes, he roughly cleared his throat and continued with the tale. "I had to identify what was left of them. It was..."

She clasped his hand and interlaced their fingers. Leaning forward, she kissed his forehead. "Baby, stop. You don't have to do this to yourself."

It was the first time she had ever used a pet name with

him. Somehow that little bit of sweetness eased the pain inside him. "I need to tell you everything. Right now. Tonight. Let's get it out there and be done with it."

"All right." Bianca kissed him, touching her lips to his with the barest bit of pressure. She caressed the back of his neck and then sat back to let him finish his tale.

He spooned another bit of ice cream into her mouth. "Before I could reach my younger brother Vladimir and my mother, they had snatched them. Vitya had gone into hiding like a coward. I didn't know what to do so I called the only man who could help me."

"Nikolai?"

"Yes." He offered her some more ice cream, but she shook her head. As he put the lid back on the cold carton, he explained, "Nikolai and Ivan had been a fixture in my life. They had lived in our neighborhood. They kept things quiet and safe. When they left for Houston, the big boss—Maksim—made sure that things stayed that way."

"So you weren't always part of, um, the family?"

"No. I stayed out of it. I did a few years in the army and went to university—"

"You went to college?" She looked taken aback. "Is that why you speak such perfect English? Did you finish?"

He shook his head. "I was close, but no."

"What did you study?"

"I wanted to be an architect. Now construction is the closest I'll get to that."

"That's not true. You could go back to school."

"It's too late for that, Bianca."

"It's not."

Certain she wasn't going to let this drop, he finally said, "I'll think about it."

She didn't look very convinced. Poking his stomach

with her big toe, she asked, "So you called Nikolai and...?"

"He sent me to see Maksim. The old man was looking for a reason to take on that crew and snuff them right out. I knew they were using me, but I didn't have any other choice. I had already lost three members of my family. It had to stop."

"What did you do?" Her voice was barely above a whisper. The fear in her eyes had him questioning what she thought him capable of doing.

"I sold myself to Maksim."

"You *what*?"

"The men holding my mother and brother agreed to a ransom, but it was too much for me to ever even dream of raising. Maksim bought me in exchange for the cash and the manpower to free them. He arranged a handoff and got them back."

"So you're like his slave?" Horror widened her eyes. "Sergei, that's not right!"

"It's not that simple."

"You belong to Maksim. He bought you. It's pretty simple, Sergei."

"I don't belong to him anymore."

She blinked. "Wait. *Wait*. Are you about to tell me that my best friend's husband *owns* you now?"

Sergei nodded stiffly. "After Maksim saved my family, I started working for the old man. It was typical enforcer stuff at first, but when he asked me to kill a man and his girlfriend for stealing, I couldn't do it. I called Nikolai and begged for his help."

"And he bought you?"

"My debt," he corrected. "Nikolai owns my debt to the family."

Speechless, she stared at him for the longest time. He

didn't know what to say so he kept his mouth shut and waited. Finally, she reached for his hand and dragged it onto her lap. Her fingertip traced the old scars on his knuckles. "So that's why you fight."

"Yes."

"To pay off your debt?"

He nodded. "And to raise money to bring my mother and brother over here."

She breathed out and shook her head. She wanted to say something but didn't. Instead, she asked, "What about your older brother? What happened to Vitali?"

"I couldn't save him. The other crew caught up with him, and they killed him."

"I'm sorry, Sergei. That's just…it's terrible." Still holding his hand, she said, "I guess it's my turn, huh?"

"You don't have to tell me if you aren't ready."

"I'm ready to tell you. It was really stupid though." She glanced toward the ceiling and blinked rapidly. "Even all these years later, I can't believe that I lost my brother because of a box of candy."

His brow furrowed. "I don't understand."

"We haven't been together long enough to talk money, but I'm a pretty frugal girl."

"Is that why you're trying to do the work around the house by yourself? Because, Bianca, it's not very frugal to have to pay a professional to come in and fix everything a second time."

"Yes, I'm quite aware of that. Some of the stuff around here I wanted to try myself as a way of proving I could do it all by myself."

Recognizing that stubborn independent streak of hers, he gave her thigh a little pinch. "You don't have to prove anything to me or anyone else. It's okay to ask for help."

She pinched him back. "I'm starting to figure that one

out."

"Good."

"I don't want you to think that I'm broke or whatever. Actually, I'm quite comfortable and have savings, mutual funds and retirement." She shrugged. "I just don't see the point of spending money on things I can get cheaper. Like my car," she said and gestured out back. "It was two years old and had less than ten thousand miles on it, but I got it for a steal. I got the house at a county tax sale auction for an outrageously low price. Same thing with my clothing. I do a lot of online designer flash sales."

He had no idea what a flash sale was. Putting together the glimpses she'd given him, he made an educated guess about the afternoon that had changed her life. "You didn't want to pay the outrageous prices for candy at the movie theater so you asked your brother to stop at the convenience store?"

"Yes. This was a few years before Mama moved the shop to its new location. The old shop was a few blocks away from a big, busy convenience store. Perry and I popped in for candy and drinks. We were along the back of the store, near the coolers, when we heard these loud, rude guys come inside."

"How many?"

"Three," she said, her fingers tightening around his. "I didn't see the one with a gun at first. I only saw the two with baseball bats. They were tearing the place up, knocking over displays and beating on the display cases. Mr. Mirwani was shouting at them. His wife was hiding behind the counter and calling the cops. Perry noticed that the door that led to the stockroom was open so he pushed me that way—and that's when they saw us."

Sergei could tell she needed some encouragement to finish so he curved his hand against her neck and rubbed his thumb up and down along the vein that pulsed wildly there. Soon, he planned to make her heart race for much better and pleasurable reasons. "What happened next?"

"The one who didn't have a baseball bat chased us. The door that led out to the alley was locked, and I couldn't get it open fast enough. Perry and the guy—Adam Blake—started fighting. My brother went down hard. Adam had his back turned to me so I picked up a broom and hit him across the back of the head."

She stopped and closed her eyes. A single tear dripped down her cheek. Sergei ached for her and slid a little closer. He embraced her and wiped the shiny wetness from her face. "Go on, Bianca."

"So I grabbed Perry's hand and tried to get him up off the ground so we could run, but he was pretty badly dazed. Adam got to his feet first and pushed me into a stack of boxes. I fell and then he was on top of me. He put his hands on my neck and started to choke me so I clawed at his face and scratched his cheek and eyelid open. That was when he hit me."

Sergei's jaw clenched together so tightly he was shocked his teeth didn't shatter.

"But then Perry jerked him off me and they started fighting again. It was such a mess and everything was happening so fast." She rubbed her temple. "Perry took another punch to the face and fell to the ground. Adam looked like he was about to stomp Perry's head so I jumped on his back. We were both slapping and spinning and shouting. Somehow I ended up against the wall. He slammed his head back and broke my nose and chipped my tooth."

Red spots clouded Sergei's vision. If Adam Blake hadn't been locked away in prison, he would have killed the man for hurting Bianca.

"He jerked away from me, and I fell to the floor. I didn't realize he had the gun tucked into the back of his jeans until he stepped away from me, and it fell. I don't know what I was thinking. I'd never fired a gun in my life but I lunged for it."

"And?"

"He got to it first. He called me...he said something really awful and aimed at my head. I closed my eyes." She closed them now, in the present, as if reliving the memory. "And then I heard Perry shouting my name. He jumped between us—and took the bullet right in the chest."

Her eyes flashed open. The shimmer of tears filled him with such sadness. He desperately tried to console her. "*Lyubimaya.*"

She sniffed loudly as he wiped her face with the bottom of his shirt. "Perry fell into my arms. Adam just looked at me. He seemed stunned. It was a complete turnaround from the vicious, bloodthirsty little bastard he had been. Then he ran out of there. Not long after, Mrs. Marwani rushed into the room and dropped down beside me. I didn't know it at the time, but Adam shot her husband on the way out the door. He died instantly."

Their gazes met, hers so wounded and his pained for the loss she had endured. Finally, she said, "In movies, they always make death this noble moment, you know? It's not like that in real life. Perry didn't say anything. He just clutched at me while he choked and wheezed. His blood spilled onto my legs and soaked my dress. He didn't say goodbye or have any last words. He just gasped...and that was it. That was the end of my brother's life."

He started to tell her that he was so sorry for her loss but the words wouldn't take away her pain. It had been so many years since Perry's murder that the days for offering condolences were long gone. Instead, he traced his thumb along the apple of her cheek and asked, "What's your favorite memory of your brother?"

Surprise flitted across her beautiful face. "I don't know." She considered his question. "Maybe the time he convinced me to go camping with him."

"You? Camping?" He didn't believe it. "Where did you put all of your hair products and makeup and clothes?"

Playfully thumping his arm, she laughed. "Yes, I know. I hated most of it. He wanted to go old school with a tent and sleeping bags. It was miserable—but somehow I ended up loving it. That was one of the last times we were together and one of the best weekends of my life."

Glad to see her smile again, he wrapped some loose strands of her hair around his finger. "Tell me what else Detective Santos told you."

"He said that the Night Wolves think I might have hired the prisoner who attacked Adam Blake. Apparently, this convict is tied in with some Albanian crew."

Sergei easily connected the dots. "And, because I'm with you, they think you used me to hire a hit." His gut clenched. "Shit."

"Yeah. I straight out asked Nikolai if the Albanians were behind the attack, but he said no."

He didn't think Nikolai had any reason to lie to her. "Then he must know who ordered the hit and why."

"I figured as much."

"Bianca," he spoke carefully, "we have to be extremely cautious until this matter is settled. You can continue working, but you have to promise me that you won't go anywhere without me or the men I hired to watch you." Before she could protest, he put his finger to her mouth. "Please, Bianca, don't fight me on this. Let me keep you safe."

She dragged his hand away from her lips. "I wasn't going to fight you. I am woefully out of my depths here. I need your help." Then, with a quirk of that sexy mouth of hers, she added, "But maybe you could give those two guys following me a refresher course."

"Sweetheart, they're going to be getting more than a refresher course when I get a hold of them in the morning." He was still aggravated beyond measure that neither man had texted or called him about Bianca's run-in with Santos.

Staring at their interlaced hands, she asked, "When do you fight again?"

He enjoyed the sight of their fingers intertwined. Her bare wrists inspired thoughts of jewelry. She needed something delicate and gold to decorate them. "The first weekend in June. It's a tournament that lasts two nights."

"There are tournaments?"

"Every year the bosses get together and put on a tournament. It's a way to introduce new fighters and score them for future betting."

"You only have to fight twice? Once each night?"

Sergei could hear the fear in her voice. "I will fight four times if I win."

Bianca caressed his knuckle with her thumb. "From what I hear, you never lose."

"I don't. It's why I'm so valuable."

"You're not a racehorse, Sergei. You're a human being. They shouldn't be making money off you like this."

Touched by her words, he admitted, "I make money off myself, too."

"To pay off your debt more quickly?"

"No, to bring Vladimir and my mother here. The last lawyer didn't work out very well." He didn't want to get into the details of how badly that experience had ended. "I need the money to pay for a new immigration lawyer and visas and—"

"There are easier ways than getting the shit beat out of you in a cage, Sergei."

"Easier, yes, but the money isn't as fast. I'm tired of waiting. I want my family here as quickly as possible."

"I don't like it."

"I don't expect you to like it."

"So what? You just expect me to stand on the sidelines and cheer you on while I pray you don't get killed?"

"I won't be killed, and I don't want you to stand on the sidelines. The fights are not the place for a woman like you."

She trailed her finger down his chest. "A woman like me, huh? What sort of woman is that?"

Sexual energy sizzled between them. Liking the turn their discussion was taking, Sergei peppered kisses along the exposed skin of her neck and jaw. "Gorgeous. Sexy. Classy."

"Keep going," she said with a smile coloring her voice.

He sucked hard on the curve of her throat and bit down gently. His dick throbbed at her excited gasp. "If I keep going, we're going to end up fucking on this table."

A mischievous glint brightened her eyes. "You say that like it's a bad thing."

Grinning, he stood up and strode toward his suitcase to dig out some extra condoms he had stowed in there rather than running upstairs for one from their stash. By the time he had grabbed what he needed, Bianca had undressed and perched like some sort of erotic wood nymph on the table. Her nipples enthralled him, and he gently pushed her back to the table so he could have better access to the places he most wanted to touch with his tongue.

"Sergei." Hearing her moan his name as he latched onto her breast made his balls ache. He sucked hard on her nipple, running his tongue over the peak, and then released it to attack the other one. She scratched at his scalp, her short nails gliding over his skin and sending shivers down his spine.

Wet and puckered, her nipples stood at attention when he was done with them. He flicked one and then the other before pinching them with enough force to make her hips buck off the table. "We should the pierce these. Can you imagine a pair of diamonds right here?"

"You're out of your mind." She hissed when he tweaked her nipple a little harder than usual. "It's not happening."

"Five months ago, you said us dating would never happen. Maybe we'll revisit the idea of piercings in a year."

"No." She ran her bare foot under his shirt. "Take this off." Her foot traveled down to his shorts. "These too."

He bent down to capture her mouth. "I think you're forgetting who is in charge here."

"Oh." She offered a contrite smile. "Right."

"I didn't say it was a bad idea." He stripped and tugged the chair closer to the table. Sitting down, he was still too tall, but it was a more comfortable angle for what he had in mind. Forcing her thighs wide open, he gazed upon the shiny pinkness of her pussy peeking out there. His mouth watered for a taste of her, and he decided not to deny himself a moment longer.

He probed the slick opening of her with the tip of his tongue. She squealed and wiggled as he started to fuck her that way. Despite her dating history, Sergei could tell she hadn't had much experience in his brand of sex. How any man could simply satisfy himself making love to Bianca in one position stupefied him. With her luscious body and sweet response, she was the hottest woman he had ever had—and the one he planned to make his one and only.

"Yes!" She pressed her pussy to his lips, encouraging him with her little moans and sighs. "Sergei, that feels so good."

He groaned against her cunt and slid his tongue through her folds to find her clitoris. Using his fingers to frame the tiny nub, he coaxed it out from its hood and fluttered his tongue over the swollen pearl. Bianca cried out and lifted her hips. He smiled against her pussy and went wild between her thighs.

She shattered in record time, her clit pulsing beneath his tongue and her pleasured cries echoing through the house. Without giving her a moment to catch her breath, Sergei thrust two fingers in her slippery channel. He attacked her clitoris with his tongue while fucking her pussy with both digits.

Slapping the table and clutching at his shoulders, Bianca let him have his way with her. He could feel her passage tightening around his fingers, squeezing him as he found the perfect rhythm with his tongue. "Sergei. Sergei. *Sergei!*"

Giving her two orgasms so quickly left him feeling rather accomplished. Grinning victoriously, he wiped his mouth on her soft belly, stood up and kicked the chair out of the way. He tugged her into a sitting position, pulled her down off the table and spun her around. One quick glance between her body and his told him she was too short for this position to work properly. Unless…

"Back on the table," he growled.

She gasped when he picked her up and deposited her

on the table. Kneeling there, she glanced back over her shoulder with bemusement. "Why am I up here?"

"Put your elbows on the table and offer me your pussy, Bianca."

She gulped but did as he had asked. He applied the condom and smiled at the perfect positioning of their two bodies now. Sometimes his extraordinary height was a real pain in the ass—and sometimes it was a real pleasure.

Gripping her hips, he dragged her back a few inches. He smoothed his hands along her thick thighs and caressed her bottom. Remembering the way she had reacted last night when he'd touched the pucker there, Sergei decided to see how hard that line was. He gathered some of the slick cream from her pussy and smeared it between her cheeks.

Her sharp intake of breath filled the kitchen. He drew leisurely circles around her anus. Tiny bumps raced across her skin like gooseflesh. Part of him wanted to know what she was thinking right now. He imagined her brain was racing with all the reasons why she shouldn't allow him to play with her like this.

Watching her carefully, he slowly penetrated her virgin ass with one finger. He had no intention of going any further than that tonight. That impossibly tight pussy of hers could barely take him. There was no way she was ready to take him here, but that didn't mean he couldn't teach her how good it could feel to stimulate her there.

When she didn't stop him, Sergei pushed in a little deeper. "Tell me how this feels, Bianca."

"Wicked," she said finally. "Sinful."

"Wickedly good or wickedly bad," he asked, slowly thrusting his finger in and out of her.

"Good," she admitted on a long sigh.

"Let's see how this feels." Lining up their bodies,

Sergei sheathed the full length of his dick. There was no stopping the groan that escaped his throat as he relished the snug, hot fit. "I can't get enough of your pussy. You're like my drug, Bianca. I crave you." He retreated almost completely, leaving just the head of his cock buried inside her before plunging deep. "I want you."

"I'm yours." She pushed back to meet his thrusts. "I'm all yours, Sergei."

The old table beneath them started to squeak and thump as Sergei increased his speed. It was going to be one very long—and very pleasurable—night.

CHAPTER ELEVEN

"I can't believe you've never eaten at Samovar." Sergei held my hand as he led me down the sidewalk to the five-star restaurant Vivian's husband owned. We were meeting friends for Benny and Dimitri's last hurrah before the baby arrived.

"Russian food isn't really my thing. Besides, when Vivi wanted to go out for dinner, the last place she wanted to go was the place she worked."

"Fair point." He paused before we reached the main doors and gave my gold hoop earrings a playful flick. "I'm sorry our first date plans had to be put on hold."

"The baby is coming any day. This will probably be the last time we get to hang out with Benny and Dimitri for a while." Laughing, I added, "Besides, I don't know about you, but Lena scares me. I wasn't about to tell her no."

He chuckled and slid his hand to my back, pulling me against him in a protective gesture. Lowering his head, he whispered, "Don't tell her I told you this, but the guys at the club she worked at used to call her the Dragon Lady."

My jaw dropped. "You're joking!"

He shook his head and smiled. "Some men are afraid of a strong woman."

"Not Yuri," I said, spotting the couple as we entered the lobby of the restaurant. The billionaire tycoon sat a few feet behind her, his ankle propped up on his knee, and watched as Lena chatted with a couple of oilmen. Living around Houston my entire life, I had developed a sort of sixth sense for picking out those types.

She took a business card from one of them and tucked it into her clutch before patting their arms. Yuri smiled at her as she approached and said something that made Lena grin. She reached down to adjust his tie, but he didn't let her draw back her hand until he had kissed each fingertip.

"Bianca!" Lena smiled at me and dragged me into a hug. Not wanting to stain my cheek with her lush red lipstick, she air kissed my cheek. "I'm so glad you guys could come." Her gaze skipped to Sergei before returning to my face. With a conspiratorial whisper, she said, "I have to hear this story."

"Later," I promised and turned to greet Yuri.

I was still shaking his hand when Nikolai appeared to take us to one of the best tables in the restaurant. Sergei's hand between my shoulder blades felt so right as we crossed the floor to join Dimitri, Benny and Vivian. I was falling fast for Sergei and becoming hopelessly addicted to his presence. When I had thrown the sheets in the wash earlier that morning, I had actually been sad to wash away the eucalyptus scent of him. Only the knowledge that my deliciously big Russian would be heating up those sheets again had eased the sadness.

I didn't think it was possible, but Benny's pregnant belly looked even bigger than it had at Erin and Ivan's wedding only a week earlier. She looked adorable in her empire waist dress and had a huge smile on her face as we hugged, but I sensed she was nearing that point in her pregnancy where she was tired and ready to get the show on the road.

How her extremely petite frame managed to bear that

load perplexed me. A bit selfishly, I realized I was probably going to lose the pool we had running on the baby. I had been sure that the baby would be a healthy seven pounds, but something told me Erin's seemingly outlandish guess of nine pounds was probably going to be closer.

Seated between Nikolai and Sergei, I shot Vivian's husband a pleasant smile. We hadn't spoken since that night outside their home. As far as I knew, Vivian remained completely in the dark about what had gone down. I wanted it to stay that way.

When Nikolai returned the smile, I couldn't help but think that he *owned* my man. *Listen to you!* I couldn't believe I was thinking of Sergei as my man. Of course, I suspected Sergei had been thinking of me as his woman since before the night he'd kicked my door down. That was simply his way.

When our waitress approached the table, I noticed a slight tightness to Vivian's mouth. It was that micro-expression of frustration that she sometimes had, and it vanished quickly. Smiling at the waitress, she addressed the stunning redhead in Russian. Whatever they said didn't seem to bother anyone else at the table so I brushed it off as one of those work things. Maybe the woman—her nametag said Lidia—had been a pain in Vivian's ass when they were both waiting tables here.

Or maybe Lidia had made the mistake of trying to come onto Nikolai...

Sergei's arm moved to the back of my chair, reminding me of that night at the wedding. "Do you want some help with the menu?"

I was relieved to see it had been printed in both Russian and English but had no idea what was good and what might be too much for my decidedly Southern palate. "Please?"

While Sergei pointed out dishes that might interest me, I kept an ear on the conversations around us. Everybody was talking business—new deals, expansions, recent successes and investment tips. Well. Everybody except for Sergei.

When I was drawn into a conversation with Benny about offering the *quinceañera* dresses, I couldn't shake the feeling that Sergei might be feeling left out tonight. He was in a weird position. Sure, he was Vivian's friend, and Nikolai treated him like family, but that didn't change the facts. Nikolai owned Sergei's body and used him as he would any other weapon in his arsenal.

As if that wasn't a bizarre enough power shift, Sergei was the only man at the table who brought in significantly less money than his partner and who wasn't a business owner of some kind. I believed Sergei was proud of my success, but was he the smallest bit embarrassed or disappointed in his career situation?

After learning he had gone to college to pursue his dreams of being an architect, I could only imagine what a bitter pill his position as an enforcer was to swallow. Did he imagine how his life might have been if his older brother hadn't been so miserably stupid?

With that uncomfortable thought rattling around in my head, I glanced up from my menu to catch Sergei staring at the waitress as she approached the table. They exchanged a smile before he dropped his gaze to his glass of water. Because he was friendly to everyone, I didn't think much of it…until Lidia walked around the table to stand behind Sergei while she took our orders.

The gorgeous, willowy waitress placed her hand on Sergei's shoulder with a touch that was much too familiar. An unwelcome idea began to form. I batted it away, refusing to even go there, and chalked it up to nothing more than friendship. Sergei spent a lot of time with Nikolai, and his boss was probably at Samovar most of the day. It was only normal that Sergei would be friendly with the staff.

Ever the alpha male, Sergei placed my order for me and made sure to tack on a glass of wine. I pinched his thigh under the table, but he one-upped me by sliding that big, rough palm of his under my skirt. His fingertips encountered the whisper-thin and exquisitely soft lace of the special panties he had given me. I had nearly died laughing when I had discovered the crotchless undies amid the gorgeous silk, satin and lace intimates, but after a little persuasion from Sergei, I had promised to give them a chance.

Recognition flashed in his dark eyes. He tried to push aside the lacy fabric to discover that secret part of me, but I squeezed my knees together, trapping his hand and denying him. Leaving his hand right there, he shot me a look that promised yet another night for the record books.

After his self-imposed celibacy, Sergei seemed to be making up for lost time. I didn't think I'd had as much sex in all the years I had been active as we had had in the last week. The man was insatiable—and inventive. Some of the things we had done together made me blush when I thought about them later. In the heat of the moment, that megawatt smile and sexy charm of his could induce me to try anything. As of yet, I hadn't been disappointed by his adventurousness or skill.

When our appetizers arrived, the conversation around the table turned to the baby and its precarious breech position. Benny was still hopeful the baby would decide to turn, but I had a feeling that kid was packed in there so tightly there was no room for maneuvering. I understood her fear of a C-section, especially the possibility of complications and recovery, but I sensed Dimitri preferred that route instead of attempting a breech delivery that might go badly.

Thinking of Benny's situation, I couldn't help but imagine myself giving motherhood a try someday. With my career in an upswing and the demands of the business rising, I assumed motherhood was a few years away. Sipping my wine, I glanced at Sergei who was deep in conversation with Dimitri and wondered what he would be like as a father.

The thought made my heart stutter. I shouldn't have even gone there—we were way, *way* too early in our relationship to even be thinking about strollers and cribs—but I couldn't help myself. After hearing how far Sergei was willing to go to save his mother and brother and having seen with my own eyes what he was willing to do to protect me, I harbored no doubts about his instincts to nurture and love.

But his current line of work was much too risky for raising a family. So many bad things could happen to him or the people he loved because of his association with Nikolai. Pushing a strange dumpling around my plate, I wondered if that was the reason Vivian seemed hell-bent on keeping her pregnancy a secret. She had already survived so much violence in her short life. The desire to protect her baby from Nikolai's enemies must have been strong.

The sound of Lidia's husky voice drew me out of my thoughts. She had stopped by to refill glasses and sweep away empty plates between courses. I watched the way she spoke to Sergei, making a point out of conversing with him in their shared language so I couldn't understand what she was saying. Her slender hand slid from his shoulder to brush the spot right above the collar of his steel blue blazer.

Is she for real? I couldn't decide if this lady was just clueless or actively trying to bait me. Sergei seemed totally oblivious to her come-on so I decided to let it slide for now. Refusing to cause a scene, I pretended not to notice and let Lena draw me into a discussion about her fledgling crisis PR firm dipping their toes into the fashion waters.

When Lidia returned with our entrees and a couple of runners in tow, she made another point of bending low to chat with Sergei. This time I actually understood one of the words that left her mouth. It was a term I often heard Vivian call Nikolai—and wholly inappropriate for the situation.

Sergei's low laughter and murmured reply hit me like an ice pick to the chest. I recognized they weren't simply on friendly terms. No, they had been much, much closer than that. So close that she felt comfortable calling him darling...

Until that moment, I had entertained only the vaguest idea of the women Sergei had dated before me. Sitting here, staring up at this knockout with a trim figure and shapely, long legs, I just wanted to cry. How in the hell did I compete with that?

The answer came quickly. I couldn't.

Lidia was a ten, and I was, on my best day, a seven. My self-confidence took a major hit, and I began to deflate. The gorgeous gold dress that I had thought looked so good on me suddenly seemed to be too clingy and tight. I thought of the way it hugged the not so firm parts of me, the spots that jiggled and needed a hefty application of Spanx.

If Sergei could have a supermodel like Lidia, what the hell was he doing with me?

All those old feelings of inadequacy began to creep up on me. I didn't even want to consider the what-ifs. I desperately wanted to believe Sergei wanted me—the real me with cellulite and flaws and a big behind—because he liked me. Faced with Lidia and the evidence that he could do and had done much better, I began to wonder how long I could hold his fascination. With all the complications I brought into his life now that my ties to the Night Wolves were front and center, would he grow tired of me and remember how good he'd had it with a beautiful woman who shared his heritage and his language?

Every fiber of my being screamed for me to publicly stake my claim on him and to put Lidia in her place, but I refused to lower myself to that level. I wasn't about to start brawling over a man—even a man I cared about as much as Sergei—in a freaking restaurant while surrounded by our friends. I had too much self-respect to do something so déclassé.

Glancing around the table, it seemed only Vivian had picked up on the strange vibes. She narrowed those icy blue eyes at Lidia but waited to say something to our waitress until the woman bent down to place Vivian's plate in front of her. Whatever Vivian hissed into Lidia's ear hit its mark. The waitress snapped up ramrod straight and strode away from the table.

"Vee," Nikolai addressed his wife in a voice I could barely hear over the clatter of silverware and the low din of conversations all around us. The withering look Vivian pinned him with dissuaded him from continuing whatever he had planned to say. Apparently, there was one person in the whole wide world who could scare

Nikolai. Unfortunately for him, it was his wife.

Choosing not to make it into a big deal, I gave my dinner a test and decided it wasn't half-bad. I doubted the flavors of Russian food would ever please my palate, but I liked the experience of trying new things. Once, I caught Lena shooting me a sympathetic look that made us both smile. It seemed only Benny had developed a true love for the exquisitely prepared dishes. Or maybe it was a pregnancy thing...

"How was it?" Sergei leaned over to speak with me and brushed his fingertips along my nape as we waited for our dishes to be cleared. With a teasing smile that made my belly swoop, he asked, "Am I going to be making scrambled eggs and toast for you when we get home?"

"No," I said with a short laugh. "It was okay. It was different, but I liked some of it."

He picked up the small dessert menu and flashed it in front of me. "Let's find something you'll enjoy."

"Oh, you're going to let me pick this time?"

"Dessert should always be the lady's choice." His smoldering gaze heated me right up. That sneaky hand of his glided along my inner thigh and reached its destination before I could stop it. The corners of his sexy mouth lifted with the hint of a smile.

Schooling my features, I managed not to react to the wicked swipe of his fingertips along the seam of my sex. There was just enough lace in the way to impede his exploration but I doubted he was going to let a little thing like that stop him. "What do you recommend?"

"Something soft, warm and sweet," he murmured, his fingertips dipping beneath the lace to glide over my clitoris.

My thighs tensed around his hand, and I had to bite my lower lip. Was this really happening? Was I sitting here in a restaurant letting my boyfriend play with my pussy? What in the hell had Sergei done to me to make me behave so wantonly? Why couldn't I stop him?

Because you don't want to…

Keeping my gaze focused on the menu, I tried to play it cool. I would die of mortification if one person at the table realized what Sergei was doing with that sinful hand of his. Glad for the long tablecloths and the wall at our back that kept us mostly hidden, I thought of Sergei swearing off desserts until after his fights. "I really shouldn't have dessert. It would be cruel to make you watch me eat."

Though the statement was meant for Sergei, it was Lidia who snorted derisively as she bent down to gather up the dishes between Sergei and Yuri. Fully aware that she was making fun of my weight, I stiffened with embarrassment. My lips parted so I could clarify my statement, but Sergei stopped me.

Without a single glance toward his ex, Sergei kept his gaze fixed on me. He trailed a finger down my cheek. No doubt he could feel the hot flush of my embarrassment. His breath tickled my ear as he moved in so close that no one else would overhear us. With his other hand, he cupped my pussy in the most possessive way. "You eat dessert now, and I'll have mine later, yes?"

Peering into his eyes, I felt some of my embarrassment melt away. "Yes."

"Perfect." He kissed my cheek and plucked the menu from my hand. Holding it up to Lidia, he didn't even look at her as he ordered something for me. The hand that had been sensually tormenting me slid down my thigh in a comforting gesture. I rarely dwelled on the numbers that lit up my bathroom scale, but Lidia had found that weak spot in my armor and jabbed her pointy stick right into it.

Sergei seemed to sense my self-confidence was under attack and wanted to soothe me with his gently petting hand.

Glad that everyone else at the table seemed oblivious to what had just occurred, I listened to the discussion of Vivian's upcoming London show.

"Bianca, did you decide if you two were coming?" Vivian absentmindedly ran her finger back and forth along Nikolai's wedding band.

I glanced at Sergei who looked surprised by the question. "It slipped my mind."

"If you want to fly over with us, there's plenty of room in the jet, and we'd love to have you," Yuri said.

"Oh! Thanks, Yuri." I smiled at the outrageously gracious billionaire. "We'll think about it."

Sergei addressed Yuri in Russian, probably to thank him for the offer, and Yuri waved his hand. In English, Yuri replied, "What's the use of having all these lovely toys of mine if I can't use them to score points with Lena's friends?"

Lena playfully rolled her eyes. "And you say I'm competitive."

"That's not all I say, *lyubimaya*." Yuri interlaced their fingers atop the table and kissed her temple. Glancing at the rest of us, he asked, "Would you like to come out to Faze after dinner?"

"Not us," Dimitri said, his arm curved protectively along the back of Benny's chair. "I have a feeling this one is going to keep me busy massaging her cramping legs and fetching antacids all night so I should turn in early."

Benny just laughed and shrugged. "You can't argue with facts."

I knew that Nikolai hated busy places like clubs and movie theaters so I was surprised when he looked to

Vivian before shooting down the idea outright.

"Is Coby playing tonight?" she asked Yuri.

"Of course," he said. Seemingly curious, he asked, "How do you know her?"

Vivian leaned to the side so her dessert plate could be set in front of her by Lidia. "We have a friend in common, Hadley Rivera, and obviously, we're both fans of electronic music."

"Then you'll have a fantastic time tonight. She's dropping some new mix tracks." Yuri's gaze slid to me. "What about it, Bianca? You want to come out to Faze?" He smiled at Sergei. "I didn't see the two of you dance at the wedding. It's a perfect night for a first dance, don't you think?"

Before I could answer, Lidia *accidentally* knocked her arm into Nikolai's full glass of wine as she placed my dessert in front of me. The deluge of rich, red wine spilled onto my lap and splashed my bodice.

Gasping, I sat back quickly, but the damage was done. Amid Lidia's apologetic blabbering, Nikolai flipped up the soaking wet tablecloth to catch the rest of the flood while Sergei snapped open his napkin and tried to sop up the mess.

I caught his wrist and stopped him from rubbing the fabric. "You should blot," I said and took the napkin from him. "Never rub."

He didn't look pleased by my correction, but I didn't have time to think about bruising his ego right now.

"I'm so sorry. I didn't see the glass." Lidia gushed with saccharine faux guilt. "I can't believe I did this!"

"It's okay, Lidochka. Accidents happen."

I blinked as Sergei's words registered in my brain. Was he seriously excusing her? And *Lidochka*? I didn't know very much about his language, but I knew those funny little endings to names were commonly applied to form pet names and show affection.

My gaze clashed with Sergei, and I instantly saw the regret in his dark eyes. Clenching my teeth together, I glanced away from him and continued blotting at my dress. Anger surged through me. *Lidochka, huh? Screw this.*

"I'll grab some towels and club soda." Scowling at Lidia, Vivian shoved out of her chair and scurried away from the table.

She had disappeared from sight before I could tell her that club soda wasn't going to be enough to help a stain this massive. Nikolai seemed to understand as he handed me a dry napkin and thrust the wet one at Lidia. "Send me the dry cleaning bill. If it can't be fixed, I'll replace your dress."

"Don't worry about it, Nikolai." I smiled at him and finished blotting up the excess. I needed to get away from the table and clear my head. Already, my heart was racing and my stomach was in knots. Playing up the nonchalance, I said, "That's the risk a girl takes when she goes out for dinner and drinks."

"That might be true at other establishments, but it's not at mine." His ice cold gaze slid to Lidia who had the good sense to keep her mouth shut. Did he suspect she had done it on purpose as I did?

I reached for my purse and rose from my chair. "Sorry, Yuri. It looks like there won't be any dancing for me tonight."

Excusing myself and shaking off Sergei's grasping hand, I made a beeline for the bathroom so I could wipe away the wine slicking my thighs and splashed on my breasts. I ignored the pitying looks from the other diners. When I got a good luck at myself in one of the beautifully framed mirrors, I understood those sad frowns. The maroon splotches ruining my gold dress looked awful.

The door swung open and Lena joined me. "Girl, that dress is beyond saving."

"Yeah," I said with a sigh. Then, with a halfhearted shrug, I added, "That's okay. I got it for seventy percent off during a flash sale."

She grabbed a handful of paper towels from the dispenser and wet them under the closest faucet. "Well, don't tell Nikolai that! Make him pay for the full cost of the dress. That lemon-faced *ved'ma* on his payroll did this on purpose."

"That lemon-faced *what*?"

"*Ved'ma*," she said again and thrust the paper towels into my hand. "It means witch."

"And you know this how?"

"I've been reading a lot of Russian children's books lately."

"Because?"

"I'm trying to practice my comprehension and language skills." She shooed me toward a stall. "You better hurry or you're going to get all sticky."

I ducked into the stall and locked the door. I heard a door a few stalls down open and close and realized Lena was multitasking. "So what's the story between that big Russian beast of yours and the red-haired succubus?"

Grinning at Lena's description of the situation, I admitted, "I'm not sure. I think they must have dated."

The image of Sergei kissing Lidia twisted in my chest like a knife plunged deep into my heart. I didn't even want to think about the two of them making love. They were so perfectly matched in height and looks. The image of me—chubby, jiggly me—in bed with the Russian Adonis seemed almost comical now.

"Apparently, that whackjob waitress didn't get the

memo that it's over. Was it a recent thing?"

I swiped the wine from my legs. "I don't think so. Sergei told me he hadn't gone on a date or been intimate with a woman since December."

"Seriously? Do you believe him?"

Even as hurt as I was by the pet name, I gave her the truth. "Yes."

"Is that when you two met? In December, I mean."

"Yes."

"Well, you've got to love a man who is committed, right?"

"Yes," I agreed softly. Was he committed to this? To us? I wanted to believe that was true, but how could he not be having second thoughts after his run-in with Lidia?

The door whined as it opened again. Assuming Vivian had finally tracked me down, I unlocked my stall and stepped out to ask her for one those towels she had gone to fetch.

Except it wasn't Vivian waiting for me. It was the red-haired *ved'ma.*

Arms crossed, she glared at me with such a haughty look on that pretty face. What in the world had Sergei ever found attractive in this woman?

"You'll never be able to make him happy."

"Oh, so that's what this is about, huh?" I gestured to my stained dress. "See, I thought maybe you were just the slightest bit jealous that Sergei was going to take me to Faze. I got the feeling you had never been invited to VIP section there so you wanted to make sure that I didn't get to go either."

Lidia rolled her light-colored eyes. "Big fucking deal. All the waitresses around here know that all they have to do is offer Yuri Novakovsky a peek at their panties, and he'll get them VIP bracelets."

I didn't buy that for one second. Sure, Yuri's playboy reputation had been legendary, but that was before Lena. He had never strayed from her. A couple didn't survive their near death experience without forming an unbreakable bond. The waitresses around here could walk around naked and Yuri wouldn't give them a second glance.

Thinking of Lena hidden away in her stall, I realized Lidia had just made an enemy she didn't need. "Honey, I think you should get back to work before you make this situation worse for yourself."

"And I think you should get real," Lidia snapped. "Do you really think you have a future with Sergei?" She guffawed. "Look at you. Once the exotic appeal wears off, he's going to get tired of fucking a fat girl every night."

Irritated, I asked, "Is that all you've got? You sure you don't want to make fun of my darker skin too? No? Just fat jokes. Well, come on. Start throwing those darts my way. I'm a big girl. I can take them."

She seemed to deflate at the realization that she couldn't bait me. Full-on nasty now, she sneered, "You'll just embarrass him. What do you think his mother will say when she meets you? She'll never approve of someone like you with her son. No, he needs a woman he can be proud of on his arm."

Someone like you? What the hell did that mean? Something told me she wasn't talking about my plus-sized figure but rather my skin color. It was the first time in years that anyone had ever made such an ignorant remark toward me. Honestly, I was taken aback by the comment.

Before I could figure out how to respond, a stall door opened, and Lena revealed herself to Lidia. The other woman's jaw slackened as the realization of the shit she had just stepped in finally hit.

Always cool and calm, Lena strode to the sink and started to wash her hands. "A woman he can be proud of, huh? You mean, like, oh, a successful small business owner who took the number one spot on Houston's *Thirty Entrepreneurs Under Thirty* list?"

When Lidia didn't answer, Lena flicked her fingers in the sink and reached for some towels. "Or maybe you mean a woman who got into one of the most prestigious fashion design programs in the world and studied abroad in Paris and Milan. How about a woman who designs couture wedding gowns that retail for thousands of dollars apiece and have been included in bridal magazines with hundreds of thousands of subscribers?"

Lidia swallowed nervously. "Well—."

"No. No. Wait." Lena held up her hand and smiled evilly. "Let me guess. You mean a woman on the wrong side of thirty who still waits tables for a living while hoping some rich man will swoop in and save her from that shitty paycheck-to-paycheck life she's living, right?"

I couldn't believe Lena had gone right for the jugular like that. Even though Lidia had been outrageously bad to me, I didn't think it was right for Lena to attack her on the same level. Was this why they used to call her the Dragon Lady? In all the time I had known her, she had never been so vicious.

"My friend over there is too sweet and classy to lower herself to your level, but, sweetheart, I'm not afraid to get dirty down here in the gutter with you." Lena grabbed my purse and slapped it into my hand. "Let's go, Bianca."

Tugging me along behind her, she glanced at Lidia. "You might want to look at the want ads in the morning. I have a feeling your time at Samovar is about to end."

Out in the hallway, we ran right into Sergei. He had a

to-go bag dangling from one hand and his blazer in the other. He stepped close and draped his jacket around my shoulders. The still warm fabric held his scent, and I pulled it tighter around my body.

The door behind us swung open and Lidia marched out of the bathroom. Dabbing at her face, she shot a pitiful look our way before scuttling away on her clacking high heels. I had to give her credit. The woman knew how to work a crowd.

"Bianca, what did you do?" Sergei stared down at me, his eyes hard and his brow furrowed. "Did you get her fired?"

"That's the first thing you ask me?" I gaped up at him in utter disbelief. "That nut ruined my dress, and you're worried about what I did?"

"Your dress can be replaced. It's not so simple to find a new job."

"Then maybe she shouldn't go around throwing glasses of wine at the people she depends on for tips!"

"It was an accident!"

"You must have taken one too many hits to the head. I think you're going blind. There was no way on God's green earth that this," I gestured to my stained dress, "was an accident."

"Why would she risk her job like that? You don't know her. She's a good person. She wouldn't do that."

"You're right. I don't know her." Shaking my head, I peeled off his blazer and pushed it back into his hands. "Clearly I don't know you either."

Spinning on my heel, I clutched my purse tightly in my hand and left him there in the hallway with Lena who, by the sounds of it, was tearing into him. Feeling numb and completely thrown by the strange turn our night had taken, I walked out of the restaurant and headed down the sidewalk. I didn't know where the hell I was going. I just knew that I had to keep moving.

Away from Sergei.

CHAPTER TWELVE

"What is wrong with you?"

Sergei frowned at Lena Cruz. "What did you say to Lidia in there?"

"What did I say?" Lena chortled loudly. "You should be asking me what your precious *Lidochka* said to Bianca."

He silently cursed himself for letting that stupid pet name slip. It didn't mean anything, but obviously Bianca thought it did. "What did Lidia say to Bianca?"

"Well, let's see." Lena held up her hand and began ticking off points on her manicured fingers. "She called Bianca fat. She insinuated that you're only with Bianca because you're satisfying some weird curiosity about black girls. Oh—and there was the part about your mom hating Bianca because of her brown skin."

Taken aback, Sergei started to protest that Lidia would never say anything like that, but the look on Lena's face stopped him. "I've known her for years. She has never said anything like that to me. She's not racist—and neither is my mother," he added with a tinge of anger.

"Why the hell are you telling me this?" Lena motioned toward the lobby. "Tell Bianca. She's the one who had to fend off your psycho ex-girlfriend. She's the one who came out here expecting you to comfort her but got an earful about making that whacko cry instead. And, FYI, Sergei, *I'm* the one who made her cry. Bianca—for reasons I will never understand—let her talk trash and didn't say one ugly thing back."

Shit. Shit!

Leaving Lena without another word, Sergei hurried to catch up with Bianca. He scanned the lobby but didn't find her. Had she gone outside? Pushing his way through the crowd, he made it onto the sidewalk. Thankful for his uncommon height, he searched both ends of the street for her.

Found you!

His gaze fixed on the back of her gold dress, Sergei raced toward her, carefully sidestepping the slower moving people packed onto the sidewalk. When he was close enough, he called out to her. "Bianca! *Please.* Stop!"

To his surprise, she actually did. She pivoted to face him. Thankfully, she wasn't crying, but the furious expression on her face scared him. He had really fucked it up this time.

Putting his hands on her shoulders, he tried to caress her neck, but she jerked her head to the side. Gulping down the pain that her rejection caused, he reminded himself that he deserved it. Hadn't he just done the same to her?

"I'm sorry, Bianca."

"I don't care. Just take me home. Now."

The urge to hash this out was strong, but he didn't think it was something that should be done on a public sidewalk. He started to slide his hand to her back to guide her back to his SUV, but she stepped forward and stopped him. Accepting her cold behavior, Sergei walked at her side until they reached the parking garage. She let him unlock her door but smacked aside the hand he offered to help her climb up onto the front seat.

Trying not to let it get to him, he let her be. Some of

the most excruciatingly tense minutes of his life occurred during the ride back to her house. He couldn't believe he had been so stupid. Maybe Bianca was right. Maybe he had taken too many hits to the head.

"How many other waitresses at Samovar have you dated?"

Sergei winced but answered truthfully. "Three including Lidia."

"I see."

"They weren't long-term, Bianca. It was two or three dates tops."

"Did you sleep with them?"

"Yes." Fearing it would come out eventually, he reluctantly confessed, "Two of them at the same time."

Bianca made a choking sound next to him. "Are you serious?"

"Yes." He refused to be made to feel bad about that. "We were all consenting adults. There's nothing wrong with what we did."

"If you say so…"

"You knew I had a life before you, Bianca. I've accepted that you had boyfriends before me. Hell—one of them handcuffed me the other night."

"I've had boyfriends, yes, but I didn't let two of them bang me at once."

He cringed at the vulgar description. "It wasn't like that."

"Whatever. You should have warned me about Lidia. I would have worn black and kept an eye on the wine glasses around me. Ugh." She made a disgusted sound. "I hope she didn't spit in my food."

"She wouldn't do that."

"Oh, so she draws the line at throwing wine on guests?"

"If that wasn't an accident, it was very stupid of her. I know the kitchen staff there. None of the runners would have let the food out of their sights long enough for her to do anything like that to it."

"If you say so..."

"Look," he said with a heavy sigh, "I was wrong about Lidia, okay? I didn't think she was like that. I never saw that side of her when we were dating."

Bianca made a frustrated noise. "Were we not sitting at the same table or something? The woman was groping you every chance she got."

He noticed the way she hadn't mentioned Lidia's derisive snort over the dessert remark. Lidia had crossed the line with that one, and he had been planning to speak to her the next time he saw her about respecting his new relationship with Bianca. Doing it there at the table would have simply drawn more attention to a touchy subject, and that would have hurt Bianca more.

Remembering the verbal assault Lena had described, he reached for Bianca's hand. To his surprise, she let him take it. Choosing his words carefully, he said, "Bianca, I like you just the way you are."

"Oh, Jesus!" Bianca jerked her hand away from his. "Can we please not do this right now? Okay? No more talking."

Despite the darkness, he could hear the pain and humiliation in her voice. If he reached out right now to swipe her face, he was certain his fingers would encounter the hot wetness of tears.

Hating himself for making it worse, he desperately tried to think of a way to fix this. As he waited for the gate behind her house to open, it occurred to him there was only one way to make this right. He had to show her how beautiful and desirable she was to him.

"You can just leave me here."

"That's not happening." Sergei grabbed the to-go bag holding her untouched dessert and slid out of the front seat before she could argue with him. He marched straight to the back door and waited for her to unlock it. Unlike the front door, he didn't have keys to this one. That was a problem he would be solving in the morning.

She stepped inside the mud room and tried to shut the door. "Good night, Sergei."

"No." Faster and stronger, he clamped his hand along the edge of the door to stop her. "That's not happening either."

"This is my house! If I say good night, that means good night, Sergei."

"You can be pissed off at me as long as you like. God knows I deserve it." He carefully pushed on the door, mindful of her feet, and forced his way inside the house. "But you still have a prowler who might be tied in with a bunch of racist thugs who want to hurt you. You asked for my protection, and I'm giving it."

She actually stomped her foot like a petulant child. "You can't just do whatever you want, Sergei! This is my home!"

"If you really want me to leave, why don't you call Kevan and have him throw me out?" Swinging the to-go bag, he flipped on the nearest light switch and started his nightly round of the doors and windows.

"You're ridiculous! You know that?"

"Yes."

She still hadn't calmed down by the time he had finished his walk-through of the ground floor. Arms crossed and foot tapping, she glared at him as he made his way to the staircase. "Are you done?"

"No." Deciding to really rile her up, he glanced over

his shoulder and said, "Unless you're waiting on Kevan to appear at the door to arrest me again, I suggest you come upstairs with me."

"What in the world makes you think I want go upstairs with you?"

He waved the bag over his head. "I've got your dessert right here—and you've got mine hidden away under your skirt."

She didn't come right away, but that was fine with him. Sergei placed the bag on the ottoman and stripped the bed of its extra covers and pillows, taking it down to the top and fitted sheets. He tossed a strip of condoms onto the mattress. Picking up the antique dressing mirror she kept in one corner, Sergei moved it in front of the bed and then toed off his shoes and removed his shirt and tie. He was peeling out of his pants when Bianca finally appeared in the doorway.

With a loud huff, she said, "You can't fix everything with sex, Sergei."

"Not everything," he agreed, "but this? Yes."

"And what is this?"

Clad in only his boxer-briefs, he held out his hand. "Come here, Bianca."

She hesitated only a moment before crossing the floor. Somewhere along the way, she had removed her shoes so her footsteps were muffled and nearly silent. She frowned at the mirror he had moved. "Why is that here?"

Grasping her hand, he dragged her close and threaded his fingers through her hair. He bent down and nuzzled her neck before peppering soft kisses on her silky skin. "I'm going to show you how sexy you are to me."

"What?" Anxiety made her voice wobble.

"You're such a strong woman, but I know you have your weak spots, Bianca. Tonight, Lidia found it, and she hurt you with it." Touching his forehead to hers, he said, "I am so sorry for that."

She gulped loudly, no doubt choking down the pain of being bullied about her weight. "I try not to let that sort of thing hurt me, but sometimes…"

"I know." Cupping her face, he kissed her tenderly, pressing all the love he held for her into the gentle mating of their mouths. He might not have been courageous enough to tell her how he truly felt, but that didn't mean he couldn't show her tonight.

Breaking the kiss, he carefully turned her to face the mirror. As if unwrapping a package on Christmas morning, he took his time undressing Bianca. She stood silently as he dragged down her zipper, unhooked her bra and pushed those lacy panties down her thighs.

Standing behind her, Sergei caressed her naked curves with his much bigger hands, all the while marveling at the pretty picture they made together. Nuzzling her neck, he nipped at her sensitive skin and whispered a promise. "By the time I'm done with you tonight, you will never again doubt how sexy and beautiful you are."

*

Oh sweet Lord.

With my legs trembling and my insides wobbling tremulously, I met Sergei's undeniably needful gaze in the mirror's reflection. Although still wounded by Lidia's attack, I couldn't deny what I saw right in front of me. Sergei moved his hands over my body like a sculptor admiring his finest work. He peered at me as if he couldn't get enough of me.

Leaving me just long enough to retrieve the bag

holding my dessert, Sergei returned to me and produced a small plastic box. He popped open the lid and let me see the triangle-shaped slice dotted with cherries and smothered in a light, fluffy cream. What was he planning to do?

He knelt in front of me and put the box on the bed behind me, just within his reach. Trailing his finger through the whipped cream, he used the blob he had gathered to paint my nipple. The cold cream made the peak pucker tightly. The starkly white cream looked so bright against my darker skin. Mouth agape with the shock of being adorned with my dessert, I stared at Sergei in disbelief. "What are you doing?"

"I'm having my dessert."

"But—oh!" I rose up on tiptoes as Sergei flicked his tongue against my nipple. He suckled my breast and licked away all traces of the cream. Heavy and aching, my breasts responded to his lightest touch. He pinched my damp nipple while painting the other one with more of the fluffy white concoction.

Sliding my fingers through his hair, I let him use me as his dessert plate, smearing my body with dabs of the whipped cream and licking and sucking it from my skin. When he tired of that sensual play, he gathered one final dollop on his finger and pushed it between my lips. "Suck it clean, Bianca."

I did as ordered, sucking hard on his rough, thick finger all the while imagining another thick, long part of him that I wanted to put in my mouth. He must have seen the flash of interest because he chuckled and placed a noisy kiss on my belly. "Soon, *milaya moya*, but you first."

Setting aside the dessert, he dragged me onto the bed and climbed up behind me. He maneuvered me into a kneeling position, grasping my inner thighs and pushing them apart. Cupping my pussy in his big hand, Sergei made sure I was watching him in the mirror. He opened the petals of my sex like a gardener coaxing apart some delicate hothouse blossom.

Brushing his lips across the shell of my ear, he murmured huskily, "You have the sweetest pussy I've ever tasted."

"Oh God." I drew in a shaky breath and tried to slow down my racing heart.

"Look at how pink you are," he said and showed me exactly what he was talking about as he glided his finger through the shiny nectar leaking from my core. "And so fucking wet." He bit down on my neck, marking me as his. "I can't wait to get my tongue right here again."

His long finger slipped inside me. My passage fluttered around him, gripping at his finger while I bucked my hips. "Sergei…"

"I've been with a lot of women, Bianca." He wasn't saying it to brag or hurt me. He seemed to be making a point. "You're the first one that ever made me so hard that I ached. You're the only one who ever tormented my dreams." He slid another finger inside me and started to thrust up into my slick heat. "This pussy is the only one I want."

Gripping his forearm, I rode his big fingers and never once broke our shared gaze in the mirror's reflection. His other hand snaked around my front. He put those fingers to good use by strumming my clit while he continued to thrust up into me. My body was on fire now, and I stood no chance against his sensual onslaught.

"Sergei!" I came hard, my body jerking against his as he used those masterful hands of his to work me into a frenzied state. The power of the climax punched the air out of my lungs. When the last waves rolled through me, Sergei gently took away his hands, and I fell forward onto the bed, my shaking arms barely holding me up.

I realized my mistake a moment too late.

Sergei gripped my hips and held me in place as he delved into my pussy with that wicked tongue of his. It had never occurred to me that a man would go down on a woman from behind, but Sergei showed me exactly why that angle of attack felt so sinfully good.

"Oh. Oh. *Oh!*" Clutching the sheets beneath me, I tried not to scream too loudly as the second climax hit me. Every time I tried to wiggle free, Sergei used his brute strength to hold me exactly where he wanted me. His tongue did things to me that were probably illegal in most states. With the wanton sex kitten inside me unleashed by him, I pressed back against his invading tongue and let him do whatever the hell he wanted because it just felt so amazing.

When I fell forward in a trembling, shuddering, limp heap, Sergei wiped his mouth on my plump bottom and reached for a condom. He sheathed himself in record time and clasped my waist, hauling me back up onto my knees. With only a slight nudge of warning, he thrust into me and slid home, burying that shockingly long cock inside me.

"Ah!"

"Take me, Bianca." He retreated and pushed forward again. "Take my cock."

Watching Sergei make love to me in the mirror was an experience I would never forget. He gazed down at my body with such appreciation and adoration and ran his hands over my skin as if he wanted to memorize every last inch of me. The glistening, rippling muscles of his chest, arms and legs enthralled me. He was utter perfection in the male form—and he wanted me.

Making love to me like this had demolished those lingering walls I erected around myself. It didn't matter what the rest of the world thought about my dress size or the number on my bathroom scale. Sergei thought I was beautiful and perfect. He made me feel feminine and desired. He reinforced my own belief that I was fine just the way I was.

A long time later, we came together, me first and him a few strokes behind. Limbs tangled atop the bed, we clung to each other while trying to breathe normally again. My body throbbed, and I shivered every time Sergei's callused palm glided over my belly and along my thighs.

"Are you convinced?"

"Yes." My throat was so raw that I winced.

Sergei chuckled with amusement and kissed my neck. "We'll be lucky if your neighbors haven't already called the cops after all that screaming."

Blushing, I buried my face against his chest. "Sorry."

"Don't ever apologize for that. It makes me feel good to know I can make you lose control like that." Kissing my temple, he murmured, "I am sorry about what happened at Samovar. I'll speak to Lidia and let her know that was unacceptable. For my own part, I promise I won't ever doubt you again."

"I'm holding you to that."

"Do you believe me now, Bianca?"

Smiling, I snuggled closer to the man who had made me feel so beautiful and desired. "Yes."

CHAPTER THIRTEEN

When I came downstairs the next morning, my poor wobbly legs barely held me up, and I expected to collapse at any moment. Sergei's sensual therapy had cured me of any lingering doubts about my desirability or his attraction to me. This morning, while showering, I had decided to let that mess with Lidia go.

I found him standing at the kitchen island prepping vegetables for omelets. Wrapping my arms around his waist, I kissed his back. "Good morning."

He lifted his arm so I could sneak under for a better angle at kissing him. Our lips lingered together for a few seconds before he brushed them against my forehead and returned to chopping a red bell pepper. "Did you sleep well?"

I smiled and made my way to the coffee pot. "I'm pretty sure I didn't move once."

He laughed. "I don't think I did either. My legs are killing me this morning."

"Mine too!" Pouring coffee into my favorite mug, I said, "Maybe I need to start working out."

"It's not a bad idea," Sergei answered carefully.

I sweetened my coffee with half-and-half and sugar and joined him at the island. I slid onto one of the stools and watched him prepare some green onions. Convinced that he accepted and adored my fuller figure, I confessed,

"I've tried losing weight, and I've been successful at it for short periods of time. I get so tired of dieting, Sergei. Counting calories and denying myself entire food groups? Squeezing in two hours of exercise every day with work and Mama? I can't do it."

"So we won't diet or do crazy amounts of exercise," he said matter-of-factly. "We'll make small, sustainable changes."

The way he said *we* made me smile and filled me with such warmth. "Like?"

"Cutting back on the sugar in your coffee," he suggested. "Switching those sodas you drink at lunch for unsweetened tea or water flavored with a lime or lemon wedge would be a good trade. You could try having a salad for lunch a few days a week. We could try some different afternoon snacks."

"Well...that does sound better than rice cakes and soup and never touching bread again," I agreed. "What about exercise? And don't even think about suggesting I start going to Ivan's warehouse of sweaty horrors!"

Sergei chuckled. "First, the only woman allowed in that place is Erin. Secondly, that's much too hardcore for you. Why don't you try walking in the evenings after work? Or we could pick out some fitness DVDs for you to try here at the house. You can work out, say, three days a week to start. When you feel more comfortable, we'll nudge it up to four and then five days."

"I guess I could do that." He was offering me sensible, realistic choices that were quite unlike some of the crash diets and insane exercise regimens I had tried over the years.

"What made you think that being so militant about your diet would work long-term?" He seemed genuinely interested.

"I don't know. I broke out those unhealthy regimens whenever I had a big social function looming. There was a time when I would have done anything to shave a quick twenty pounds off my body. Nowadays, I'm more worried about the business and Mama's rehab. Losing weight is a low priority."

"I don't think it should be your main priority in life right now, Bianca, but I do think it should be a priority to get healthier." He looked at me with an expression that betrayed his fear that he might have overstepped his boundaries again. "I don't care if you lose a single pound, *milaya moya*, but I do want you to be around forever."

"Forever, huh?" His words touched me in ways I could not even express.

"I worry about you, Bianca. Your mother nearly died because of high blood pressure and diabetes. You've been lucky, and you're still very young. There's time to make changes now that will help us enjoy a long life together."

"If you'll help me, I'll try really hard." I doubted I would ever be truly thin but healthier? That seemed like a goal I could attain with some dedication and my very own personal trainer.

"I'll help you. I'll do anything for you."

I swallowed nervously. "Anything?"

He suddenly had a wary look but nodded. "Yes. Anything."

"You want me to make changes that will make me healthier so we can be together forever. Well—you need to make changes, too." I gulped again as I realized what I was asking of him. "I'm not saying that you have to choose *them* over me, okay? I know that's a battle I can't win for myriad reasons. No, I'm just—I'm asking you to think about exit strategies."

Sergei picked up the knife and started slashing at

mushrooms. "I already am thinking of exit strategies, Bianca."

"You are?" His admission caught me by surprise.

"I have been thinking of how to get out ever since I was forced into this life. Now, with you, I want out much sooner. I'm trying, Bianca." He gazed at me with such yearning. "I'm doing everything I can. I'm laying the groundwork—but it's going to take some time."

"How much time?"

He shook his head. "I don't know." He hesitated. "It could be a few years, two or three." Sadness rounded his shoulders, and he returned to his chopping. "If you can't wait that long, I—"

"I can wait." I reached across the island and held out my hand. He stared at it in disbelief but finally placed his palm atop mine. "I will wait for you."

"I don't deserve you, Bianca. You are so fucking far out of my league. You're the woman every man dreams of finding, that one woman who makes him better by simply allowing him into her life." Squeezing my fingers, he said, "Nikolai calls Vivian his sun. I never really understood why he chose that pet name for her, but I understand now. It's melodramatic, I know, but she brings light into his dark life." Lifting my hand, he leaned forward to kiss it. "You're my light, Bianca."

My lower lip wobbled, and my eyes stung as his incredibly romantic confession washed over me like the warmth of sunshine. "Thank you."

He winked at me and went back to making us breakfast. Clearing his throat, he said, "So, while you're at work today, I'm going to tackle some projects around the house. I have some plumbers coming over to switch out the water heater and give me an estimate on the pipes. I'm going to measure the bathroom and sketch out some ideas for you about the renovations in there..."

Listening to him rattle on about the ways he planned to tackle all the problems around my house, I couldn't stop smiling. I didn't know how we were going to make this work, but I had faith that we would figure it out somehow. Replaying the sweet things he had said to me, I decided that Sergei was worth it. He was worth fighting for.

* * *

Sorting through tile samples the next morning, Sergei felt his phone vibrate in his pocket. Bianca had wandered off to look at faucets and antique-style tubs so he assumed it was her trying to find him in the massive home improvement store. He dug the phone out of his pocket, glanced at the screen and sighed. It wasn't Bianca. It was Nikolai.

"Yes?"

"Sergei, we have a problem, and I could use your help."

He wanted to point out that this was the second Sunday in a row that he had been called in to deal with a problem, but he didn't. "I'm picking out bathroom tile with Bianca. It will be at least an hour unless—"

"That's fine. There's no rush. Kostya is just getting started. Come to the ice house."

The phone call ended, and Sergei grimaced with distaste. Of all the ways he wanted to spend his Sunday afternoon, this wasn't one of them. After spending the morning at the gym with Paco, he had been planning to rip out some tile, make love to Bianca—probably twice— and then grill some steaks. Whatever awaited him at the ice house was going to ruin his entire day.

"Boo!" Bianca poked him in the side and laughed.

Pushing away thoughts of the phone call, he grinned down at her and kissed the top of her head. "Did you find the tub you want?"

"I found a few I like. They gave me some brochures. I figured you would be able to help me figure out which ones would fit best..."

They finished picking out tile samples that complemented some of the paint colors she liked and left the store. He waited until they were headed to her house to tell her. "Look, Bianca, I need to go see Nikolai."

She sighed softly. "I won't ask why."

He hated himself for putting her in this position. "I don't know when I'll be home. It might be late."

"Okay."

"I'm sorry, Bianca. I truly am. I didn't want our day to end like this."

She clasped his hand and dragged it onto her lap. "I said I would wait for you to get out. So this is me waiting and believing that all this crap will end someday."

"It will, Bianca." He wished he could give her a date, but he refused to break a promise to her.

When they reached the house, he was surprised to find Arty, one of Nikolai's most-trusted captains, sitting across the street with some of his crew. At first, he thought they were there for him, but then Arty lifted two of the three fingers on his right hand to his eyes and gestured toward the house. Sergei understood the silent message. Nikolai had arranged for Bianca to be watched.

On one hand, Sergei was relieved to have someone like Arty, a man who had survived some horrible gang wars, taking care of Bianca. On the other, Sergei knew what this meant. Whatever he had been called away to help with involved the Night Wolves. Nikolai expected blowback, and he expected it to land here.

Rubbing the back of his neck, Sergei leaned across Bianca and popped open his glove box. The sight of his handgun made her gasp. When he reached for her hand, she tugged it back. "No freaking way, Sergei!"

"Bianca," he said firmly. "I would feel better knowing you had this."

"And I would feel better knowing my boyfriend isn't tangled up with the Russian mob, but you know what they say about wishes and horses and poor folks."

He didn't actually, but he let it slide. "Have you ever fired a gun?"

"No."

"We should fix that."

"Like hell!"

"Bianca—"

"No, Sergei."

Exhaling roughly, he pointed the weapon away from them. "This is the safety. This is how you flick it on and off. It's loaded. You have ten rounds so use them wisely."

"You are crazy if you think I'm taking that thing into my house."

"Then you'd better call for a straightjacket because it's happening." Sergei tucked the pistol into her purse. "Let's go."

She didn't get out of the SUV immediately. For a moment, he wondered if he was going to have to toss her over his shoulder and carrying her back inside. With a dramatic huff and slam of the door, she exited the vehicle and stomped her way up the front door. He followed her inside, checked the house and handed back her purse.

"I'll be back later. Don't let anyone inside the house that you don't know. Those men outside? The ones in the car? They're watching the house so they might get out and sit on the porch or walk around the yard, especially if I'm not back by dark."

She made an annoyed sound. "What are my neighbors going to think?"

"Probably that you have very bad taste in men," he answered honestly. Certain she was pissed at him, he kissed her cheek and left the house. He had only gotten as far as the porch before she called out to stop him.

Gripping the front of his shirt, she hauled him down for a deep, passionate kiss. "You had better be careful doing whatever the hell it is you're about to do."

Touching his lips to her forehead, he promised, "I'll be back."

The long drive to the ice house did little to dissipate his anger and frustration with his situation. This wasn't going to get any easier. Soon, Bianca would begin to resent Nikolai for calling him away. What was that going to do to her friendship with Vivian? It wouldn't be good.

By the time he reached the ice house, he still hadn't figured out a way to speed up his exit plan. The old building located between two small towns had once been exactly what its name said it was—a house that sold ice. Later, the building had housed a bar and grill. Now, it was a shadow of its former self, all rotten boards and overgrown weeds.

No one ever drove out the lone private road that led to it. Nikolai had seen to that by snapping up all the land around the ice house for his private use. Sergei shuddered to think what secrets Kostya had buried out here.

He wasn't all that surprised to see some of Besian's men loitering around outside, smoking and bullshitting with one another. He nodded at them as he entered the ramshackle building, ducking his head to avoid an injury from the low-hanging beams and short doorways. He crossed the dusty floor to the back room that had once housed the freezers and stopped cold at the sight of Kostya peeling out of his black leather apron.

The cleaner had a reputation around Houston—hell, probably around the fucking world—for his work. Sergei didn't think the man enjoyed hurting other people. In fact, Kostya seemed to be able to wholly divorce himself from the reality of it to avoid the moral complications of his work. Sergei had suffered the misfortune of watching the man use his skills on too many occasions to count, but he had never seen Kostya take it nearly as far as his black, soulless reputation would have him expect.

Sometimes Sergei suspected Kostya's theatrics got him more cooperation than any amount of bloodletting. The black leather apron, the gloves, the shoe covers, the kits filled with torture gear—it made for a convincing show. Most of the time, a couple of pulled teeth, a cut here or there and a good beating got a man to spill his secrets.

The plastic covering the floor crinkled beneath Sergei's boots. He quickly surveyed the scene before him. Nikolai and Besian stood nearly shoulder to shoulder and stared at some poor, naked bastard strapped to a chair. He had been worked over a bit but there was hardly any blood to be seen. Some spatter from a few punches but nothing outrageously violent.

In the back of his mind, Sergei recognized that thought was more than enough evidence that it was time to get out of this life.

The swastika tattooed on the younger man's chest held his attention. So. He was one of *them*. At the same time Sergei spotted the ugly tattoos, the man became aware of him and looked like he was going to piss himself. Whether it was his size or his reputation around the underworld for being a brutal fighter in the cage, he couldn't say.

Glancing at Nikolai, he said, "Boss."

"Ah, Sergei, come here. I want you to meet our new friend. His name is James, and he's got some photos I think you'll find very interesting." Nikolai waved a cell phone.

"No," the man said nervously. "Look, please. I'm just the guy they gave the recon mission. That's it. I never meant to hurt her."

At the mention of *her*, Sergei went rigid. He crossed the floor in four quick strides and snatched the phone from his boss' hand. Running his thumb across the screen, he nearly puked as images of Bianca appeared. Swipe after swipe filled the screen with her beautiful face. In a few of them, Vivian was even present.

Slapping the phone back into Nikolai's hand, Sergei stormed toward the other man and kicked the chair right off the ground. The man grunted loudly as the chair slammed his bound wrists to the floor. Putting his boot against that ugly fucking tattoo on the man's chest, Sergei pressed down with some of his weight. "Why are you following my woman?"

The man coughed and wheezed so Sergei let up enough for him to draw in a breath. He moved the toe of his boot to the man's throat. "What do you want with Bianca?"

"Darren," he coughed the name. "Darren says she's the key. She has to pay."

He pushed down harder. "The key? To pay for what?"

Eyes bulging, Darren gagged, and Sergei let up. The younger man inhaled a shaky breath and started sobbing. "She should never have tried to kill Adam!"

Sergei's entire body went ice cold at the realization

those white power freaks actually believed Bianca was behind the attack on Adam Blake.

"She didn't," Besian cut in loudly. "I know it and that devious fucking prick Darren Blake knows it, too."

James started to choke as Sergei's weight crushed his neck.

"Don't kill him yet, Sergei. He's still useful to us." Nikolai waved his hand in that imperious way of his.

Sergei removed his boot from James' throat and hefted the chair and the man tied to it back into position. He stood behind him and waited to see what the two bosses wanted.

"See, Sergei," Besian pulled a lighter and cigarettes from his pocket, "what young James there doesn't know, is that I've had a rat inside their gang since January. After they killed Afrim, my loan shark," he added. "The thing is, James, I know for a fact that Darren hired a man who used to run with my crew to kill his own brother. He was hoping the blowback would catch my outfit."

Besian retrieved a cigarette and tucked the pack back into his pocket. "Do you know why Darren really wanted to kill Adam?"

James shook his head. "N-no."

Besian lit up and inhaled a long drag. On his noisy exhale, he said, "That's the thing about brothers. They have a way of fucking up long-term plans." Smiling evilly, Besian gestured toward him. "Isn't that right, Sergei?"

Clenching his jaw, Sergei didn't answer.

"No?" The Albanian boss shrugged and pointed the bright red cherry of his cancer stick at the bound skinhead. "There's a story there, James. One that would interest you, but we don't have time to convince Sergei to tell us about his big brother." He sucked on his cigarette again. "See, my guy inside the prison tells me that Adam

Blake has been rethinking his racist ways. I hear that he's considering making a deal to join a RICO case against your gang."

"That's bullshit! Adam would never turn his back on us."

"That's for fairytales, kid." Nikolai's gaze slid to Besian's cigarette in a way that seemed almost longing. His stare landed on James again. "When the only thing that binds men together is hatred? There can be no loyalty."

As if to make his point, Nikolai pointed to Sergei. "Do you think that man left the love of his fucking life to come here and deal with this shit because he hates me? Because he's afraid of me? No." Meeting his gaze, Nikolai asked, "Why are you here, Sergei?"

Was it Sergei's imagination or did the boss sound genuinely uncertain? Was he aware of Sergei's doubts? Of Sergei's desire to get out and move on with his life?

"I'm here because you saved my life. I'm here because you saved my mother and my brother." He swallowed hard. "I'm here because I swore to serve you."

"You see, James? That's loyalty. That's why your bullshit gang will die out just as quickly as it flared right up. One—you have nothing binding your men together except hatred, and a foolish hatred at that. Two—your men lack brotherhood. You don't bleed or sacrifice for one another. And three? You're stupid and you take unnecessary risks…like following my wife home from church." Clicking his teeth, Nikolai advanced on the man. "That was *incredibly* stupid of you."

"They told me to follow the girls and figure out their Sunday routines. It's the only time they're both alone. When they're at church," James said, sobbing now. "I was only taking pictures!"

Crouching down in front of James, Nikolai held out his hand. Kostya placed one of his wicked looking knives on it. Dragging the sharp point down the white supremacist's chest, Nikolai asked a very simple question. "How far are you willing to go for your brothers, James?"

"Wh-what?" the younger man nervously stammered.

"Are you willing to bleed for them?" He dug the knife in just enough to make the other man hiss. "What if I said that I would let you go back to your crew right now and offer them peace with my men and his?" He gestured to Besian. "What if I told you that you could warn them of the RICO case and the war I will bring to their door if they don't leave my family alone? All you have to do to earn that chance is to make a sacrifice. What do you do, James?"

He didn't answer. The cowardly bastard was actually thinking about it. Sergei's nose wrinkled with disgust. No matter how much he wanted out of this life, he would have given his last ounce of blood to save any member of this family.

"If I say no?" James asked quietly.

"We put you in a car and you drive to a safe house in San Antonio with two of Besian's men. They'll hold you there until our plans play out—and then you're free to go on with your life."

"Seriously?"

"Yes."

Sergei knew that tone of voice. Nikolai was absolutely serious. He would let this prick walk out of here and escape whatever wrath and hellfire were coming. Was it the baby that had brought on this newfound mercy? Marrying Vivian had softened the boss a little around the edges. Would becoming a father change him too? Something told Sergei the boss would even more ruthless in his dealings with others if it meant keeping his wife and child safe.

"I want the safe house."

With a deep sigh of disappointment, Nikolai rose to his feet. "Yes, I thought you would." Flicking his fingers, he said, "Come along, Sergei. We have business in Houston."

"Wait. Aren't you going to cut me loose?"

Nikolai considered the knife in his hand. "Besian, is the car gassed up?"

"Yes."

He slapped the knife against the other boss' chest. "Then make sure he can still drive when you're finished with him. There's no reason your men should tire themselves."

"Wait! *No!* You said I could leave untouched."

"*He* said you could leave untouched." Besian made the distinction. "You should have been paying more attention when my friend there gave his speech about being stupid…"

With Kostya hot on their heels, they left the ice house to the sounds of James screaming. Sergei didn't want to imagine what the Albanian was doing to the guy. If he absolutely had to guess, he would put his money on Besian defacing James' tattoos.

"When this done, get started on the packages, yes?"

"*Da.*"

"And make sure it's clean, Kostya." Nikolai scanned the area. "We'll have to sell this place soon and find a new spot."

"I'll start scouting real estate." Motioning back toward the ice house, he promised, "It will be perfect."

Nikolai clapped the other man's shoulder. "I know it will. Sergei? Let's go."

Sergei held up his hand. "I don't have my gun." At Nikolai's incredulous look, he explained, "I gave it to Bianca before I left."

"There's an extra in my car," Kostya offered. "It's clean. Take it."

"Thanks." Sergei found the weapon in question, checked it and carried it back to his SUV. He hadn't planned on driving the boss anywhere so being armed hadn't been a top priority. Thankful that Kostya was always prepared, he slid behind the wheel and glanced at Nikolai. He wanted to ask about the packages Kostya was preparing but didn't. Instead, he asked, "Where are we headed?"

"To see Alexei."

Because there were about fifty Alexeis they both knew, he quickly narrowed it down to the two most likely. "Alexei at the car wash or Alexei at the dealership?"

Nikolai smiled and fastened his seat belt. "Alexei Sarnov at the dealership."

"Right." Sergei backed out of his spot and turned onto the private road. "Are you picking up a Ferrari or a Bentley?"

The boss chuckled. "Neither. We're going there to get Alexei to return a favor he owes me."

Sergei wondered at the favor Nikolai hoped to extract. Alexei Sarnov's time in the family had been before his. In fact, he suspected the only reason Nikolai had brought him over and paid for his debts was because he had been down one big, strong man and Sergei had fit the bill. He had heard rumors of Alexei's departure from Nikolai's crew but no one seemed to know the truth. Maybe Ivan and Kostya but those two never gossiped.

What Sergei did know to be absolutely true was that Nikolai had helped Alexei buy his first luxury dealership.

Now Alexei's company owned dealerships up and down the interstate that catered to Houston's elite. On top of that, he owned two trucking companies and had his hands in some other businesses around town. Like Ivan, Alexei had done extremely well for himself and was one of Sergei's role models.

Nikolai tugged out his lighter and rolled it back and forth between his palms. Had that cigarette of Besian's given him a craving?

"Do you know Kelly Connolly?"

The question took him by surprise. "Sort of. When I'm with Vivian, I run into him. He's a nice guy. Why?"

"His father owes half a million to Besian. I hear the old man is in deep with John Hagen for even more."

Sergei swore under his breath. "Does Kelly know?"

"He does now." Nikolai flicked the lighter open and closed. "Vee overheard me talking to Dimitri about it this morning. She's asked me to intervene on Kelly's behalf." The tightness in the boss' voice told Sergei he wasn't thrilled by the request. "Apparently, Besian made Kelly an offer he isn't likely to refuse."

Sergei had to hear this. "Yeah?"

"Paulie, his fighter, is still in hospital after that wreck. I hear Besian's second string fighter is absolute shit so he wants Kelly to replace Paulie in the tournament."

Sergei's gaze skipped from the roadway to his boss and back again. "No shit?"

"Yes. Did you ever see him fight?"

"Kelly?" He shook his head. "No. I heard that he did okay in some of the smaller matches. I'm not saying he doesn't have heart. He was a Marine, and you have to respect what he survived over there, but this? He's not up to this."

"I don't think he is either." Nikolai snapped the lighter

shut and tucked it away in his pocket. "Vee will never let me hear the end of it if her friend gets hurt. I can't very well ask Ivan to train him because, obviously, I want you to win, and you need his full attention when he gets back from his honeymoon."

"So you're going to ask Alexei to train him?"

"Yes."

"Huh."

"I know." Nikolai wiped a hand down his face.

"He's a good trainer. I've seen him around the warehouse. If anyone can get Kelly into shape this fast, it's Alexei."

"For Kelly's sake, let's hope so." Nikolai adjusted the air conditioner vent to hit him with a blast of cold air. "I didn't fire Lidia, but if she pulls a stunt like that again?" Nikolai made a clipped sound and made a chucking motion with his thumb. "She's out on her ass and that kid of hers can learn what it's like to live off food stamps."

Sergei found the remark unnecessarily harsh. "I've never seen her like that."

"Of course you haven't," Nikolai said matter-of-factly. "You were the prize she wanted. She saw you as the answer to all of her problems. Before you? It was Arty."

"What? Three-Fingered Artyom?"

"Yes." Nikolai looked at him with surprise. "They dated all last spring and summer. Then you came sniffing around in the fall, and she dropped his ass. It was a cold move. Arty loved that woman. Hell, he still loves her."

Guilt gripped Sergei. "I never would have asked her out if I had known she was dating Arty."

"She kept it quiet. I always had the feeling she was keeping him around as her backup plan. Then your better offer came along—"

"I never made her an offer," Sergei interjected. "We

dated. That was it."

"She talked around Samovar like you two were getting married—"

"No." He emphatically slashed his hand through the air. "That was never in the cards for us."

"But it is with, Bianca?"

Sergei grunted and shrugged. "We'll see."

They drove for another ten minutes or so without speaking. Finally, Sergei asked, "*Nochniye volki?*"

"I'm handling it."

"And me?"

"You take care of Vee during the day, protect Bianca at night, and train for the tournament. Paint some walls. Put up new tile. Go to Bianca's cousin's wedding on Saturday night. That's it. Nothing changes for you."

Surprised but simultaneously glad that Nikolai was cutting him out of the loop on this one, Sergei thought of those ominous photographs. "Do you think they're going to try to kidnap Bianca?"

"Yes." Nikolai didn't even try to lie. "Unfortunately for them, they aren't going to get the chance. In a few days?" The boss drew his line across his throat. "It's over."

Gripping the steering wheel, Sergei's stomach knotted as he imagined how much danger Bianca was in now. He prayed Nikolai was right and that this would all be over very soon.

CHAPTER FOURTEEN

"So, Sergei, Bianca told me that your mother is a seamstress. Is that right?"

Sitting in the second row of seats in his SUV, I inwardly cringed as my mother continued her interrogation of Sergei as we drove from the church where Lulu and Corey had just been married to the reception hall. She had finagled her way into the front passenger seat, probably to keep me from running interference.

Ever since he picked the two of us up at her apartment, Mama had been after him like the CIA. He had struggled with her odd inflection and delayed speech in the first few minutes but now he seemed to have her little quirks down pat. They were chatting away like two old friends. I couldn't decide if that was a good thing or a bad thing.

"Yes, she is." He flashed her one of the trademark smiles that Mama seemed to just eat right up. "I'm hoping that she'll be able to retire after she comes over here."

"Oh, that will be so nice. Is she coming soon?"

"I hope so."

Mama seemed to sense that was a touchy subject for him and backed off. "I hear you've been doing some work around Bianca's house. She showed me the pictures of the bathroom you two have been remodeling. The tile is gorgeous."

"Thank you. It's been quite a learning experience for both of us." He glanced at me in the rearview mirror. The hungry glint in his eyes made me blush. Oh, he'd definitely taught me a thing or two about using sawhorses for things other than holding up wood!

"That's nice," she said. "Real nice."

"Bianca and I were discussing the carriage house out back, actually," he remarked. "She's going to have some contractors come in to do some different bids than the last time. She's thinking of turning it into an apartment."

"Really? To rent out?"

"Maybe," I said, not wanting to commit one way or the other yet. "I have to check the zoning rules and see what my homeowner's association says about that sort of thing first."

"Well, just make sure you can make back that investment, sugar."

"I will, Mama."

I had warned Sergei that she wouldn't like the idea of me renovating the space with her in mind so I shot him a look that said to cool it with this topic. She liked her independence and wouldn't want to feel like a burden to me even though I would have loved to have her close.

When we reached the reception hall, I noticed the way Sergei got out of the SUV and scanned the area around us with his hawkish gaze. Ever since being called away on Sunday, he had seemed so tense any time we were out in public. He hadn't told me what had happened that day, and I sure as hell hadn't been brave enough to ask, but I got the feeling it had something to do with the those white supremacist nutjobs.

Twice, he had asked me to go with him to the shooting range, but I had nixed that idea. I had seen first-hand what guns could do and wanted no part of it. I got the feeling he thought I was being naïve and unsafe, but this was one issue where I refused to bend.

One thing I had been nosy about was this business with Kelly Connolly. I had known the former bodyguard and Marine for years. He and Perry had played baseball together in high school. We had run into each other a little more than a year ago and seemed to always be bumping into each other around the city's hot spots. Vivian liked him—as a friend and nothing more—so we always made sure to invite him out when he was in town and not on assignment with Dimitri's private security firm.

Vivian had let me know about this ongoing mess with his gambling addict and drunkard father. When she told me that Kelly might possibly have to fight Sergei in the upcoming tournament, I couldn't believe it. Sergei had been reluctant to tell me the details but he had confirmed that it was true.

I didn't like it at all. Somehow not knowing the identities of the men Sergei would fight made it more palatable. Thinking of my Russian hulk beating Kelly to a pulp was just too terrible to imagine, but I harbored no illusions that Kelly could beat Sergei. My man was simply too powerful and too ruthless to lose. I worried that Kelly might get in a few good shots that could really hurt Sergei. No matter how many times he promised that he would be fine, I didn't buy it.

Breaking me free from my troubling thoughts, Sergei opened my door first and helped me down. He didn't miss the chance to caress my bottom or give it a loving pat before kissing my cheek and heading to the cargo area of his SUV to grab Mama's walker. I had wanted her to bring her wheelchair, just in case, but she seemed to be doing very well with the aid of her walker and making use of available seating.

I stood back as Sergei used those burly arms of his to gently help Mama out of the SUV. He was exceedingly patient with her and looked ready to pounce at the first sign of wobbliness on her prosthetic leg. "Are you good?"

"I'm fine, honey." Mama patted his hand. "Now give my purse to Bianca. Fuchsia just isn't your color."

"Yes, ma'am." Smiling, Sergei slipped the purse strap off his arm and held it out to me. After I had slipped the second purse on my shoulder, he took my hand and tucked it into the curve of his arm. Glad to have him with me this evening, I entered the reception hall with a grin on my face.

Our mismatched trio didn't turn nearly as many heads as I had expected. We made our way through the receiving line with only one really awkward encounter with Kevan. Mama must have sensed the weird vibe because she made a production of needing to find a seat. I was only too happy to hurry her along to our table.

We had been seated with my mother's two widowed older sisters and their two sons, both college basketball players, and their girlfriends. Shawn was pre-med and Trey was studying business. One of the girlfriends was studying fashion marketing. The other one wanted to be a lawyer.

Once the introductions were out of the way, the inevitable questions about Sergei started. He neatly replied that he worked in construction and managed to wrap up that issue. Of course, then my aunts wanted to know where he was born and why he had come to Houston. Where does your mother live? Do you have any family here? Do you go to church?

I wanted to crawl under the table and hide. Sergei took

it all in stride and seemed only too happy to chat them up. In the same way he had impressed my mother, he won over my Aunt Sara and Aunt Penny. I didn't miss the shy yet flirty smiles from the two girlfriends across the tables. Something about Trey and Shawn's looks had me suspicious.

Did they know what Sergei really was? Had they seen him fight perhaps? In the last week, I had done a little digging and learned that there was heavy betting action from the universities in town. Vivian had informed me that select frats had exclusive invites to the matches because most of the members had such deep pockets. The thought of Trey and Shawn betting their hard-earned money on fights didn't make me happy. Maybe I needed to chat with the two of them later…

Although this wedding reception wasn't anywhere near as rowdy as Erin and Ivan's, it was still a beautiful evening. The food, the flowers, the cake, the band—everything was top-notch. When the dance floor opened after the first and parent dances had been completed, Sergei leaned over and cupped my face in his massive hand. "You owe me a dance, *milaya moya.*"

"Yes, I suppose I do."

Sergei led me out to the packed floor and held me close. The differences in our heights made things interesting. I considered dragging over a chair to stand on so I could rest my cheek to his shoulder. Glancing around, I noticed that quite a few of the men in attendance tonight were tall with shorter dates. None of them were as big as Sergei, but then, he seemed to be a true one-of-a-kind.

After a few dances with me, Sergei found himself dancing with Aunt Sara and Aunt Penny. He was a good sport about it, even when Aunt Sara got a little tipsy from all that champagne and pinched his taut backside. I thought poor Trey was going to fall out of his chair when he spotted his mother getting so fresh.

"Eye bleach," Trey said and shoved out of his chair. "I've got to find me some eye bleach." Slapping his hand against Sergei's back, he said, "Man, come on. Let's take a break from this estrogen-fest, okay?"

When Sergei glanced at me to see if I minded, I waved my hand. I had a feeling he needed the escape and would enjoy meeting some more male members of my family. He had been such a doting date all afternoon and evening and had earned some free time. I doubted he would have found the conversation at the table very interesting anyhow.

Alone with my gossiping aunts and mother, I sipped some champagne and watched the dance floor. My gaze landed on Kevan who danced unsteadily with a woman I didn't recognize. He had clearly had too much to drink. I wondered why none of the groomsmen had cut him off and put him in a corner to sober up with some coffee.

Kevan rudely groped the breast of the woman he danced with, and she rightfully slapped at his hand. I waited to see if someone would save him from himself, but no one stepped forward. He wandered off the dance floor and disappeared from my view. I had a feeling he was going to get himself into trouble. Should I chase him down and see if he needed a ride home?

"I like this one, Bianca."

My Aunt Penny's remark interrupted my thoughts. Not sure what she meant, I asked, "Ma'am?"

"Sergei," she said with a lift of her chin in his direction. "He's sweet as pie."

"Well, I don't know about that." Would she say the same thing if I told her he made his living enforcing for the Russian mob?

"I know," Aunt Penny replied confidently. "I can tell a good man when I see one. That one? He's good all the way through."

"And handsome!" Aunt Sara commented with an envious sigh. "He'll make some beautiful babies with you, Bianca."

"Oh, sweet Lord!" Laughing, I put up both hands and rose from my seat. "On that note, I'm out of here. Mama, do you want some cake?"

"No, honey."

Leaving my two aunts and my mother cackling together, I shook my head and made my way along the edge of the dance floor to the cake station. I recognized the delicate sugar flowers as the work of a baker I respected and anticipated the first bite of her perfectly moist and not too sweet Italian cream cake.

Plate in hand, I turned to leave the table—and slammed right into Kevan. Somehow I managed not to get cake on either one of us. "Kevan! Whoa!"

"Sorry, Bibi." His sour beer breath wafted over me, and he leered at my chest. "You look real pretty tonight."

"Thanks, Kevan. Um—how much have you had to drink?"

He flapped his hand. "It's okay. I can't get into trouble for drinking."

"Because you have a designated driver?" I asked hopefully.

He puffed out his chest. "Nope. Because I've got a badge! There's nothing I can't get away with," he stated proudly. "Just you wait and see!"

I didn't like the sound of that at all. "Kevan, I don't know what you're planning to do with all that super police power of yours, but it had better not be something that hurts me."

His expression turned angry. "You hurt me."

"How?"

"You broke up with me."

"Really, Kevan? What are we? Fifteen? Adults stop dating all the time. It's not like we were serious."

"Maybe you weren't, but I was." His voice rose in pitch and volume as he got more agitated. In his drunken state, I didn't know what he would say so I decided to carefully extricate myself from the situation.

"Well, I'm sorry I wasn't more clear when we started dating, Kevan. I never meant to hurt you, but I wasn't looking for anything serious."

Holding my cake plate to the side, I stepped around him and headed back toward the table where my mother was now watching me with concern. Unfortunately, my plan to escape Kevan without causing a scene didn't work. He followed close behind me, running his mouth and drawing unwanted attention.

"But you're looking for something serious now, huh? With *him*?" He snarled angrily. "What's he got that I don't, huh?"

I didn't touch that one. No, I kept my eyes forward and my feet moving. *Please, just turn around and go back to your friends.*

"I thought you were something special, Bibi. I thought you were worth waiting for, but now I realize that you're just a no-good slut."

The last word echoed in the reception hall. The music had lowered to a mere whisper as the DJ had been preparing to make an announcement of some kind so just about every freaking person in the ballroom heard my ex-boyfriend call me that awful, ugly name.

Amid the gasps of outrage, I saw my mother pushing

herself out of her seat to give Kevan a piece of her mind. My aunts were right behind her. Trey and Shawn were striding across the dance floor with pissed off expressions. Hoping to head off a fight that would only ruin the bride's night, I turned to tell Kevan to take it outside—but I was too late.

From heaven only knew where, Sergei had swept in behind Kevan. He tapped the police officer on the shoulder. "Hey."

Kevan's face registered the recognition of Sergei's deep voice. Whirling around with his fist raised, he swung at Sergei. It was such a dumb move. With the ease of a seasoned fighter, Sergei reared back and popped Kevan right in the face. Kevan's head snapped back—and he dropped like a sack of freaking rocks.

Jaw dropped, I stared at Sergei. *Holy. Shit.*

And then all hell broke loose. People were clapping and shouting and whistling. The bride started caterwauling as Corey rushed to defend his friend. Two of the groomsmen joined him, but Sergei held up a warning finger. Over the noise of the crowd, he calmly warned, "You three had better think twice before you come at me, because I can do that all night long. No one talks to Bianca like that, understand?"

The groom nodded. "Yeah, man. I get it." Staring down at Kevan, he shook his head. "He overstepped the line. He had this one coming."

Although Corey had diffused the situation, the bride demanded we be thrown out of the reception. I didn't blame my cousin Lulu for wanting us out of her celebration. Even so, it was embarrassing as hell to be tossed out like that. As Sergei helped my mother into his SUV, I kept glancing around, half-expecting the police to pull up at any moment to arrest him for assault.

There were only a handful of words spoken between Sergei and Mama on the drive back to her apartment. I sat in the backseat, stared out the window and tried to sort out my conflicted feelings. As the shock of seeing Sergei flatten Kevan began to fade, I grew increasingly more upset. Having someone call me a slut in front of hundreds of my family and friends was beyond humiliating. I hated to think what they were all saying about me right now.

And Sergei? What were they saying about him? Knowing my two loud-mouthed cousins, Trey and Shawn were probably spinning all sorts of stories about him. Corey and Kevan's friends were all police officers. No doubt they were running Sergei's name right now and finding out all the sordid details of his life to spread around the wedding. By this time tomorrow, he would probably have a reputation that included three stints in the federal pen, a murder rap and outstanding international warrants!

Why had he reacted with his fists first? Didn't he understand that he was asking for trouble? With his connections, knocking out a police officer was the very last complication he needed. Was this the way it would always be with him? Punch first, ask questions later?

We arrived at the apartment complex, and after Sergei helped me get Mama inside, he stepped out into the breezeway between apartments to make a phone call. I figured this was one of those things he needed to report to his boss. Once Kevan sobered up, he was probably going to make problems for Sergei and his friends.

"Don't you be mad at him," Mama said as I helped her into her nightgown. "He defended your honor."

"I'm a grown woman, Mama. I don't need a man to punch out someone else in defense of my honor."

"Maybe you don't," she conceded, "but sometimes it needs to be done. Kevan was out of line. He had no right to speak to you like that. What do you think Perry would have done?"

My lips parted but I didn't have the answer. Shrugging, I admitted, "I don't know."

"He would have done the same thing Sergei did. There is no way he would have allowed any man to say such a nasty thing."

"Maybe, but that doesn't make it right."

Mama sighed and settled into her favorite chair in the living room. "Well...don't you be mean to Sergei. He's a nice boy, and I like him."

"All right, Mama." I glanced around the living room. "Do you want me to get your meds?"

She shook her head and patted the phone on the end table next to her. "I'm about to call Agnes. She'll come out and get me situated for the night. You go on home."

The door to the apartment opened and Sergei stepped inside. Abashed and clearly regretful, he crouched down in front of my mother. "I'm sorry, Mrs. Bradshaw. I didn't mean to ruin your evening."

"You didn't. Kevan did that, not you." She bent down and whispered something to Sergei that I couldn't hear. The two of them sharing secrets just irritated me to no end.

"Night, Mama." I kissed her cheek and hugged her. "I'll call you in the morning."

"Okay, honey. Good night. I love you."

"I love you, too."

Out in the warm, still night, Sergei smartly didn't say a single word. We rode to my house in complete silence and still hadn't uttered a syllable by the time we entered the house. Sergei trailed me into the entryway and watched me kick off my shoes and drop my handbag in its usual spot on the table there.

Finally, he found the courage to speak. "Baby, I'm sorry."

"Don't even start with the baby and *milaya moya* stuff, Sergei. You're not going to fix this one by seducing me and making me forget why I'm upset with you."

"What was I supposed to do, Bianca?" He seemed genuinely at a loss.

"Nothing."

"Nothing?" he repeated in disbelief. "Bianca, that man insulted you."

"So? You think that's the first time someone has ever insulted me? News flash, Sergei! It happens all the time. Remember Lidia?" The sour look on his face told me he did. "I didn't punch her lights out even though I was sorely tempted."

"This was different."

"Was it?'

"He called you a—." As if unable to even bring himself to utter the word in my presence, Sergei shook his head. "No one says that about you. No one! You're my girlfriend, and I'll fight any man who says something so nasty to you."

"You can't just go around whacking people because they piss you off, Sergei. That's not the way it works in the civilized world. Maybe in the underworld that's how you guys settle things, but you can't do that in my world."

"Is that what this is about? You think I don't know the difference? That I can't tell when a man deserves to be hit and when he doesn't?"

"Does any man ever really *deserve* to be hit, Sergei?"

"Hell yes! If they insult you, they deserve more than that."

Agog at his strident defense of me, I asked simply, "Why?"

"Why?" he echoed. "Bianca, you're mine. You belong to me. I protect what's mine." He swallowed in a way that seemed almost nervous. "I love you, Bianca. I will love you until the moment I draw my last breath, and even then, I'll probably go on loving you until the end of time."

The air between us sizzled. I couldn't breathe as his admission of love wound itself around me like a warm embrace. It wasn't the scary thing I had imagined it to be. No, it was quite the opposite. Instead of dreading the way those three words would change things between us, I relished them. It occurred to me that I had been waiting for him to say them all along. For the first time in my life, I didn't want to play it safe or easy. No, I wanted the most impossibly complicated thing in the world. I wanted Sergei. Because...

"I love you, Sergei."

His face slackened with shock. A second later, he grinned. "Yes?"

Nodding, I smiled at him. "Yes."

"*Lyubimaya.*" Utilizing his brute strength, Sergei lifted me off the floor and captured my mouth in a tender kiss. I wrapped my arms around his shoulders and my legs around his waist. He used the nearest wall to brace my back while he attacked my mouth with increasingly passionate kisses. "Say it again, Bianca."

His breathless plea made my heart flutter. God, this man loved me so much. All he wanted was for me to love him back. That was it.

Caressing his face, I peered into his proud, handsome face. "I love you, Sergei."

"I'll do right by you, Bianca. Whatever it takes, I'll get out and give you the life you deserve."

Taken aback by the vow he had just sworn to me, I claimed his mouth. It wouldn't be that simple, and I feared what it would cost him, but I knew he wouldn't break that promise. Somehow, some way, he was going to get out of the mob and build a future with me.

Dotting his lips along the ticklish curve of my neck, he said, "I think we should take this to the bedroom. This is the sort of thing a couple celebrates with a marathon of lovemaking, isn't it?"

"Oh, I really hope so."

A teasing smile lit up his face. "I thought you said I couldn't fix this one by seducing you?"

"Apparently, I was wrong." I kissed his neck and nipped at his jaw. "Take me upstairs, Sergei. Show me how much you love me."

He laughed and easily carried me up to the second floor. "It might be years before I let you out of bed."

"Promises, promises..."

CHAPTER FIFTEEN

Humming softly to myself in the stockroom, I pressed the button on the automated racks that carried our bridal inventory and waited for the next dress on my list to approach. After the magic of my weekend with Sergei, I hadn't really wanted to come into work today, but running a small business, even with the amazing staff here, required my presence. We were knee-deep in the busiest part of the wedding season so this was the time when it was all-hands on deck.

The rack slowed to a stop, and I ran my fingers along the tags attached to each hanger until I found the simple sheath. Plucking it free, I transferred it to a rolling rack of gowns I was preparing for an afternoon appointment. The bride-to-be was two months pregnant and preparing for a quickie South Padre Island ceremony. She wanted something light and flirty with enough coverage in the front to provide some camouflage. Thankfully, we had about a dozen different gowns in stock that were ready to go with only minimal alterations.

A door squealed behind me. Thinking it was one of the consultants, I didn't pay it much attention. There were seven of them on the floor right now, and it was common for them to dart into the back if their first four or five picks didn't make the bride swoon.

"Bibi?"

Startled by Kevan's voice, I spun around and frowned at him. "What are you doing back here?"

Dressed in his police officer uniform, he gestured to his bruised cheek and jaw. "I came to apologize for what I said." His downcast gaze telegraphed his regret and embarrassment. "I shouldn't drink like that. It brings out the worst in me."

"Clearly," I said tightly.

"I didn't mean it, Bibi. I know you're not...you know."

"Well, that's nice, Kevan. Unfortunately, an entire room filled with our friends heard you call me that so saying you're sorry now doesn't exactly fix that, does it?"

"No," he answered quietly.

Those feelings of humiliation washed over me. "You called me a slut in front of my mother, Kevan."

He cringed. "I am sorry, Bianca. If I could go back—"

"Yeah, I know."

Holding out his hands, he said, "I didn't press charges against your—against Sergei."

"Wow. That's so gracious of you."

He frowned at me, the expression drawing attention to his fat lip. "He hit me and knocked me out. I could have had him arrested."

"So why didn't you?"

He prevaricated. "Well..."

"You know what I think? I think you knew that you were in the wrong, and you didn't want everyone at work to know how damned nasty you were to me." When he didn't agree or disagree, I added, "I don't condone what Sergei did. I don't like that he solved that problem with his fists, but I know why he did it."

Kevan seemed to be waiting for me to explain the why of the situation, but it wasn't any of his business. He sighed roughly. "You know he's trouble, Bianca. That man is tied up in some really bad shit. You don't need that in your life."

"I know what I do and don't need in my life, Kevan."

"And you need him?"

"Yes."

Clicking his teeth, he shook his head and glanced at the far wall. Blowing out a noisy breath, he said, "We'll just have to agree to disagree when it comes to him."

"Yes, I suppose we will."

"Look, I don't like the way things are between us. We used to be good friends. You counted me on for everything. I'd like to get back to that."

"I'm not sure we can get back to the way things were, Kevan."

"I'd like to try." He hesitated. "Maybe I could bring dinner and we could paint that bathroom you've been talking about doing."

"We painted it this weekend." Flashes of the steamy tryst I had shared with Sergei atop that drop cloth came to mind. Watching those rippling muscles of his as he had rolled paint up and down the walls had done crazy things to me. In between coats, we had found a few very pleasurable ways to kill time. This morning in the shower, I had still been scrubbing paint off my skin—but oh! I rather liked the do-it-yourself tricks Sergei was teaching me.

"I see." He didn't sound happy, but that wasn't my problem. "What about your prowler? Have you had any more run-ins with him?"

"No." Thinking of the way he had kept information from me, I asked, "Is there a reason you didn't tell me about the attack on Adam Blake?"

His eyes widened. "You know about that? Bibi, I was just trying to shield you from the ugliness of it. There's nothing to be gained from knowing all that nonsense."

"That's not your decision to make, Kevan. Did you know that the Houston PD has someone following me around now because they're worried those skinheads are going to come after me?"

"What? You're sure?"

"Yes, I'm sure. I spoke to Detective Santos about it. He couldn't believe you hadn't told me about the attack on Adam Blake."

Kevan's eyes narrowed. "What else did he say?"

Not wanting to get into specifics with Kevan, I shrugged. "That's it. He told me to be careful and get a dog, a security system and a gun."

"So you went out and got a Russian mobster instead?"

I slid both hands out in front of me. "Okay. We're done here. Goodbye, Kevan."

"Bibi, one of these days you're going to realize what a mistake you've made. You're going to need me."

"I doubt that, but thanks for the warning." I watched Kevan leave and stood there shaking my head at what a bizarre turn our friendship had taken. I accepted that I wasn't totally blameless here. Obviously I hadn't been careful enough and had failed to let Kevan know that I hadn't been after anything serious. That was one-hundred percent my fault. Even so, that didn't give him the right to be a total jackass about this.

Pondering whether to cut ties with Kevan or find a way to move forward, I finished selecting dresses for my bridal appointment. Out on the floor, I wheeled the rack to the dressing area I would be using and made sure the space was prepared for my client's arrival.

"Hey, Bianca?" Our receptionist Mindy poked her inside the dressing room I was tidying. "There's a guy at the front desk who wants to speak with you. He said he's a contractor. Something about a bid on a garage?"

"Oh. Um—tell him I'll be right out." Surprised by the visit from a contractor, I primped the flowers in the dressing room, wiped down the mirror and hung a fresh robe for the bride. I got sidetracked on the way to the reception desk by a consultant who needed some help with a plus-sized bride who wanted a specific mermaid gown. The sample size was much too small for her, and she looked about ready to burst into tears.

"Go pull the Arianna design from my collection, Jackie. The sample size should be a close fit." Rubbing the bride's bare arms, I smiled at her in the mirror. "The dress Jackie is bringing is one of my designs. It's a bit simpler than this gown you're wearing, but it will give you an idea of how you'll look in the mermaid silhouette."

"But I can get this dress in the right size?"

"Absolutely," I assured her. "If this is the dress of your dreams, Jackie will get someone over here to measure you. Once the deposit is paid, the designer gets the order, and they'll start making a dress especially for you."

She stared at herself in the mirror, her gaze critical and one I recognized all too well. "I just want to be really pretty on my wedding day."

"Sweetheart, you will be. I promise you. We'll make sure that your wedding dress is perfect." Rubbing her back, I said, "You're already beautiful. It's our job to accentuate that."

Smiling, she nodded. "Okay. Thanks."

Jackie returned with the mermaid gown from my design collection so I excused myself from the visibly calmer bride. Out in the reception area, I spotted a man in jeans, rugged boots and a blue work shirt. When he turned toward me, I managed to put a name to his face. Extending my hand, I greeted him. "Marcus, right?"

He seemed relieved that I remembered him. "Yes, ma'am."

"What can I do for you?"

"I had a phone call earlier from a man named Sergei Sakharov. He wanted me to come by to take a look at your carriage house." He hesitated. "I wanted to make sure everything was on the up-and-up with that call."

A little miffed that he had made assumptions like that, I explained, "Sergei is my boyfriend. He also owns part of a contracting business, but they work mainly in retail. You know, shopping centers, restaurants. He's taken over the remodeling projects at my home."

"Okay." Marcus offered an apologetic smile. "I didn't mean to step on your toes. I know you're a young woman living alone, and I wanted to make sure some general contractor wasn't trying to scam you."

"That's not the case, I assure you."

"Good. I'm glad. Well—I suppose I'll get back in touch with Mr. Sakharov and see when would be a good time for me to come by and adjust my bid on the project."

"Great, and thanks for stopping by."

After the contractor left, I couldn't shake the weirdness of that run-in. Glancing at my watch, I realized I didn't have time to call Sergei and chat with him about it. Later, I promised myself, and got ready for my bridal appointment.

Of course, one appointment turned into three and then I had a design consultation that ran over its allotted time. Between inventory questions, following up with Gladys in our billing department and promising Maggie in alterations I would look into squeezing some more seamstresses into the budget, I barely found the time to eat the snack Sergei had packed me. The selection of bite-sized fruit chunks and the small container of mixed nuts wasn't exactly the bag of cheese puffs I had been craving, but he was right about it satisfying me much longer.

I was walking into the house when my phone rang. Clamping it between my ear and shoulder, I answered while pushing the door shut with my foot. "Hello?"

"How was work, sweetheart?"

Sergei's voice made me grin and left me feeling all tingly. "It was great. You?"

"Same old story," he said with a chuckle. "I kept Vivian out of trouble so I'll put a point in the win column for today."

Knowing what a pain she could be, I figured that was about as good as it would get for him. "Are you coming home for dinner?"

"No, I'm heading to the gym. After, I promised Nikolai I would help run an errand."

"Oh?"

"It's nothing like that, Bianca. It's for Kelly Connolly."

"I see." Considering what I knew of Kelly's current predicament, I doubted I wanted to hear any more details of what this errand might entail. "Will you be late?"

"Probably," he said, already sounding tired.

Not wanting to burden him with Kevan's appearance at the shop and the contractor's strange visit, I kept those stories to myself. "I'll wait up for you."

"You don't have to do that."

"I want to, Sergei. I've missed you today."

"I'll try to get home as soon as possible. I need to stop by my apartment to pick up some clothes."

The mention of his apartment spurred thoughts of a topic we hadn't even come close to opening for discussion. Ever since the night he had kicked my door in to save me from my shower curtain, Sergei had basically been living here. It definitely wasn't something I had ever planned on happening, but the thought of not having him here every night, even if I didn't have this prowler issue and the Night Wolves scratching at my front door, made me really sad.

"Maybe you should pack some more clothes and bring them here. You can have the closet in the guest room across the hall for now." With all the clothes I had packed into the master closet, there simply wasn't room for him in the bedroom we were sharing.

Sergei's end of the line stayed quiet for a while. "Are you sure?"

"Yes." I wasn't. In fact, my palms were getting sweaty just thinking about making this first step toward cohabitation. "It's the best solution for our current situation. Just bring whatever you need, and we'll find a place for it here."

"All right. I have to go. I'll see you later."

"Be safe."

"I will, *milaya moya*. I love you."

Those three simple words still hadn't lost their magic. "I love you."

After ending the call, I made my way to the kitchen and sorted through the mail I'd grabbed from the box out front. I thought about dinner but wasn't in the mood to cook. I considered having something delivered, maybe a pizza or some Chinese.

Glancing out the front windows, I spotted the dark car that followed me everywhere. Sergei had introduced me to Arty a few days earlier. He was a nice guy, a bit older than Sergei, and soft-spoken. Something Sergei had told me about Arty made me curious.

With an evening to fill, I decided to be friendly and left the house. I had made it halfway down the sidewalk before Arty was out of his car and coming toward me. Looking concerned, he asked, "Is something wrong? Do you need my help?"

"Everything is fine, but I think I do need your help."

"Okay. What can I do for you?"

"Sergei said you recently helped your mother and sister come over here. I wondered if you might be willing to come inside and tell me how you did it. You know, the law firm you used, the steps and all that." Sweetening the deal, I added, "I'll order something for dinner so you don't have to sit out here and eat in your car."

He seemed surprised by the offer but nodded. "Yeah. Okay."

"Great."

While Arty returned to his car to grab some things, I headed back to the house. Sergei had his own exit plan in the works, but I was looking at the big picture. He was never going to be happy here until his mother and brother were safe here with him—with us. Whatever I could do to make that happen, I had to try.

* * *

"What are you reading?"

Sergei glanced at the rearview mirror and found Nikolai staring at him with interest. They were parked outside Connolly Fitness, the gym Kelly's older brothers owned. Word on the street was that the loan shark John Hagen would receive half of the building if the loan on it wasn't repaid. Sergei had no doubt that Hagen would force them to sell in order to get the building and the land beneath it.

"Property records and blueprints for Bianca's home,"

he answered. "There's something funny about that carriage house out back."

"How's that?"

"The dimensions aren't right."

"It's an old building. The carpenters who put it together didn't have to meet codes, Sergei."

He made a humming sound of agreement. "That's probably it."

"You don't sound convinced."

"I don't know." Sergei hesitated before admitting, "It feels strange in that building."

"Strange?"

"Yes, strange." He wasn't about to tell the boss that he got the worst knot in his stomach when he was in the place.

"Maybe it's the fumes from old lead pipes and paint," Nikolai suggested. "Unless you think it's something supernatural."

He could hear the teasing tone in the boss' voice. "*Nyet.*"

"So then what?"

"I don't know."

"I think you're overly stressed. You're juggling Bianca, your duties with Vivian, this threat from *nochniye volki*, the prowler, the tournament—it's too much, Sergei." Stretching out his legs, Nikolai exhaled a long, slow breath. "When the tournament is finished and this mess with those white power bastards is done, I want you to take Bianca on vacation. Go to London. Go to Paris. Go visit a beach. Just—go away for a while."

Sergei twisted in his seat for a better look at his boss. "You're serious?"

"You've earned it." Glancing out the window, he said, "Ah. Here they come."

Sergei leaned down to see out the window and spotted Kelly Connolly and his two brothers leaving their gym. He opened his door, climbed out of the driver's seat and walked around to the other side of the vehicle. Arms crossed, he waited for the three brothers to see him.

Kelly strode toward him, and they sized each other up carefully. If the man made it through enough matches, they would face off in the cage, and then Sergei would have to hurt him. Probably badly. Maybe even irreparably. He hated the thought of it, but there was nothing to be done.

Without a word, he opened the door to the middle row of seats and gestured for Kelly to get inside. He remained outside the vehicle while the boss handed over information about the man who was blackmailing Kelly's girlfriend. It was the last bit of help Kelly would get from the Russian camp on this matter. Sergei hoped he used it wisely.

When it was done, Sergei watched Kelly rejoin his brothers before sliding behind the wheel. Nikolai asked to be dropped off at Samovar. Once the boss was off his hands, Sergei drove to his apartment to gather some clothing and other necessities. He wondered at Bianca's invitation to keep more of his things at her place. Was she feeling out the possibility of offering him a more permanent spot there? Were they ready for that step?

Navigating the busy night streets, Sergei contemplated their relationship. It seemed they were moving outside the prescribed timetables that most couples followed. He trusted they would find their own way and left it at that.

When he turned down the alley behind Bianca's house, he killed his lights and crept along the narrow path. Staring at the old, rotted out carriage house, he didn't even see the shadowy figure moving across Bianca's backyard at first. Easing on the brakes, Sergei put his SUV in park and watched the spot by the gazebo. Amid the shadowy darkness, he spotted the man-sized form moving closer to the house.

Spurred into action with thoughts of protecting Bianca, Sergei opened the door and slid out of his vehicle. He jogged to the back gate, put both hands on the sturdy iron frame and vaulted over the top. The hard landing jarred his ankles, but he ignored the jolt that rattled his knees. Eating up the ground with his long strides, Sergei hurried to intercept the prowler before he could reach the back door of Bianca's house.

He launched himself at the man, wrapping his arms around him and taking him down to the grass. "Got you!"

The prowler fought back hard, twisting and kicking to escape Sergei's clenched arms. A knee to Sergei's belly made him growl, but he simply squeezed harder. The man got a hand free and slapped at Sergei's face. They rolled around in the backyard, punching and scratching and shouting.

The back door slammed open, and Bianca rushed onto the back porch. "Sergei!"

"Get back inside!" His broken concentration allowed the man to jam his elbow into Sergei's ribs and break free. "*Shit.*"

Sergei snatched at the prowler's ankle. The man slipped on the grass and went down hard. The prowler kicked wildly, and his shoe came off in Sergei's hand. The man scuttled like a bug across the grass and finally managed to get into an upright position. Sergei shoved off the ground and made chase.

Before they reached the gate, another man appeared in the alleyway. He jumped over the gate and became illuminated by the streetlights. Sergei had never been happier to see Detective Eric Santos in his life.

"Houston PD! Hands in the air!" Weapon trained on the prowler, Eric forced the other man to stop. "Sergei, hands up, too. Don't move until I sort this out."

Happy to oblige, Sergei held up both hands and tried to catch his breath. The prowler looked like he might try to bolt but he finally put up his hands. Eric advanced on the prowler and quickly cuffed the man. "You armed, Sergei?"

"No. My weapon is in my vehicle."

"Sergei!" Bianca raced toward him. "Are you okay?"

"I told you to go back inside." He reached for her hand and dragged her behind him, shielding her body with his, just in case.

"I did." She embraced him from behind and kissed his back. "I called 9-1-1. They're sending two units right now." She peeked around him to look at the prowler. "Eric? What are you doing here?"

"I decided to drive by to check on your place. It's been quiet with the Night Wolves, but I don't trust them. That's when I saw a car parked a few blocks down the street. I decided to come down the alley and spotted Sergei's SUV. I figured there was only one reason he would abandon his car down there."

"Is he one of them?" Sergei needed to know who the prowler was and what he was doing here.

"Let's find out." Eric dragged the black ski mask from the man's head—and Bianca gasped.

"Kevan! What in the hell are you doing here?"

Sergei wanted to know the same thing. Eric, however, didn't seem nearly as surprised. Staring at the detective, he asked, "Did you know?"

"I suspected," Eric admitted reluctantly. "I've been keeping tabs on Bianca so I have her file and her brother's file flagged in the system. Kevan has been doing a lot of digging in cases he has no business seeing. I had a bad feeling and followed him one evening. He came here, a block down, and just sat there all night."

"Why, Kevan?" Bianca stepped closer to her ex-boyfriend and tugged her robe tighter around her body. "Why would you do this to me?"

"I think I know," Sergei said through gritted teeth. "He's obsessed with you, and he knew the only way to get you back was to make you scared. He knew that if you had a prowler, you would call him for help. He kept coming back to scare you because he wanted you to invite him back into your life."

"But you didn't," Kevan spat angrily. "You called *him*. You let *him* help you." The disgraced police officer shook his head. "You're so stupid, Bibi. Don't you have any idea how dangerous he is? He's going to get you killed."

"How dangerous he is? You're the one who nearly gave me a heart attack! You're the one who made me think the Night Wolves were creeping around my house to take me out in a revenge killing."

"I'm trying to save your life."

"Yeah, well, you better start thinking about how you're going to save your career," Eric interjected. Sirens wailed as they neared the house, and the detective sighed. "You really fucked yourself on this one, Kevan."

Holding Bianca against his side, Sergei stood with her while they answered questions and gave their reports. He still couldn't quite believe that it had been Kevan all along. In a way, he was relieved that it was something so ridiculous and not the Night Wolves, after all. It was one less threat to Bianca's life.

But, as they slid into bed together a few hours later and Bianca worked her way down his body, kissing and licking and then finally sucking his cock deep into her mouth, he couldn't stop thinking about something Kevan had said.

He's going to get you killed.

What if Kevan was right? The thought of Bianca being hurt because of him deflated his erection. His chest ached, and he found it hard to breathe.

"Baby?" Bianca abandoned the amazing blow job she had been giving him and nibbled her way back to his chest. "Are you with me?"

"Yes." He was glad for the darkness that hid his taut, worried expression. "Come her, *milaya moya*."

She straddled his hips and let him drag her mouth down for a sensual kiss. Their tongues danced as he drank from her lips to quench his thirst for her. Palming her breast, he brushed his thumb across her nipple and enjoyed the mewling, kittenish sounds she made.

"I love you so much, Bianca."

She sifted her fingers through his short hair as he suckled her breast. "I know you do."

"I don't ever want the bad things in my life to touch you." He kissed the spot just above her heart.

"They won't."

She sounded so sure. Her unshakable belief in his ability to protect her and keep her safe filled him with such conflicted emotions. On one hand, he loved that she trusted him so completely. On the other, he was terrified that her life was in his hands. One wrong move, and he would lose everything.

Grasping her hips, Sergei rocked his body until his cock nudged between her slick folds. The fat head of his dick slipped inside her, and they both groaned. Sucking in a sharp breath, Bianca lifted her bottom and pulled off his unsheathed erection. "Sergei, you forgot to put on a condom."

"I didn't forget." He wanted to be inside her without anything between them. "Let me make love to you, Bianca. Let me come inside you."

Even as he begged for the chance to mark her with his seed, to share something with her that he had never shared with any other woman, he fully expected her to say no. When Bianca pressed down on his shaft, allowing his naked cock to slide deeper inside that sweet, snug pussy, he lost the ability to breathe. Mouth agape, he curled his toes against the mattress and marveled at the slick, wet heat enveloping him. "Bianca!"

She whimpered at the sound of him groaning her name and put both hands on his chest for support. Rocking slowly, she swirled her hips and rubbed her clitoris against his body. "Oh, Sergei." She exhaled with such pleasure in her voice. "I love you so much."

Gliding his worshiping hands along her breasts and then cupping her backside, he thrust up into her. He bit his lip and prayed this experience would go on forever. He wanted to draw it out and savor every single second of this coupling. The bed creaked beneath them as Bianca's pace hastened, and she chased her climax.

Wanting to help her find release, he licked his thumb and placed it against her clit. She gasped and pressed against his thumb, urging him to stimulate her. "Make me come, Sergei."

Wanting to give her so much more than that, he swirled his thumb over the little pearl there and delighted in the rhythmic clenching of her pussy around his cock. At the first fluttering spasm, he grinned triumphantly and listened to her coming apart atop him. "Sergei! *Sergei!*"

There wasn't a sweeter sound in the world than Bianca coming on his cock. When she fell forward against him, he flipped their positions, shoved her thighs even wider apart and thrust deep and hard into her cunt. She cried out and clawed at his biceps. "Oh! Oh! *Oh!*"

She came again, her pussy squeezing him and driving him fucking wild. Lowering his body, he planted his hands on either side of her head and plundered her mouth. He took her with long, unhurried thrusts, plunging into her again and again, and holding his orgasm at bay as long as possible. He felt that familiar buzz in his lower stomach and knew it was time.

Burying his face in her neck, he slammed as deep as possible, pressing the head of his cock right up against the entrance of her womb, and allowed the waves of ecstasy to crash over him and drag him down in their pleasurable depths. Shuddering and petting each other, they clung together in the stillness of the night and traded gentle, tender kisses.

Sergei finally found the strength to roll off her. He curled up to her back and wrapped his arms around her. She wiggled her bottom until she found a comfortable position and sighed contentedly. He kissed her cheek and wondered if she was thinking the same thoughts he was.

They had just played with fire—and there were only two possible results, one that would change things between them forever.

CHAPTER SIXTEEN

"Are you staying late tonight?"

I glanced up from my sketch pad to smile at Gladys. "Yes. I'm a little behind on this design, and I need to sort through some fabrics. I've also got to get into the stockroom and start culling floor samples for the clearance sale."

"You want me to stay?" Though Gladys headed up the business side of the shop, she had started out as a consultant when Mama first opened the doors. She was always willing to pitch in and help wherever she was needed.

"No. Go home. I've got it."

"Okay, honey. If you're sure."

"I'm sure. Would you mind locking the employee entrance behind you?"

"Not at all," she said with a smile. "I'll see you in the morning."

"Good night."

Alone in the store, I got comfortable at my desk and sketched out some bodice details. Designing would always be my first love, but running the shop while Mama recovered had grown on me. She had been hinting at the idea of selling me the business so she could retire completely. I had been wholly against it, but lately I found myself wondering if it wasn't time.

Done with my sketches, I decided to get a head start on sorting through the floor samples in the back. I had been putting off the task for a few weeks, but we would be getting new shipments for the recently debuted spring collections. I would need the space on the racks. Besides, our bi-annual clearance sales were huge draws and brought in lots of business.

I had only picked four dresses off the racks when my cell phone started ringing. Sergei's handsome face filled my screen and I swiped my finger across his forehead to answer. "Hello?"

"Hey, baby." His rumbling voice made my knees weak.

"Hey, what are you up to?"

"I'm waiting for the boss to come out of a meeting. After I drop him off, I thought I would pick up something for dinner and meet you at the shop. If you're still staying late?"

"I'm in the back right now, picking out floor samples."

"Okay. So I'll pick something up and then maybe I can help you."

"You? Help me sort wedding dresses?"

"Sure. Why not?"

"Um…well. Okay."

He laughed. Then, more seriously, he said, "Bianca, about last night…"

We hadn't yet discussed the way we had made love without protection. I sensed he was guilt-ridden over it now that the lust-filled moment had passed.

"I don't regret it, Sergei."

"No?" He sounded surprised.

"No." Running my fingers along the protective plastic covering the dresses, I asked, "Do you?"

"No. I feel guilty about pressuring you, but I'm glad that I shared that experience only with you."

"You shouldn't feel guilty. I—"

The crunch and squeal of metal interrupted me.

"Bianca, what was that?"

"I don't know." I had lowered my voice to a whisper on instinct. "It sounds like it's coming from the loading docks in the next room."

"Hide." He gave the order immediately. "Be very quiet. Don't say a word. Not even to me. Just hide. We're not far away."

Glad that I had left my high heels in my office, I padded softly to the farthest corner of the backroom and squeezed my body behind three overlapping racks of dresses. I had never been more thankful for our abundant stock than in that moment.

"If you're hiding, press a button."

I tapped a key on my screen.

Sergei exhaled with relief. "Nikolai is with me. He's calling Kostya. He's closer than us. Just stay hidden."

Clutching my phone to my chest, I curled my body into the tiniest ball possible and waited. My ears perked to every strange noise. A loud, screeching yawn ricocheted through the building. I pinpointed it to the loading dock for sure and held my breath. It was hard to hear over the blood pounding in my head, but I picked out three distinct sets of running footsteps.

Oh, God.

Trying not to freak out, I convinced myself I was safe here in my hiding place. Sergei would get here quickly. He would save me.

Because the shop was so big, and I had left lights on in most of the back offices, it seemed like the men who had broken in were concentrating their search there. Were they looking for money? For merchandise to sell? Or was it something far more sinister? Were they looking for me?

Dread gripped my stomach. A sixth sense told me the boogeymen of my nightmares had finally caught up with me. Those white power freaks were here. They'd come to get their revenge—and I was all alone.

Footsteps echoed in the cavernous back room. The space was huge, running three-quarters of the length of the building, so they had a big area to search before they found me. I squeezed my fingers into tight fists and bit my lower lip so hard I could taste blood.

"That bitch is in here. Toss this place. Find her."

The male growl made my blood run cold. I closed my eyes and prayed. *Please. Please hurry, Sergei.*

There were three men in the room now, all of them flicking through the racks and dumping boxes. It was only a matter of time now. I had nowhere to run. I was cornered and screwed beyond belief.

"Gotcha!"

The dresses and racks shielding me were thrown aside. Heart racing and mouth dry, I leaped to my feet and held up my hands. My phone fell to the floor and bounced. "No. Please! *Please!* Don't!"

The skinhead who had discovered me stepped aside and let another man, one who bore a scary resemblance to Adam Blake, grab me. I screamed bloody murder, but it was no use. The brother of the man who had killed Perry had me in his hands, and he wasn't about to let me go.

With his fingers snarled in my hair, he dragged me kicking and screaming into the room next door. One of his cronies produced zip-ties, those plastic cuffs riot cops carried, and used them to bind my ankles together. They forced my wrists high overhead and bound those together. A dress rack was brought over, and my trapped wrists were strapped to the long horizontal bar. The painful position made my shoulders burn so badly.

Sobbing hysterically, I wanted to beg for my life, but I knew it was pointless. I was outnumbered and couldn't bargain with these men. They absolutely hated me. I could see the disgust burning in their eyes as they stared at me.

"Do you know who I am?" The one who looked like Adam Blake stared expectantly at me.

I nodded and sobbed. "You're Adam Blake's brother."

"Darren Blake." He tugged a knife from a sheath in his boot and trailed the super sharp tip down the front of my blouse. The fabric split open to reveal the lacy cups of the delicate pink bra Sergei had given me.

"Why are you doing this?"

Darren laughed in my face. "*Why are you doing this?*" He mocked me in a sing-song voice that made my skin crawl. "Because I fucking can! Stupid bitch."

I flinched at his cruel words.

"I know your boyfriend and his boss have James. I sent him out to follow that skinny, blue-eyed gash, but he never came back."

I suspected his vulgar description was meant for Vivian. "I don't know anything about Sergei's business. He doesn't tell me those things."

"I don't care if you know or not. That's not why I'm here." The edge of the blade pressed against my neck, and I held my breath. "You're the reason my brother is turning his back on his family."

"Wh-what?"

"Adam told me that your face haunts him." His lip curled in a menacing sneer. "I can see why. I've seen some ugly fucking n—"

He didn't get the rest of that filthy, nasty, horrible word out of his mouth. The sharp puff of bullets fired from a silenced pistol interrupted him. The man standing behind Darren crumpled forward as two bullets ripped through his head. The other skinhead reacted instantly and raced toward the back room, escaping death for now.

Kostya stepped through the doorway and lowered his gun. He fired twice more, hitting Darren's kneecaps and dropping the man to the floor. Writhing and screaming with pain, Darren clutched at his bleeding legs while Kostya kicked aside the knife the evil man had been carrying. The frighteningly quiet Russian glanced briefly my way as if to ascertain that I was in no need of immediate help and then strode calmly into the back room.

"No! No! No!"

Another two bullets were fired, and the pleading from the third man stopped.

A few seconds later, it was Sergei's panicked voice that echoed in the shop. "*Bianca!*"

He burst into the room with Nikolai right behind him. They quickly scanned the space, taking in the dead man in front of me and Darren's tortured cries. Sergei raced toward me while Nikolai went to stand over the skinhead leader.

Whipping out a knife from the back pocket of his jeans, Sergei sliced through the awful plastic ties squeezing my wrists and ankles. He gathered me in his strong arms and cradled me close. I hugged him so hard and sobbed against his neck. The soothing scent of him broke through my fear and convinced me I was safe.

"You need to get her out of here. Now," Nikolai ordered.

I made the mistake of glancing over Sergei's shoulder. Kostya had wrapped the third man in one of the plastic dress bags and carried him on his shoulder like a rolled up carpet. I assumed the other dead man would soon get the same treatment. I didn't even want to think about what they were going to do with Darren.

"Do you have a security alarm?" Kostya lowered his burden to the floor and waited for me to answer.

"Ye-yes."

"I will need the code."

"It's in the top drawer of my desk. On a pink sticky note," I added, still so very dazed by my horrific experience. Staring at the carnage, I asked, "What are you going to do?"

"After I clean up this mess," Kostya gestured around him, "I'll stage a break-in. We'll steal some dresses and some equipment. You don't need to worry."

Swallowing hard, I burrowed into Sergei's protective embrace. "What time am I leaving?"

Kostya frowned at first but then nodded with understanding. He glanced at his watch. "Fifteen 'til eleven, okay? Leave your car and the keys. I'll drive it back to your house so our neighbors see it come home at the right time. That way you both have alibis, yes?"

Kostya produced my phone from his pocket and handed it to Sergei who was staring at Darren. I had never in my life seen such fury on any man's face. I knew that if I let go of Sergei, he was going to kill Darren. It would be bloody and brutal—and it would change the man I loved forever.

"Take me home, Sergei. Please."

My softly pleading voice seemed to break through that haze of bloodlust. He swept me up into his arms and carried me out of the shop. I didn't know how I was supposed to come back here in the morning and pretend nothing had happened. Could I seriously play along with the break-in story?

You don't have a choice.

I accepted that there was no decision here. Those men were going to kill me. They might have even raped or tortured me before they slit my throat or stabbed me.

Still…guilt held me in its cold clutch. What if I had called 9-1-1? Would they have gotten there in time to save me? Would they have ended the attack on me in a different way?

Tormented by those thoughts, I didn't even realize we had reached my house and were parked in front of the carriage house until Sergei touched my hand. "Bianca?"

I rubbed my face and felt the bile rising in my throat. "I need to take a shower."

"It will help." He sounded as if he spoke from experience. "Let's go inside. I'll fix you some tea, and then you can sleep."

I doubted I would ever get a full night's sleep again.

* * *

Sergei couldn't sleep.

His mind insisted on playing the scene he had discovered at Bianca's shop on an endless loop. His queasy belly churned relentlessly. The tea he had been drinking all night threatened to erupt at any moment.

Rubbing his face between his hands, Sergei leaned back against the leather chair and propped his aching feet on the ottoman. He had two fully loaded guns within arm's reach and sat between the bed where Bianca slept and the door where any trouble might appear. She had tossed and turned fitfully before finally succumbing to exhaustion.

And it was all his fault.

While Sergei conceded that Darren Blake's beef with Bianca had started years ago, he also believed that Darren had specifically targeted Bianca for his deceitful machinations and power plays because of her ties to him and his ties to Nikolai. Whatever plans Nikolai and Besian had for the skinheads would put an end to that problem—but what about the next gang war?

And there would be another one. There was always another one. Nikolai tried so hard to keep the city's underworld quiet, but there were always outside forces that couldn't be controlled. Sergei refused to put Bianca in harm's way ever again.

"Sergei?" Bianca's sleepy, sweet voice interrupted his troubled thoughts.

Shifting his gaze toward the bed, he realized sunset was upon them. Had he lost track of time so easily? He took in her rumpled hair and the cotton nightgown with its feminine softness and pale shade of purple. It dawned on him that this was the last time he would ever see her like this so he tried to imprint the vision on his brain forever.

"Yes, *milaya moya?*"

"You didn't come to bed."

"No." He gestured to the door. "I wanted to make sure you were safe."

She tugged the sheet higher. "Am I safe now?"

"You will be." Numbness spread through his body, starting at his aching, breaking heart and arcing out from there with pulsing bursts. "When I'm gone."

She frowned. "Gone?"

Lowering his feet to the floor, Sergei pushed himself into a standing position. He reached back and unhooked the gold medallion his mother had given him many years ago. His throat was so tight he could hardly breathe but he forced himself to speak. "It's over, Bianca. We can't do this anymore."

She blinked rapidly. "What?"

"I'm leaving. Forever," he added, in case she hadn't understood him. "This?" He gestured between them. "Us? It's over. We're done."

"But I love you." Her whispered words cut more deeply than any knife possibly could have.

"And I love you," he answered honestly. "Because I love you, I have to leave you. I never wanted this life for you. I love you too much to condemn to this."

"But I—"

"No, Bianca." He held up his hand to silence her. Moving close enough to touch her, he grasped her small hand and pressed his medallion onto her palm before curling her fingers closed around it. Certain he wouldn't survive a final kiss, he picked up his weapons and moved to the door. "I'll pick up my things after you've gone to work."

"Sergei…"

Taking in her beautiful face one last time, he smiled at her. "You deserve so much better, Bianca. I know you'll have no trouble finding a better man than me."

Broken and battered inside, Sergei spun on his heel— and left behind the woman he would love until he drew his dying breath.

CHAPTER SEVENTEEN

Standing in the lobby of Samovar a few days later, I toyed with the gold medallion of Saint Sergius that I hadn't taken off since Sergei had broken up with me. I gazed at one of Vivi's paintings that hung in a prominent position there. It was one of the pieces she had done during her freshman year of college. Viewing the moody canvas today, I had a different feeling of the art piece now than I had four years ago.

Of course, four years ago, I wasn't suffering from the most wretchedly broken heart. My eyes closed briefly as a fresh wave of pain swept over me and tried to drag me under the melancholic currents that had been trying to drown me since Sergei walked out on me. Squeezing the medallion in my hand, I tried to get a grip on my emotions.

I still had a hard time believing he had done that. When the initial numbness had passed, I had been enraged by the way he had turned his back on me and walked right out of my life. Later, when I had calmed down, I had finally grasped the motivation for his harsh and unexpected reaction.

He loved me so much he refused to put me at risk. There was no way we could pretend that his life in the underworld would never touch mine. That childish, optimistic dream had been crushed under the weight of two dead bodies and one badly injured skinhead who had I feared would never be seen alive again.

"Bianca?"

My eyes widened at the sound of Lidia's voice. Of all the people I never wanted to deal with again, she ranked right up there at the top. Sighing, I reluctantly turned to face her. Instantly, I noticed the way she wrung her apron in her hands. "Yes?"

"May I speak with you?"

"Sure." I followed her to a quiet corner of the lobby. "Well?"

Her gaze lingered on the medallion dangling from my neck, but she said nothing about it. She smoothed a few wayward strands of hair behind her ear. "I wanted to apologize to you for the other night. What I did to you and what I said to you was wrong, and I'm sorry."

Her apology caught me off guard. It seemed sincere so I accepted it without reservation. "Thank you."

"I'm a jealous person by nature. It's not an easy thing for me to admit, but it's true." She swallowed nervously. "I wanted Sergei for myself. He wanted me once, and I thought he would be the one to marry me. When he met you—well—all that changed."

This would probably go down as the most awkward conversation of my life, but I decided to push through it. "What about Arty?"

Surprise crossed her face. "You know Arty?"

"It's a long, convoluted story." I waved my hand. "He told me that you two had dated for a while."

"We did." Her expression softened, and I could tell she still had feelings for him. "He's a nice guy, but I treated him badly."

"So apologize to him," I suggested. "You're right. He

is nice. I'm sure he'd be willing to sit down with you and listen to whatever you need to say."

"Maybe," she said uncertainly. "Why are you being so nice to me after the mean things I said to you?"

"We're all human, and we all make mistakes. My mother is always preaching grace, and I think it's a good place to start in any relationship." I touched her arm and smiled. "I don't think you're a bad person. I really am sorry about the way Lena came after you."

She shook her head. "I deserved that. It was a lie. What I said about Yuri," she explained. "He was a big flirt before her. He'd come in here and tease all of us. Sometimes he even took the prettier girls out for a nice time, but then he met Lena and all that stopped." Her mouth slanted, and she shrugged. "It's hard to see other women get what you want. It makes a woman cold inside."

"Only if you let it," I reminded her.

"Yes," she agreed quietly. Her gaze flicked to the door behind me where a large lunchtime business party was coming through the doors. "Come on. I'll take you back to see Nikolai."

I followed Lidia to the offices in the rear of the restaurant, rapped my knuckles against the door and waited.

"Yes?"

I opened the door and peeked inside. "Nikolai?"

"Bianca!" He stood up and gestured toward the chairs in front of his desk. "Come in. Have a seat."

I shut the door behind me and shook his hand before taking one of the chairs. "Thanks for seeing me."

"It's no problem. Would you like something to drink? Water? Coffee? Tea? Vodka?" He said the last with a teasing smile.

"No, I'm fine, but thanks."

He returned to his chair and leaned back. "Have you been to see the baby yet?"

I smiled at the reminder of Benny and Dimitri's baby. Sofia Natalya Stepanov had made her debut early yesterday morning. In the end, Benny had undergone a planned C-section to bring her nine pound, two ounce bundle of joy in the world.

"No, I'm going later today. I figured Benny was tired yesterday after having surgery in the morning. I would have stopped by this morning, but I didn't want to run in to Vivian and Sergei."

"Oh. Right." A flash of regret touched his face. As quickly as it appeared, it vanished. "Sofia is the prettiest baby girl I've ever seen."

"Yeah?"

"So pretty," he repeated. "She has dark hair like Benny but blue eyes like Dimitri."

"I think all babies have blue eyes when they're born."

"These will stay blue, I think." Rapping his fingertips on his desk, he said, "About the repairs to your shop..."

I waved my hand. "It's done. The contractors were in and out in a day."

"If there was any other way, Bianca—"

"It's fine, Nikolai." I really didn't want to talk about what had happened that night or the aftermath that followed. Kostya's impeccable staging had easily fooled the police and insurance company. Thankfully, the redundancies around the shop had allowed us to continue serving our brides with only the tiniest hiccup. The mob cleaner had only taken or destroyed dresses that hadn't been spoken for by customers.

"It's not fine. It never should have happened." He ran his fingers through his sand-colored hair. "I waited too long to act and you very nearly paid the ultimate price."

I didn't dare ask him what he had waited too long to do. The news had been filled with stories of a major fire at the auto shop the Night Wolves operated out of and of a shootout at some bar they owned outside of the city when the Feds had raided them to round the rest of them up. The only casualties had been those racist scumbags so there didn't seem to be much outpouring of concern over the gang violence.

"He misses you," Nikolai said, his words seemingly out of the blue. "I've never seen him like this, not even when he had to leave his mother and brother behind."

Hearing that Sergei missed me bolstered my courage. I had never faced off with a mob boss before so I needed every drop of bravery I could squeeze out of me. "That's why I'm here."

"You want him back?"

"I never asked him to leave."

Nikolai sat forward. "You didn't break up with him?"

I shook my head. "He left me."

"To protect you?"

"Yes."

Shaking his head, Nikolai swore softly in his mother tongue. "He's always been such an honorable bastard." Turning his attention to me, he asked, "What can I do to help you?"

"You can start by telling me exactly how much outstanding debt you hold for Sergei."

"Why?"

I reached into my purse and retrieved my checkbook and pen. "Because I intend to buy him from you."

Nikolai blinked. "Are you serious?"

"Yes."

The mob boss stared at me for a few very unnerving

seconds before bursting into laughter. Head thrown back, he stared at the ceiling and chuckled. "God, Bianca, I always knew you were a dark horse."

Bristling at his amusement, I insisted, "I'm serious, Nikolai."

He lowered his head and peered intently at me. "I know you are."

"How much?"

"It's a lot, Bianca."

"Well, luckily for you, I have deep pockets."

"Is that so?"

I was probably tipping my hand too early, but I didn't think Nikolai would cheat me. "When Daddy was killed, the drunk driver who plowed into him survived, and our family took him and his insurance company to court. We received a big payout that Mama invested wisely. Later, when Perry was murdered, my mother sued the Blake family. They settled with us by giving us some pieces of land down in south Texas. You've heard of the Eagle Ford Shale?"

"I have."

"So you know what sorts of royalties we have pouring in then," I replied. "Name your price, Nikolai. I'm not walking out of here until I own Sergei."

The mob boss reached for a slip of paper and clicked his pen. He scribbled a figure and slid the paper my way. "Don't start writing that check yet, Bianca. You can't just give me money like this. It will attract unwanted attention."

I understood what he meant. Glancing at the paper, I kept the shock from filtering across my face. "How do we do this?"

Nikolai seemed to be mulling it over. A smile started to lift the corners of his mouth. "I have just under sixty acres of land in Waller County that I need to move."

"What? Over near Hempstead?"

"Close by," he said. "It would be better if this land stayed in the family."

"Uh-huh," I replied unhappily. "I suppose I don't want to know why."

"Probably not," he agreed. "I can promise you that the land would be...cleaned...before it came into your possession."

"So I buy the land—"

"And you get Sergei, free and clear."

"Do you mean that?"

"I need him to fight on Friday and Saturday," Nikolai answered honestly. "There's too much money involved, including his own, to risk that. After Saturday, he's all yours."

The mention of Sergei's money tied up in the fights made me think of his family. "That's something else I wanted to discuss. How do I get Sergei's family over here?"

I might have imagined it, but it looked as if Nikolai's pale eyes actually warmed toward me. "Vladimir could easily immigrate under a job's visa with Dimitri's company, but it's Sergei's mother that has the hardest time coming over here because she's only a seamstress. Until Sergei becomes a citizen, he can't sponsor her immigration. The brothers don't want their mother left behind." He hesitated. "Did he tell you about the last lawyer?"

"No."

"The bastard scammed many Russians and Ukrainians here in Houston. He tucked tail and ran before I could get my hands on him. Sergei lost a ton of money and time to him. He's starting over now, and it will take time, even if Sergei gets citizenship soon. Unless—"

"Unless what?"

"There are ways to jump the line, but it costs money, Bianca."

"Legal ways?"

He nodded and opened a leather address book. Plucking free one of the Samovar business cards sitting on the corner of his desk, he turned it over and jotted down a name, phone number and address. He slid the card toward me. "This guy works for a firm that Yuri uses. He's safe and totally above board. He'll get Sergei's family here—for a price."

"Thank you." I tucked the card into my purse along with my checkbook. "Which realtor do I need to visit to get this ball rolling?"

"The land isn't officially for sale yet. I'll have Vee call you when it's time."

I narrowed my eyes. "Is this your way of holding onto Sergei longer?"

"No, this is my way of making sure we're all protected in this transaction. When Sergei is finished on Saturday, he's all yours if you still want him."

"I do want him."

"I can tell." Nikolai rose from his chair and walked me to the door. Touching my cheek, he smiled down at me. "I'm glad it's you, Bianca. You're the only woman brave enough to fight for him."

"He's worth it."

"Yes, he is." Nikolai patted my back. "It was nice doing business with you, Miss Bradshaw."

"And you, Mr. Kalasnikov."

Feeling some of the tension leave my body, I made my way outside and fished my phone out of my purse. Scrolling through my contacts, I found Erin's number.

She was phase two of my plan.

A bit breathlessly, she answered, "You've reached Mrs. Ivan Markovic. How may I dazzle you today?"

I couldn't help but laugh. "Boy, you're really milking that newlywed thing."

"Bianca! Hey, you want to go see the baby with me later?"

"Sure. You want me to pick you up?"

"Yeah. That's great."

"Listen, I wondered if you might help me with something."

"Is it about Sergei and the fights this weekend? Ivan said that you two were on the outs, and, honestly, I'm so shocked. When Lena told me you two were together, I thought for sure this was it, you know? Anyways. I'm rambling. Basically, I am totally at your disposal. Whatever you need, I'll do it."

I laughed at her babbling offer of help. "I knew I could count on you."

"You know it! Look, give me an hour to get dressed and then come get me. We'll go see the baby and then grab an early dinner. How does that sound?"

"Like a good plan," I said and firmed up the details. Dropping my phone in my purse, I headed for the parking lot down the block. Determination blossomed inside me. Sergei thought the only way he could protect me was to cut me out of his life—and his heart—forever. Little did he know that he was about to meet his toughest opponent yet.

I loved that man, and I wasn't giving him up without one hell of a fight.

CHAPTER EIGHTEEN

Head throbbing and hands burning, Sergei tried to drown out the noise of the crowd and get his nerves under control. In a very short time, he would walk down the dimly lit hall of the meatpacking plant to the metal cage to face his third opponent. Last night, he had won his first two fights, but he didn't feel the usual surge of male pride that followed hard won victories.

No, he didn't feel anything but that deep, hollow, soul-sucking ache in his chest. The pulsing emptiness of it reminded him of the only thing he had ever truly wanted and the one thing he simply couldn't have.

Ivan lumbered into the makeshift locker room like the great big bear that he was. He dumped a second bucket of ice into the sink before coming over to the bench where Sergei sat. His trainer and mentor crouched down in front of him and put his hands on either side of Sergei's face. "Let me see that cut."

Sergei looked up at the dingy ceiling tiles while Ivan prodded the slit on his cheek. "It's fine."

"For now," Ivan said unhappily. "This is what happens when champions get sloppy and forget to block."

"*Da.*"

Cracking his battered knuckles, Ivan exhaled a pent-up breath and took the spot next to him on the bench. "I know you're in pain, Sergei. I know that you miss your woman, but that is no excuse for putting your life at risk. You have to get your fucking head right—or I'll throw in the towel right now."

Sergei's gaze snapped to Ivan's face. "You wouldn't."

"I will."

"But the money—"

"Fuck the money, Sergei." Ivan shook his head and ran his finger along one of the tattoos decorating the back of his hand. "The only reason I train you now and keep one foot in this dirty business is because I wanted to keep you safe. If you're not going to look out for yourself in that cage, then I'll do it for you."

Sergei thought of the cash he had tied up in bets. "I'll be safe."

"You had better be or else I'll kick your ass all the way to the hospital."

Sergei snorted. "*Da.*"

Ivan slapped his hand against Sergei's back. "I'm sorry about the girl. I know it hurts."

Sergei stared at the opposite wall. If any man could understand what he was going through, it was Ivan. "It was stupid of me to think that I could have something normal."

"It's not stupid to have dreams or to want better things, Sergei. How the hell do you think I got where I am in life? I let myself dream of how it could be someday." Ivan hesitated. "But I never let myself fall in love when I was still deep in the family."

"That was smart."

"No, it was simply good timing. If Erin had walked into my life back then? There's no way I could have ignored what I feel for her. It would have been hard not to cross that line, but I would have tried. I would have reminded myself that she deserved something better.

Even now, I struggle with the idea of tainting her life with my sins."

Sergei glanced at Ivan. "She loves you. I don't think she cares."

"If she does, she's made peace with it. God knows I don't deserve her selfless love, but she never stops giving it." Ivan squeezed Sergei's shoulder. "You're a good man, Sergei, but you can't have everything. At some point, you have to choose—Nikolai's family or your own."

After having a taste of freedom and a glimpse of the possibilities, Sergei had never wanted to break free more. "How?"

"I don't have that answer, Sergei. It's different for all of us."

"Do you miss it? Do you ever feel guilty about walking away?"

Ivan considered the questions. "I miss the brotherhood, but I don't miss the violence or the gut-gnawing fear that came with every night. And guilt?" He shrugged. "In the early days, yes, I felt guilty about walking away from the only life I had ever known and leaving everyone else behind. Now?" He shook his head. "I get to go home every night to Erin. I get to climb into bed with her and make love to her and dream about the babies we're going to have without worrying that I might get shot or stabbed at work."

Ivan rubbed the back of Sergei's head. "If you get the chance to get out, take it, Sergei. Then run like hell."

"You might get that chance sooner than you had expected."

Sergei's gaze jumped to the doorway where Nikolai leaned against the frame. How long had he been there? Obviously long enough to hear Ivan's advice.

Sergei didn't want to cause any problems, especially

not tonight, and he didn't want Nikolai to doubt his loyalty. "I'm your man, boss."

"No, Sergei, you're not."

His stomach rolled with anxiety. That was the sort of statement that usually preceded a man getting clipped. "What do you mean? Is this because I took Vivian to see Hagen?"

Two days ago, Kelly Connolly's girlfriend had come to Vivian's studio seeking help. When Vivian had asked him to drive her to see the loan shark Hagen, he had argued with her, but she wasn't easily swayed once her mind was settled. Rather than risk letting her go alone with the girl, he had taken Vivian and escorted her inside. Needless to say, the boss had been less than pleased to find out about their excursion.

"No. It's about this." Nikolai pushed off the door frame and reached under his suit jacket to retrieve something hidden in the pocket there.

Sergei saw only a flash of something dark before it was presented to him on Nikolai's palm. His heart skipped a few beats as he stared at the *chotki* resting on the boss' hand. The Orthodox prayer rope was the gift that was given to men who got out of the family with the blessing of their boss. Certain he was hallucinating, Sergei didn't dare touch it. "I don't understand."

"Your debt has been settled. You're a free man, Sergei. After the fights, you can walk away with no strings attached."

"Settled? But—how?"

Nikolai shot him a look. "How do you think?" When Sergei didn't answer, the boss said one name. "Bianca."

He nearly fell off the bench. "Bianca?"

"Apparently, she's rather wealthy." Nikolai studied him. "Did you know?"

266

He shook his head. "She said she was comfortable. I never thought—but why?"

"Because she loves you," Nikolai replied matter-of-factly. "She wants a future with you. If you're out of the family, there's no risk to her. You can be together."

"And you said yes?"

"You came into this family under duress. It wasn't your choice, Sergei. When that debt was paid, I planned to let you go. Bianca merely accelerated the timetable." Then, with a careless shrug, he added, "Her offer came at a useful time for me. The land we needed to unload? We made a fair trade. She gets you and the land. I get the money and the peace of mind that goes with having that land stay in the family."

Dazed, Sergei took the *chotki* from Nikolai. "I don't know what to say."

"You should probably start by telling Bianca thank you."

"I will."

"That will have to wait," Ivan interjected. "You fight soon, Sergei. It's time to clear your head. This first fighter is garbage, but I think Kelly Connolly will make it to the finals. He has heart, and he's fighting for something real. He's fighting for his family. What are you fighting for, Sergei?"

Kissing the rope beads that gave him the freedom to walk away and start anew, Sergei experienced the strongest surge of hope. "I'm fighting for *my* family."

* * *

"Are you sure we'll be able to get inside?" I warily eyed the double doors of the abandoned meatpacking plant where the tournament was being held.

"Yes," Vivian said, clutching my hand a little tighter. "One of the perks of being Nikolai's wife is that no one has the balls to tell me no."

"We're going to get into so much trouble for this," Lena warned as she pushed Erin forward. "I can already hear Yuri's lecture."

"I thought Kolya was going to stroke out when he found out about my trip to see Hagen but this? He's going to blow a freaking pupil when he sees me."

"Yeah, well, Ivan is probably going to toss me across his knee and smack my backside for this stunt." Erin kept close as we weaved our way through the noisy throng.

Lena snorted. "I knew that dirty Russian of yours was a kinky bastard."

We reached the door, and Vivian took point. The two bouncer type guys there recognized her instantly. They seemed uncertain about the proper protocol and wavered a moment too long.

"Are you going to open the door or do I need to call my husband to come get me?"

They profusely apologized for making us wait and hurriedly wrenched the double doors open to let us pass through and shut them quickly behind us. We all wrinkled our noses at the awful stink that permeated the place. It was stale and musty and reeked of sweat, alcohol and worse. Men clumped together in groups in the wide hallway and leered at us.

"Okay, I know this is really kindergarten, but let's hold hands and stick to the buddy system," Lena suggested.

"Which way do we go now?" I wondered as my eyes adjusted to the dim, shadowy lighting.

"I guess we follow the noise," Vivian said and led us forward.

Following our intrepid leader, we made our way down the creepy passage and into a massive open space. From the ragged, old bloodstains on the concrete floor, I deduced this had once been the main butchering floor. *Gross.*

A huge crowd of men surrounded a tall metal cage, the sides lined with chain-link fencing. I swallowed hard at the sight of it. Sergei, my Sergei, would soon be locked inside there. The only way out was to put down the other man or make him tap out in surrender.

"There are the bleachers Danny told me about," Vivian said and pointed to spots that seemed to be reserved for the betting heavy hitters and VIPs. "Let's go there. It's probably the safest place for us."

"That's not saying much," Erin said nervously and glanced around the rough crowd. "Now I know why Ivan said this place was forbidden to me."

Holding hands, we moved as one solid unit toward the bleachers. As we neared the metal stands, Kostya stepped in front of us. He frowned at our group and shook his head. Without saying a word, he gestured for us to follow him. He pointed out a row of seats. Once we had taken them, he growled, "Don't move."

We didn't dare.

Kostya assigned two men to watch us and then took off through the crowd, shoving guys out of the way to force his way through. He was probably running off to tattle on us. When Nikolai, Dimitri and Yuri appeared a short time later, all three of them wearing sour, disapproving expressions, I figured my instinct was right.

Like the freaking queen of the underworld, Vivian rose from her seat ever so calmly and gestured to the open spot next to her. She held out her hand in silent invitation for Nikolai to join her. His eyes narrowed to slits before the slightest, almost imperceptible smile lifted one corner of his mouth. For all his intimidation and ruthlessness, it was clear to anyone watching that Vivian owned him, body and soul.

When he sat down next to her, he curled his arm around her waist and hauled her tight to his side. Cupping her face, he said something that made Vivian lower her gaze almost submissively. He traced her bottom lip with his finger and then claimed her mouth in a very public and very possessive kiss.

Yuri shook his head as he took a space next to Lena. He seemed to know better than to try to rein her in while in public. After seeing Lena in action, I doubted Yuri wanted a taste of the Dragon Lady's waspish tongue where others might overhear. Not that he seemed to mind her feistiness. I suspected he found it rather sexy.

Looking every bit the tired new father, Dimitri sat between me and Erin. He sighed and patted both of our knees. Addressing Erin first, he said, "Ivan told me to tell you that you are to stay here with me until he's finished tonight. I'm not supposed to let you out of my sight." He glanced at me. "You either, Bianca."

"I'm not going anywhere," I promised.

Loud rock music blared out of speakers mounted around the warehouse. They seemed to signal the start of the first fight of the night because men moved into better positions around the cage. Up here on the elevated bleachers, we had an unimpeded view. My stomach started to churn violently. Could I really sit through this?

But I had to do it. I had to let Sergei know I was here for him and that I would do whatever it took to make a future possible for us.

The man who came out of the tunnel first looked pretty tough. He was a good-sized man, close to Ivan in height and build, and had a grizzled appearance. I zeroed in on the pudginess at his hips and decided he had nothing on Sergei who was lean and mean and all muscle.

"He fights for one of the outlaw motorcycle clubs," Dimitri explained, leaning close enough that I could hear him over the crowd. He touched his arm to indicate the tattoo the fighter had there. "He's a Bandit."

I noticed the group of loud, leather clad men who cheered him on. Their vests were embellished with the same tattoo. They didn't seem like a crowd I wanted to cross.

When the crowd went wild, I glanced to the tunnel again and spotted Sergei coming into view. He wore red trunks and nothing else. I had hoped that his hands would be taped for protection, but his bare knuckles were clearly visible even from this distance. The nearer he came to the cage, the easier it was for me to see him under the bright lights illuminating that central space.

He hadn't shaved in days. The slight beard covering his cheeks was a strange sight for me because I had only ever known him to be clean-shaven. I noticed the faint bruising along his jaw and the ugly cut under his eye. It would be yet another scar that he would bear.

Inside the cage, he advanced to his corner while Ivan made the walk outside the fence to take up his coaching spot. Standing there, waiting for his match to begin, Sergei searched the bleachers—for me. Our gazes met across the distance, and my tummy flip-flopped. He slowly brought two fingers to his lips and kissed them before holding them out toward me. Grinning, I mouthed the only three words that mattered right now. *I love you.*

Rolling his shoulders, Sergei faced his opponent. I started to breathe faster as an announcer came out to get the fight started. There were very few rules that he listed.

I understood then how outrageously dangerous these matches were. When the referee waved his arm to signal the start and a bell clanged, I thought I was going to vomit. My stomach lurched painfully as the man I loved rushed his opponent.

At the first traded punches, I nearly passed out. Dimitri seemed to sense my wooziness and put his hand on my back. He gently rubbed circles there and gave me the support I needed to keep going. This was so much worse than the one punch I had witnessed Sergei throw at Lulu's wedding.

Earlier, Erin had explained that part of the reason Sergei was so damned good at this was because he understood showmanship. The people who bet on these fights wanted their money's worth, and he made sure they got it. That's why everyone loved him. He had the stamina to give them the bloody street brawls they wanted and the skill to avoid getting seriously injured.

The nasty fight inside the cage was worse than I had ever imagined it would be. The bloodthirsty crowd cheered every time Sergei landed a blow. By the time the second round started, the floor was already splattered with blood. When Sergei took a hit to the ribs, I cringed. I wanted this fight over with, like, right now.

Just as the second round neared its final seconds, Sergei connected with a powerful jab that sent the other man whirling to his left. He wavered on his feet before falling forward. Sergei actually caught his opponent on the way down, preventing a nasty head wound, and gently lowered him to the concrete floor.

Relieved that it was over, I jumped to my feet and whistled and hollered. The other guy's trainers rushed into the cage to help him. I heard someone shout for an ambulance but I had a feeling there wasn't one coming.

All around me, people yelled and clapped and went wild.

Sergei walked to the fence, gripped it in his massive, brutal hands and stared right at me. One long finger crooked and made a come-hither motion. Powerless to refuse the man who owned my heart, I slowly made my way out of the bleachers to meet him at the cage.

So many eyes were trained on me as I pushed my way through the crowd. Lena had suggested we wear black dresses and gold embellishments so we could be seen as one cohesive unit, much like the gangs and crews of men here. More than one loud catcall and high-pitched whistle cut through the noise of the crowd. Considering the way Sergei looked at me, I could tell he approved my curve-hugging black dress and the golden belt that nipped in my waist.

He bent down until we were eye to eye. His gaze zeroed in on the medallion around my neck. "Come here," he ordered huskily.

I gingerly rubbed his bruised, bloodied fingers and leaned forward until our foreheads touched through the fence. "I really love you, Sergei."

"I know what you did for me, Bianca. I'm going to spend the rest of my life making sure you never regret it."

Smiling up into his loving face, I said, "Just get through this last fight so we can go home and put all of this behind us, Sergei."

"Done." Kissing my fingers, he gave one final instruction. "Stick close to Vivian. No one will touch you if you're with her."

"I will." Noticing Ivan's impatient stare, I backed away from the fence. "Good luck."

Sergei nodded and left the cage. Ivan trailed him into the tunnel, and they disappeared from view. I rejoined my friends and managed to sit through Kelly's fight.

Watching a friend was just as bad as watching the love of my life. Knowing Kelly had been forced into this tournament to save his family just made the whole thing impossible to stomach.

Kelly's opponent, a stocky fighter, landed some powerful kicks, including one that caught him in the ribs. I winced and silently urged Kelly to watch that guy's leg. The two fighters traded punches, and then Kelly stunned me by taking the man to the ground. The guy shouted with pain as his shoulder slammed into the concrete.

Catching his opponent's arm between his thighs, Kelly jerked hard. I thought for sure he was going to dislocate the guy's shoulder. Unable to watch, I averted my gaze and listened to the crowd for clues.

Next to me, Dimitri leaped to his feet. He had come to cheer on Kelly. It wasn't that Dimitri didn't support Sergei, but Kelly was his employee and in an incredibly untenable position between his father and the two loan sharks who owned the old man. "Come on, Kelly. Harder. *Harder.* Yes!"

I looked up and saw Kelly untangling himself from the other fighter. He tried to help the man who had surrendered, but the guy spit at him and shot him the finger. *Jesus. So much for sportsmanship!*

The break between fights wasn't nearly long enough. My stomach was still in knots when Sergei and Kelly marched back into the cage. With so much trepidation, I watched the two men stand across from each other while the referee spoke to them. They knocked together fists, and Sergei said something that made Kelly's stoic expression slip fractionally.

And then the battle began.

The two earlier fights hadn't been anywhere near as brutal as the brawl that occurred before me now. Kelly managed to sneak in the first punch, but Sergei's answering blow knocked Kelly back a few feet. Blood sprayed from the contact between their bodies, and I grimaced at the awful sight.

Kelly shook it off and avoided taking another hit. He punched Sergei in the ribs and slammed his knee into Sergei's belly. I saw my man's rough and pained exhale and felt tears pricking my eyes. A second later, Sergei snatched Kelly's leg and jerked the former Marine off his feet. Kelly hit the concrete ass first but he was quicker than Sergei and managed to avoid being pinned down.

The air horn blasted, signaling the end of the round. Both men returned to their corners to receive attention from their trainers. In no time at all, they were brought back to the center of the cage. The second round began, and I wasn't sure how much more of this I could stomach. Only the knowledge that Sergei needed me to show my support kept my butt parked on that bench.

Inside the cage, they were kicking and punching. One of Sergei's powerful kicks left Kelly limping as they entered the third round. I don't think Sergei expected Kelly to last that long. My big, handsome Russian was breathing hard and looking frustrated.

The two men traded hits and kicks. Sergei stumbled backward after one good kick from Kelly, and the bodyguard jumped on the advantage given to him. He wrapped his arms around Sergei and shoved him into the fence.

"No!"

I watched in awe as Sergei used his incredible strength to free himself from the hold. Sergei slammed his elbow into Kelly's ribs, and the former Marine looked like he was going to die. He gasped for breath and wobbled on his feet. Out for blood, Sergei tripped Kelly and followed him down to the concrete floor where they grappled in the most brutal way.

"Oh god!"

I flinched when Kelly punched Sergei repeatedly in the temple. Sergei lost his grip on Kelly, and the other man escaped his hold and clambered to his feet. Sergei spat a mouthful of bloody saliva toward one side of the cage and wiped the back of his hand across his bleeding face.

The two men charged each other again. Sergei landed a punch that made Kelly totter. Sergei kicked Kelly right in the ribs and the man started to guard his right side. I witnessed a definite change in Sergei. Like a predator who spotted a weakness in his prey, he pounced on Kelly. With a punch and a choke hold, he brought Kelly down to the floor.

With my hands in a prayer position, I pressed them to my lips and looked on in horror as I fully expected Sergei to kill Kelly. Our gazes clashed—and the bloodlust seemed to fade from Sergei's eyes. He lowered his lips to the former Marine's ears and said something only the other man could hear. He repeated his words again, and this time Kelly reacted.

Weakly, Kelly tapped Sergei's arm three times before passing out cold. Eyes closed with relief, Sergei inhaled a long breath and carefully placed Kelly on his side. He crouched over him protectively until Jack and Finn Connolly made it to their brother's side. Only then did he back away and leave his opponent.

While the referee held Sergei's hand high and everyone around me celebrated, I simply smiled and held his gaze. It was over. He was out of the mob—and now he belonged to me and only me.

CHAPTER NINETEEN

A loud snore from the passenger seat of my car made me smile. I reached over to rub Sergei's leg as I pulled into the driveway behind my house and waited for the gate to close behind me. "Sergei? Baby, we're home."

"Huh?" He bolted upright and then hissed with pain. Putting a hand to his ribs, he groaned. They weren't broken, but clearly they still hurt like hell. "I didn't mean to fall asleep."

"Sergei, you've had a long day. It's okay." I carefully touched his arm. "I didn't mean to startle you."

Yawning, he tried to stretch but was impeded by the cramped quarters of my car. "We've got to get you something bigger than this if you're going to drive me around town. This is worse than an airplane seat."

"Hey, now," I said with mock hurt. Running my hands over the leather, I remarked, "This is luxury, baby."

"Luxury, huh? No, luxury is coming home with you tonight and knowing I never have to cross *that* line again." He cupped my face in his battered hands and nuzzled his mouth to mine. "I'll never be able to thank you enough, Bianca."

"Well, I can think of a few ways you can start," I murmured against his broken lips. "But you don't have to repay me in any way. I did this for us. This was an investment in our future."

He gestured to his bruised mouth with his swollen hands. "You might have to give me a few days of deferment on paying this debt. I won't be much good to you until some of this starts to heal."

An invisible band squeezed my chest like a vise. I hated that he was in pain and wanted to make him feel better. "Let's get you inside. You need to shower and take some more anti-inflammatories. Then I'll give you a massage like Ivan described to me."

Even so beat up, Sergei still couldn't control his raging lust for me. "I've got something I'd love to have you massage."

I wanted to be annoyed with him but I couldn't stop smiling. "You are a very dirty boy. Now, unfold yourself from that front seat and march up to the house."

"God, you're so sexy when you give orders." He leaned over and planted a lingering kiss right on my mouth. "All right. Let's see if I can get some blood flow back into my legs."

I rolled his eyes at the overly dramatic description of my cramped—to him—front seat. "Normal-sized people fit just fine in this car. Thank you very much."

"*Milaya moya*, you know me better than that. I'm big all over."

Shaking my head at his nonsense, I slid out of the driver's seat and tried to ignore his flirtatious laughter. The guy needed to rest and heal, but I had a feeling he was going to try to get my panties off me the first change he got. Not that I was going to put up much of a fight about it…

Inside the house, I offered to make him something to eat, but he declined. I tried to take his heavy gym bag from him, but he refused to let it go. After a glass of milk and some anti-inflammatories, Sergei went through the house to check the doors and windows. Amused, I followed him on his nightly round. "You must have taken a hard hit that scrambled your memory. I don't have a prowler anymore, and the Night Wolves are long gone."

"So?" He shot me a look that said his overprotectiveness was never going to fade. "Those aren't the only bad things that exist in this city. Believe me," he muttered. "I know."

Certain that he did, I waited for him to finish and then led him upstairs to my—our—bedroom. He dropped his gym bag on the ottoman, and I realized how much I had missed seeing it there. My closet door was open, and he backed up after walking by it to take a better look. Flicking on the light, he studied the newly reorganized shelves and bars. "Bianca?"

Coming to stand beside him, I reached out to touch some of the clothes he had left behind. "They were in dryer. I started to hang them up in that guest room closet but then I decided I would move everything I wasn't wearing this season across the hall and move your things here." I swallowed anxiously. "Where they belong."

He put his hand on the wall and turned to gaze down at me. His eyes were suspiciously shimmery. "Are you serious?"

"Yes." I slid my hand under his shirt to gently caress his chest. "I want you here with me."

"People will say I'm taking advantage of you and your kindness and generosity."

"I don't care what people say."

"No?"

"No." Then, just because I liked teasing him, I added, "Besides, I like to keep my investments close."

He grunted but bent down to kiss the top of my head anyway. "I have a feeling this is going to be a piece of ammunition you'll use against me for years to come."

"Well, yeah!" I said with a laugh. "It was a lot of money." I cautiously embraced him, minding his bruised sides, and savored the heat and strength of him. "But you were worth every single penny, Sergei."

"I'll make you happy, Bianca. I swear. I'll spend every fucking second of the rest of our lives doing whatever I can to make you smile."

"I'm holding you to that promise." Leaning back, I peered up at him. "Come on. Let's get you clean. Then? Bedtime."

Just as I had expected, Sergei tried to seduce me once we were naked and in the shower together. Thankfully my shower was too small for him to get anywhere with that. I playfully batted away his fondling hands and made him hold still while I scrubbed all the parts of him I could reach. He tackled his hair, face and neck because he was much too tall for me to adequately clean those areas.

The pink water and blood-tinged suds swirling around our feet and rushing down the drain left me nauseated. I reminded myself that this was the life I had saved him from and that this would never, ever happen again. In time, his abused body would heal, but I imprinted the sight of all that blood in my brain so I would always remember where we started our journey together.

"Don't put that on," Sergei admonished as we dried off after our shower.

I stared at the chemise in my hands. "But this is one that you bought me."

"I haven't seen you or felt you in days, Bianca. I want to feel your naked skin on mine tonight." He slashed his hand through the air in that imperious, alpha male way of his. "No clothes at night for at least a week."

"Yes, master," I said with a roll of my eyes. Secretly

thrilled, I dropped my chemise on the counter and followed him out of the bathroom. Sergei made quick work of tossing the decorative pillows from my bed. For tonight only, I chose not to scold him for being so messy, but I pushed aside the pillows that fell between the bed and the bathroom, just in case one of us had to get up in the middle of the night. A fall and a trip to the emergency room weren't appealing in the least.

"On your stomach," I said, remembering the way Ivan had described the massage. "I'll start with your back."

Looking dead on his feet, Sergei crawled onto the bed and did as instructed. I selected the only unscented lotion I had and climbed onto the mattress. Mindful of Sergei's many bruises and injuries, I carefully massaged his tight, knotted muscles. Every now and then he grunted or hissed and shifted beneath me. I followed his short directions and adjusted my technique to give him the most relief.

"Turn over, baby."

Sergei rolled onto his back and flexed his calves. "Start with my legs?"

"Sure." I helped him stretch his taut muscles in the way Ivan had showed me, holding his heel in my hand and applying gentle pressure to his toes. Sergei winced but started to slowly relax as the cramps left him.

With my palms slicked by lotion, I massaged his massive calves, all the while marveling at the unbelievable strength beneath my hands. Although Sergei wasn't going to fight for money any more, he wasn't about to let himself go. I had a sneaking suspicion Ivan would try to cajole him into joining him as a trainer for those legit mixed-martial arts fighters on his roster. Now that Sergei had options, I hope he explored all of them.

"*Unnnhhh.*" Sergei let loose a guttural groan when I

began to run my thumb up and down the sole of his foot. The more pressure I applied, the more he seemed to enjoy it. I didn't miss the way that big cock of his started to grow. Amused by the reaction, I used both hands on his sensitive foot, working my thumbs in slow circles along his arch. His erection throbbed to life, standing tall and proud, and weeping glistening drops of pre-cum.

Deciding to indulge my naughty side, I leaned forward and sucked his big toe. An explosive string of curse words shot from his mouth. Sergei lifted up on his elbows to watch me. He groaned and inhaled a shuddery breath. "You're killing me, Bianca."

"How?"

His eyelids lowered, hooding his dark, dangerous eyes. "You know how. Don't tease me, *milaya moya*. I'm on the edge tonight."

"Who's teasing?" I placed his foot on the bed and began to kiss my way up his sturdy legs. Pushing his thighs apart, I slid down onto my belly and dragged my tongue up and down and side to side along his heavy sac.

Cursing again, Sergei fell back to the pillows and spread his thighs even wider. "Suck me, Bianca. Put me in your mouth."

Smirking at the power I held over this Russian giant, I gave him what he wanted. My poor baby had suffered through one hell of a week. Surely he deserved some pleasure now.

I licked all over that huge cock of his, gathering the little bit of pre-cum from his slit before pulling him into my mouth. He groaned and reached down to caress my hair, urging me on with softly whispered compliments. Letting saliva pool on my tongue, I slicked down the impressive length of him and wrapped my lips around his wide shaft. He was so amped up tonight. I didn't think it was going to take him long to explode.

Hungry for his cum, I used my hand to stroke the bottom half of his erection while I concentrated all my oral efforts on the most sensitive part of him. As my hand moved up and down, my mouth followed the same path, stimulating him in ways that made Sergei cry out and whisper my name like a litany.

When I took him deep into my mouth, letting him nudge that hot, wet alcove at the back of my throat, Sergei lost control. He thrust up just a little bit, rubbing against my tongue and pushing himself right over the edge. I drank down his cum, moaning happily around the pulsing shaft stretching my lips, and reveled in the sound of my name shouted from his lips.

After I licked him clean, I peppered feather-light kisses up his belly and chest. Looking sleepy and so relaxed, Sergei placed his hand against my cheek and grinned at me. "You are so fucking amazing at that."

"I've never really liked doing it," I admitted. "Not until you," I added, when his brow furrowed. "You make it seem like a gift. You appreciate it."

"You have no idea how much," he said, kissing me tenderly. Tangling his fingers in my hair, he issued a gruff command. "Show me how much you like sucking my cock, Bianca."

Heat rushed into my face. I wanted to shake my head and say no, but those dark eyes of his enthralled me. Reaching between my thighs, I let my fingers ride the curve of my pussy to gather the evidence of my arousal. Lifting my hand, I showed him the shiny wetness clinging to my fingers.

Sergei stunned me by grasping my wrist and dragging my hand to his mouth. He licked my fingertips and growled with appreciation. "I've missed the taste of your pussy so much."

"Sergei!" I wondered if I would ever get used to the dirty things he said. Probably not...

"On your side," he ordered. "And open your legs for me."

"Sergei," I said uncertainly. "You're in bad shape. You need to rest."

"I need to feel your thighs wrapped around my head while I tongue-fuck you, Bianca. Now get on your side and give me what I want."

Trembling with white-hot currents of anticipation and excitement, I did exactly as told. Sergei slid down the bed and rested his head against my inner thigh. The position we were in allowed him to get what he wanted without having to rely on his tired arms to hold up his weight.

The first flick of his heavenly tongue on my throbbing clitoris made me want to sob with relief. *Finally!* Eyes closed, I surrendered to Sergei's skillful oral assault. He nibbled my clit and ran his tongue around it in slow circles before suckling me with long, slow tugs that made my freaking toes curl. Just as he promised, he probed my soaking entrance until I started to see stars.

When his tongue returned to my clit, I lost it. Shrieking his name, I rocked my hips and smiled as the blissful bursts of pure joy radiated through me. Even after my orgasm died, Sergei continued to swipe that wonderful tongue of his through my folds. Apparently he hadn't been joking about missing my taste.

Crawling back up beside me, Sergei burrowed close and rested his head on my shoulder. For the first time ever, I was the one cuddling him. I understood that he had survived some wild emotional turmoil this week. Pressing all the love I had for him into my embrace, I wrapped my arms around him and held him tight until he drifted off to sleep. It didn't take long for me to follow him into the realms of peaceful slumber.

But a strange sound woke me sometime later.

Confused and disoriented, I glanced at the bedside clock. It was late, almost three in the morning. I winced as my neck protested the odd position I had fallen asleep in and pushed up onto my elbow. Beside me, Sergei muttered something and flopped onto his back, his long arms slapping against the mattress.

I heard the sound again. It was a muffled thump that perplexed me. Certain it was coming from out back, I decided to investigate. I squashed the instinct to wake Sergei. Grabbing his shirt, I slipped into it and some panties before grabbing my robe from the chair in the corner. On tiptoes, I quietly left the bedroom and headed downstairs. The house was dark and still as I made my way to the kitchen and then into the sunroom. I heard the thumping sound a third time and pinpointed the noise's origin.

It was coming from the carriage house.

Curious now, I unlocked the back door and reached for the handle. The sudden awareness of another person's body heat made the fine hairs on the back of my neck rise. A hand closed over my mouth as a scream of panic erupted from my throat.

"Sweetheart, hush. It's me." Sergei's harsh whisper echoed in my ears.

Sagging with relief, I leaned back against his bare chest. The stiff sensation of denim tugged at my robe. He lowered his hand and kissed the side of my neck. Giving my bottom a swat, he hissed, "Don't ever do this again. When you hear something, you wake me up."

"You were tired."

"And you're stubborn," he retorted tightly. "Stay here

while I go see what the hell that is."

"No way. I want to know what it is."

"Bianca—"

"Sergei, I'm going." I could just imagine his frustrated expression, but the darkness prevented me from confirming my suspicions.

Growling, he gently pushed me behind him and thrust my phone into my hands. The feel of cold metal stunned me. Was he armed? Of course he was. Sergei wasn't going to investigate a strange noise without a way to defend us.

"Stay behind me. At the first sign of trouble, call 9-1-1 and run."

"Yes, dear."

He snorted and dropped a kiss to the crown of my head. "Come on."

Holding my hand, Sergei led me out of the house. We both skipped the step that squeaked and hopped down onto the grass. Sticking to the shadows and glad for the new moon that left the sky an inky black, I followed him across the yard to the carriage house. The dilapidated structure seemed so sinister in the darkness. Sergei had joked once that I should rent the space out to film students as a horror film set. I had to concede now that he was right.

The thumping sound grew louder as we neared the building. Peeking through one of the grimy windows, we spotted the glow of flashlights and a battery-operated lantern. A man with his back to us attacked one of the masonry walls. I had no idea what he thought he was going to find back there, but I sure as heck wanted to find out.

I felt Sergei relax next to me. Whatever this guy was doing, he wasn't here to kill or attack us. He just wanted whatever was behind that wall.

Sergei tugged me along beside him but wouldn't let me through the door. He pushed me down by the adjacent wall and put a fingertip to my lips. I understood his instruction and gave his hand a squeeze to let him know I would stay put.

Stepping up to the doorway, Sergei used the building as a shield for his body. In that deep, rumbling voice of his, he issued one clear order. "Turn around slowly with your hands in the air, or I will shoot you."

I strained to hear the movements inside the carriage house. The man there must have done exactly as Sergei ordered because he stepped away from his shielded spot for a better look. With his gun aimed and ready to fire at the first sign of trouble, Sergei held out a hand. "Come here, Bianca. Do you know this man?"

Joining Sergei, I blinked a few times to let my eyes adjust to the new sources of light. When my gaze settled on the dirty, dusty man, I gasped. "Marcus?"

"Who is he?" Sergei asked more forcefully.

"He's one of the contractors who put in a bid on this place. The one who said he grew up around here," I clarified. Confused, I threw my hands wide. "What are you doing?"

A man on the verge of a breakdown, the contractor Marcus scratched his fingers through his hair and wiped his filthy hands down his face. Sweat had mixed with the dirt and dust to form muddy rivulets that arced across his face. "Please," he begged. "Just let me get my father, and I'll go."

"Your father?" Sergei and I echoed in unison.

Marcus stepped aside and gestured to the brick wall behind him that he had partially dismantled. Gasping, I jumped back and clamped both hands over my mouth to stifle a scream of sheer terror when I spotted the desiccated, mummy-like skeleton entombed there. Even Sergei who seemed so unflappable exhaled with shock and murmured with disbelief in Russian.

His moment of shock quickly passed. Sergei didn't take his eyes off Marcus who he now viewed as a threat. "Bianca, give me your phone and go back to the house right now."

I didn't argue with him. I handed over my phone and backed out of that carriage house ever so slowly. Once I was free from that big old house of crazy, I pivoted on my heel and raced back to the sunroom. Staring out the windows there, I bit my lip—and waited.

*

Of all the things Sergei had expected to find out here in this creepy fucking building, a dead body locked away behind layers of bricks hadn't been one of them.

"I noticed the dimensions weren't right," he said finally. "When I compared the specs from the bids to the old blueprints, I discovered the discrepancy." Staring at the man, he asked the only question that mattered. "Why is your father in that wall?"

Marcus rubbed the back of his neck and dropped his crowbar in defeat. "Does it matter?"

"It might," Sergei said, still uncertain what course of action he would take. "Give me a reason not to call the police and have you arrested for murder."

"The house was never supposed to be bought by anyone outside of the family. Mother and I thought we had everything squared away with an attorney who was supposed to look after the trust and keep the tax bills paid. After Mother died, I left Houston and moved to

Seattle with my family. I didn't even know the place had gone up for auction because of taxes until it was too late."

"So you tried to put in a bid with Bianca for renovating this place so you could get the body before it was discovered," Sergei guessed. "I wondered why your company was so new and had no references. I thought you were a scam."

Marcus shook his head. "I am a contractor in Seattle. I had a business here years ago so it was easy enough to fake some business cards and letterhead." Swiping his hand out in front of him, the desperate man insisted, "I never meant to scare her. I tried to come in one night, a few weeks ago, but there was this cop who ran me off so I high-tailed it out of here."

So Kevan had gotten the idea to play a prowler after Bianca had seen Marcus and reported him.

"I drove by other times, hoping I could get in here and do what needed to be done, but there were always men watching the house or you were here. I didn't see your SUV tonight so I assumed it was safe."

"Obviously not."

"No," Marcus agreed.

"You still haven't answered my question. Why is your father in that wall?"

Marcus didn't want to answer. Sergei recognized the shame that turned the man's eyes so bleak. Eventually, the contractor said, "He was a really bad man. He hurt my mother all the time. Sometimes he would hurt me. After he caused my mother to lose a baby, I decided he would never hurt her again. I caught him trying to rape her—and I snapped."

Sergei didn't say a word as the chilling tale poured out of the man's mouth. Now he knew why this place always gave him a bad feeling. That body entombed in the wall belonged to a monster.

"I was only thirteen. I didn't know my own strength. After it was done, Mother helped me wrap him up in a tarp. I brought him out here and...well." Marcus ran his hands over the uneven seams of the bricks. "That secret has been buried here for forty-two years."

"No one ever wondered where he had gone?"

"Everyone assumed he had walked out on us. He was a known womanizer and a gambler. Some people thought he might have been killed for his debts." Marcus hesitated before nervously inquiring, "What are you going to do with me?"

Sergei considered his options and decided there was only one way to end this quietly. He used Bianca's phone to dial a number he had memorized.

"Who the fuck is this?" Kostya's snarled answer made Sergei wince.

"It's me. I need your help."

"Sergei? What's wrong? Is someone after you and Bianca?"

"No, we need a different kind of help. Disposal," he said carefully.

Clothing rustled in the background. "Give me twenty minutes."

"Come around the back of Bianca's house. I'll open the gate for you."

"*Da.*"

Marcus stared at him with apprehension, and Sergei realized the man hadn't understood a single word of the Russian he had been speaking. "My friend is coming to help you. He's a cleaner. You understand?"

Marcus nodded weakly. "Yes. Why are you helping me?"

Sergei didn't reply because he didn't have an answer to

that one. He honestly couldn't pinpoint the reason. Motioning toward the wall, he said, "You had better start digging. It will be sunrise all too soon, and I want you—and that—out of here before first light."

The contractor didn't have to be told twice. He went back to work, busting out the bricks that entombed his father and stacking them neatly to one side. Uncertain whether the man could be trusted, Sergei kept his gun on Marcus. He didn't want any surprises, not tonight when the whole wide world of possibilities had been unfurled in front of him.

When Kostya arrived, the cleaner stood in the doorway and took in the macabre scene. "Fuck me. This is a first."

Sergei glanced at Kostya. "Truly?"

Nodding, Kostya entered the carriage house to survey the ongoing work. "One hour tops, and I'm out of your hair."

Coming in under his estimate, Kostya helped Marcus remove and wrap the mummified body in forty minutes. A perfectionist, Kostya checked the wall cavity for any spare parts or evidence. He had Marcus load the tightly wrapped parcel into the back of his SUV. Holding the contractor's gaze, he said, "I'll bury it properly."

Marcus shrugged. "I don't care what you do with it."

The cold reply didn't surprise Sergei. After Kostya left, he walked Marcus out to the gate. Gripping the front of the man's shirt, he dragged the contractor up on his toes and gave one final warning. "If you ever come back here again or if even one fucking whisper of this gets out to anyone, I'll come for you. Then you'll be the one wrapped in plastic and blankets. Understand?"

"Yes." Marcus gulped. "I'm leaving Houston right now. You'll never see me again."

"That's a promise you had better keep." Sergei released the man's shirt and pushed him outside the gate. He waited until the man disappeared down the alley before going back to the house. Weary and haggard, he washed his hands at the kitchen sink, checked the doors and trudged upstairs.

Still wearing his shirt, Bianca sat on the edge of the bed and nervously swung her feet back and forth. "Well?"

"It's done. Kostya took care of it."

"Oh."

"Yes."

"Do I want to know why Marcus was using my carriage house as the family crypt?"

"No." He didn't want to talk about any of that. Pointing to his shirt, he said, "Take that off. Naked for a week, remember?"

With a huff, she peeled off the shirt and tossed it at him. "Happy?"

"I am now." He gazed at her luscious body and started to plan all the ways they would spend their Sunday afternoon.

She moved under the covers on her side of the bed, and he switched off the lamp. Sliding in next to her, he hauled her tight against him. Content to hold her, he caressed her arm and wondered at the bizarre end to an already stressful day.

"So I was thinking about that carriage house—"

"Don't worry," Sergei cut in. "I plan to have someone out here to raze that whole fucking thing as soon as possible."

"Thank God! Because, wow, I can't even stomach looking at it again."

"I feel the same way."

"So I had two prowlers, huh?"

"It seems that way. Kevan ran off Marcus that first time and then he took over the prowler's identity to scare you so he could stay close to you."

"This is so screwed up," she murmured. "I want to get back to my normal, boring life."

"You will," he promised.

"What about Darren Blake?"

She asked in a way that made him think she had figured out that answer for herself. "He can never hurt anyone else ever again."

"And the Night Wolves?"

"They were shut down from the inside." He didn't tell her that Nikolai and Besian had hidden James away so he could provide the evidence the Feds needed to round up those skinhead bastards. As far as Sergei knew, the younger guy was recovering from some plastic surgery in Mexico as a VIP guest of Romero Valero. It had all been neatly wrapped up by Nikolai and Besian in a way that used the Feds to do the heavy-lifting.

She drew lazy shapes on his chest for a while. "You know, maybe we could look into building a proper mother-in-law quarters out back."

"For your mama?"

"No, for yours."

Sergei reeled with surprise. "Mine?"

"Mama is talking about moving in with Aunt Penny and Aunt Sara. They have their eyes set on one of those new houses in that seniors-only housing development by the country club. She seems really excited about it so I was thinking maybe we could do something for your mom."

"Bianca, my mother is stuck in Russia. It could be years before she's able to immigrate."

Yawning, Bianca snuggled close and hooked her leg

over his. "Don't worry about that. I have a plan."

"A plan?"

"*Mmhmm*," she murmured sleepily.

Though he wanted to interrogate her, Sergei held his curiosity at bay. She had fought tenaciously to save him. Heaven only knew what wonders she would work for his mother and Vladimir.

Throwing up a silent prayer of thanks for Vivian's devious theft during the wedding reception, he cradled Bianca close and dreamed of the bright future ahead of them.

EPILOGUE

"What do you think of this hotel?" I spun my laptop screen around so Sergei could see it. "It's close to the gallery where Vivian will be showing her paintings. It has some suite options that will work better for us since we'll be a group of four."

"It's nice. If you like it, I like it." Sergei winked at me before threading zucchini chunks onto skewers. We were preparing to host our first barbecue together as a couple, and he was finishing up some of the food prep.

"Did Vladimir finalize the plane tickets?"

"Yes, they'll be flying into London the day after we get there. We'll have four days together before they head back."

"Perfect." I selected the suite we needed to house all four of us and started the reservation process. "Don't forget that the lawyer rescheduled your meeting for tomorrow morning, Sergei."

"I haven't forgotten."

"And you've filled out all the citizenship paperwork, right?"

"Yes, *milaya moya*." Amusement filled his voice. "I've also got an appointment with Yuri to figure out how to set up the money for the investment Mama will make in my construction business."

One of the loopholes the new lawyer had suggested

was to turn Sergei's mother into an investor with money she wanted to use create jobs here. Sergei planned to use the cash he had been socking away from his fight purses to fund her investment. If that didn't work, Sergei was only a few steps away from completing his citizenship. He could legally sponsor his mother once he had those papers.

Once the lawyer had Sergei's mother's situation sorted out, it would be relatively straight-forward to get Vladimir over here. The former Spetsnaz commando had easily snagged a job with Dimitri's firm so he would qualify for immigration sponsorship through the Lone Star Group.

The process wouldn't be simple or quick but it would be successful. Until then, Sergei and I had agreed that he would meet with his family every couple of months in Europe. He didn't feel safe returning to Moscow so it was the best compromise.

"Are you going to tell your mother about...?" Sergei eyed me carefully as he jammed chunks of red onion onto the skewers.

My hand drifted down to my belly. Like a true alpha male, Sergei had planted his seed inside me with just one try. I still couldn't quite believe it was true. My period was only a day late when had I tested on a whim. The double lines had stunned me. A blood test the next morning had confirmed the result. We were going to have a baby.

Even though I knew we had flirted with danger, I never in a million years thought it would happen after just one single time. Obviously I should have paid better attention to the statistics in sex ed class!

"Not tonight," I said finally. "That's something I want to share with her when it's just the two of us."

I wasn't quite sure how she was going to take the news. She would be disappointed that I had gotten myself into trouble, as she would say, without being married. Eventually, though, she would come around and support me. I could already imagine what a doting, coddling grandmother she would be. Once Sergei's mother made it over here, she would probably be just as bad. Our child was going to be so spoiled.

"The three of us," Sergei corrected. "I want your mother to know I take my responsibility seriously."

"And your mother? Have you told her?"

He shook his head. "I'll tell her in person when we go to London later this month."

Abandoning the skewers, Sergei walked around the island and spun my barstool so that we were facing each other. His big hand curved protectively against my belly. "I know this is still a shock, and it's not ideal timing, Bianca, but I love you." He rubbed his hand over the place where our baby was growing. "It's been four days, and I'm already in love with this baby. We'll make it work."

Sliding my arms around him, I closed my eyes and breathed in the familiar scent of him. His soothing heat and strength assuaged the lingering fears. "You're right. It isn't ideal, but I keep telling myself that we'll give this baby a good life."

"We will," he assured me. "I'm out of *that* life now. Your business is booming. I'll spend more time actively working at the construction company instead of simply taking a cut. I'm going to pick up some extra work with Ivan, too." He gestured around us. "We'll tackle the priority projects around here and get the house ready for the baby. It will be okay, Bianca. You'll see."

Loving the way Sergei could calm me down and reassure me so easily, I caressed his handsome face. The future promised some big changes for us, but I was ready to meet them. We were starting our journey together, and I couldn't wait to see where the path would lead us.

SERGEI

AUTHOR'S NOTE

Thanks so much for reading SERGEI (Her Russian Protector #5)! I hope you enjoyed Sergei and Bianca's story.

The next books in the series will release in 2014 and include NIKOLAI, Volume 2 (Her Russian Protector #6) a sequel that picks up a few weeks after this book ends, ALEXEI (Her Russian Protector #7) and KOSTYA (Her Russian Protector #8.)

If you haven't read In Kelly's Corner yet, you can pick up a copy of that book right now to get his side of the fight story. Big brother Jack is up next in the *Fighting Connollys* series with In Jack's Arms.

You can check out my website, Facebook page or sign up for my newsletter for updates and notices on upcoming releases. I also offer Free Reads featuring couples from my books on my website.

ABOUT THE AUTHOR

When I'm not chasing after my wild preschooler, I like to write super sexy romances and scorching hot erotica. I live in Texas with a husband who could easily snag a job as an extra on History Channel's new Viking series and a sweet but rowdy four-year-old.

I also have another dirty-book writing alter ego, Lolita Lopez, who writes deliciously steamy tales for Ellora's Cave, Forever Yours/Grand Central, Mischief/Harper Collins UK, Siren Publishing and Cleis Press.

You can find me online at www.roxierivera.com.

ROXIE'S BACKLIST

Her Russian Protector Series
Ivan (Her Russian Protector #1)
Dimitri (Her Russian Protector #2)
Yuri (Her Russian Protector #3)
Nikolai (Her Russian Protector #4)
Sergei (Her Russian Protector #5
Nikolai Volume 2 (Coming 2014)
Sergei Volume 2 (Coming 2014)
Kostya (Coming 2014)
Alexei (Coming 2014)

The Fighting Connollys Series
In Kelly's Corner (Fighting Connollys #1)
In Jack's Arms (Fighting Connollys #2)—Coming January 2014!
In Finn's Heart (Fighting Connollys #3)—Coming March 2014!

Seduced By…
Seduced by the Loan Shark
Seduced by the Loan Shark 2—Coming Soon!
Seduced by the Congressman
Seduced by the Congressman 2

Erotica
Chance's Bad, Bad Girl
Halftime With Craig
Tease
Eddie's Cuffs 1
Eddie's Cuffs 2
Eddie's Cuffs 3
Disturbing the Peace
Quid Pro Quo
Search and Seizure